ROAD KILL

TEXAS HORROR
by
TEXAS WRITERS
Vol. 7

edited by

WILLIAM
JENSEN

HellBound Books Publishing LLC

A HellBound Books LLC Publication

Copyright © 2022 by HellBound Books Publishing LLC
All Rights Reserved

Cover photo courtesy of Linda Unger

Cover design by E. R. Bills for
HellBound Books Publishing LLC

www.hellboundbookspublishing.com

No part of this publication can be reproduced, stored in a retrieval system, or transmitted by any form or by any means, mechanical, digital, electronic, photocopying or recording, except for inclusion in a review, without permission in writing from the individual contributors and the publisher.

All contents in this anthology are works of fiction. Names, characters, places and incidents are imaginary. Any resemblance to actual persons, places or occurrences are coincidental only.

Printed in the United States of America

TABLE OF CONTENTS

Foreword

"Everything was quiet. The houses. The lawns. The roads. No pedestrians, no traffic. It was as if the world had been conquered by some sleeping death and now just the structures and the skeletons remained."

It's timely, eerie, and relevant. It's COVID, post-COVID and postmodern Ovid.

For the first time since this annual anthology's inception, a literary scholar isn't just one of our number. He's leading the procession, and, pardon the pun, it's one hell of a spectacle. The quoted lines above are excerpted from his acclaimed debut novel, *Cities of Men* (2017), which I highly recommend. We know places in Texas where the silence is oppressive, where the surrounding expanse is ominous, and where the whole world seems to have "been conquered by some sleeping death and now just the structures and the skeletons" remain. These locales haunt as well as remind us. They inspire and instruct. This volume covers lots of ground, and there are stark totems throughout, but we shouldn't kid ourselves. The Lone Star State isn't what you make it. It's what it makes you.

Bravo, Mr. Jensen. Bravo.

E. R. Bills

Introduction

TEXAS GOTHIC

It can be argued that all literature is regional literature. It is difficult to imagine Tolstoy's *Anna Karenina* in Los Angeles or Key West; similarly, can one picture the short stories of John Cheever reset in Kentucky or Arizona? Characters react to setting because setting is another character. Texas is a heck of a place because it contains so many characters. The Big Bend country, the Piney Woods, the Rio Grande Valley. Those are just three pockets so different from one another that help make the "big wonderful thing" that is the Lone Star State. The stories set here range from indigenous tribes to conquistadors, vaqueros, cowboys, and people working in skyscrapers and driving the interstates from Dallas to San Antonio and Laredo and beyond. It's a giant and a half. And every corner has a tale.

Horror is just a different spin on stories about place. Sometimes the conflicts we have with our homes, our states, and our regions frighten us. What place isn't haunted? New England has its puritan poltergeists, the South has the ghosts of slavery. Even sunny southern California has its cursed coasts with crimes that remain strange and unsolved. How many different types of phantoms and monsters can you think of that terrify your neck of the woods?

This anthology brings the terror of Texas to your front door. A wide array of voices cover the things that go bump in the night, from the days of the Texas Republic to the fast streets of Houston; this collection contains freed slaves moving west, women fighting for their bodies, racial tensions, unnamable supernatural forces, and numerous fears of what waits for us in the dark.

Hayden Gilbert's "Ax-Squatch," reinvigorates a well-known Lone Star cryptid behind the pine curtain, and Carmen Gray's "Remembering Refugio" shows how love can overcome fear as well as history. John Kojak invents new urban legends in "The Boogie." Patrick C. Harrison III and Cedrick May explore legacy and strife in Texas following the Emancipation Proclamation in their stories "The Devil Witch of Hanging Oak," and "Ambush and Blood for a Hoodoo Cowboy." Tytus Berry's "Definitive Act" reinvents a classic narrative for the modern era. Jonathan Duckworth's "Got the Spirit but Lose the Feeling" captures the angst and paranoia of growing up in small Texas towns where nothing is truly what it seems. Jacklyn Baker's "Blue Moon" is about a young woman who finds herself unexpectedly pregnant with terrifying consequences. Josh Rountree's "We Share Our Rage with The River," may focus on the early colonizers under Stephen F. Austin, but his story is timeless with its chills. Thomas McNeely and Patrick Torres examine legacies, regret, and memory in their macabre pieces, "The Visitor," and "Secrets That Keep Us." Madison Estes tackles the grotesque double standards of gender in "Pestilence." Nathan Machart's "The Old Man of the Ground" probes the unknown and unnamable, and Christian Riley's "The Retribution of John Ramsey" goes into mysterious realms of the Hill Country during prohibition. And *Road Kill* co-creator Bret A. McCormick takes a more humorous approach to the supernatural with his delightful tale of "The Book Sniffer."

This edition of *Road Kill: Texas Horror by Texas Writers* is also incredibly fortunate to feature work by the great Katherine Anne Porter. Her story "The Grave" has layers upon layers, and it is an exploration not just of death (and the fear of death) but of innocence, destruction, and time. Porter, a giant of Texas letters, reminds us that narratives of dread and the grotesque can be more than shocking anecdotes. Her fiction, like that of Faulkner, confronts ideas of legacy, heritage, and place. Just as Nathaniel Hawthorne, Edith Wharton, and Henry James explored repression and guilt with their horrifying fictions, a new generation of writers continue to examine the foreboding relationship between the individual and setting by way of ghouls, spirits, madmen, madness, and the undead. Texas is special; it deserves a special campfire tale. These stories you're about to read delve deep into the complex heart of the Lone Star State and remind us that sometimes the scariest place is home.

William Jensen
Texas State University, 2022

Nescio qua natale solum dulcedine captos
Ducit, et immemores non sinit esse sui.

Ovid

Pestilence
Madison Estes

My legs dangle off the edge of the gynecologist's table. Sweat glues my bangs to my forehead. It must be a hundred degrees in here, and the pink tissue paper gown the nurse gave me starts to slide up my crack. Pamphlets with lovely, comforting headlines like, *Living with HPV*, *What You Need to Know about HIV and AIDS* and *How to Protect Yourself from STIs* greet me from across the room. I think of puppies, my biochem project, anything but those texts. As much as I try not to, I replay them again in my head.

I miss being inside you.
Been thinking about what I want to do to you all day.
You're still on the pill, right?
I wanna eat that ass. You into that?

The last one made me dry heave. I didn't even know people really did that, outside of porn. I couldn't read anymore after that because Brian came back to my place once he realized he'd left his phone. He thought his secret was safe because he had a password-protected lock screen, but I snuck a peek at him entering the code when I started to get suspicious of all his late nights with the boys. I thought I was being paranoid, but weeks of sexting and dozens of naked pictures between him and a girl named Jasmine confirmed my suspicions. The next day I scheduled an appointment to get checked out.

When the doctor comes in, she smiles and seems to be just the right amount of cheerful and professional for someone who is about to look up my coochie. This friendly, middle-aged woman introduces herself and starts asking me about my sexual history.

"How many partners have you had in the past year?"

I want to tell her, *"Look, I've only been with one person, but it might as well have been a dozen, because every person he had sex with increased my chance of getting an STD. I didn't consent to all these risks, I just believed my boyfriend when he said he wanted to be with only me, and that we didn't have to use a condom because we were being exclusive."*

Instead, I mumble, "Just one."

"Did you use protection?"

"No. I'm on the pill." Her lips turn downward. Medical professionals aren't supposed to be judgmental, but there's a concern-bordering-disappointment look in her eyes that reminds me of my mother.

"We were supposed to be monogamous," I say.

She frowns harder.

"Monogamy is for penguins."

I want to tell her that research has shown that some female penguins may have one to three partners in one season and some males may have one or two partners, but I hold my tongue. She doesn't want to hear *Animal Planet* facts, and I don't want to be here any longer than necessary. I put my legs in the cold metal stirrups and scoot down toward the edge of the table. I try to ignore the paper gown crawling further up my ass. She swabs my vagina. My eyes shoot to the tile ceiling. Thin black marks spot the white ceiling, hundreds of them, spiraling, like bacteria swimming under a microscope. I don't want to see these spots that look like the germs that are probably inside of me. I wish they had put a T.V. on the ceiling so I could watch something mindless like *The Big Bang Theory* and pretend this wasn't happening to me.

The pelvic exam is worse. She doesn't heat up the speculum before she inserts it, and she uses the wrong size and it hurts more than losing my virginity to a guy I was smart enough to wear a condom with. I want to scream, but I bite my fist instead. She's punishing me. She's punishing me, and maybe I deserve it for being so stupid.

I can't wait to be inside you again. You're the best I've ever had. Tomorrow night?

I haven't prayed in several years, but I say a prayer now. God, please let everything be okay. Don't let me be infected. I'll do anything.

"We're almost done here," the gynecologist says, noting my discomfort. When I look down I nearly scream again, because it's not the nice woman I met moments ago, but a hooded figure in a white robe between my legs, peering down at my opening. Something icy penetrates me, even colder than the stirrups. My chest feels too tight to yell, so I whisper, "No. Stop. Please."

Why didn't I say that sooner? Why didn't I say that to Brian before I let him have sex with me without a condom?

I squeeze my eyes shut from the pain, and when I open them, the robed figure is gone. The gynecologist disposes of her latex gloves and gives me a sympathetic smile.

"We should get the results back in two weeks," she says. "Try not to worry in the meantime."

As I drive home, I pass almost a dozen churches. It's impossible not to when you live in South Texas. I stop at a pitiful, run-down church because it is the only one with a door open in the middle of the week. When I get to the front, I see that the door isn't open but missing. The church is deserted, the congregation likely dispersed among the various other religious organizations in the community. That's probably for the best. I don't need confession or support right now; I need God.

I go to the altar and pray for God to have mercy on my body and soul.

As I toss and turn in my bed, trying to sleep, the shrouded figure returns. It brings three others with it, all in different colored cloaks: white, red, black, and pale green. I open my mouth to scream, but nothing comes out. My chest constricts. I can't move. The black veiled figure removes its hood, revealing an oblong skull, triangular and definitely not human. It turns its head to the side, examining me. A dozen square teeth peek out in a lopsided grin. I don't recognize what it is at first because it's so thin that it reminds me of dinosaur skeletons I once saw on a museum field trip. It's only when one of its hairy hoofs emerges from the cloak and touches one of the others that I realize what they are.

The four horsemen.

I didn't think they would literally be part-horse, like a reverse centaur. They don't speak to me or each other. They communicate in hoof gestures and neighing. They seem to get on the same page and spread out across the room.

I'm not in my bedroom anymore. I'm in a hospital. There are three other beds lined up in a row, with a girl on each. One of them looks half-starved. Her ribs protrude. Her waist is a sheet of paper. Her cheeks are sunken in like a mummy. One of the horsemen puts his black hooves between her thighs and spreads her skinny legs. She doesn't resist. Her eyes roll back into her head like she's going to pass out as he enters her. Somehow I know, perhaps from all the Sunday school lessons that were drilled into my head as a child, that this is famine.

She is famine.

The next girl is a petite blonde who fights the cloaked figure taking her on the bed. Her eyebrows furrow in distress as it stomps her chest, leaving hoof prints all over her breasts. Its red robe falls to the floor. Red is supposed to mean something, but I can't remember what. Blood, maybe. Or carnage. Violence. I see blood between her legs, scratches all along her arms and torso from where his hooves are pushing her down into the mattress. She scratches him back. They are fighting; they are at war.

She is war.

The last girl doesn't move. Doesn't open her eyes. The horseman drops his pale green cloak to reveal human-like legs, but his genitals look more horse than man. The long pink organ protrudes from its brown sheath. I feel sick. Bile rises in my throat. What is she? I go back to my Sunday school days, coloring in pictures of Noah's ark, answering trivia questions about Adam and Eve, receiving that abstinence ring that I should have taken more seriously, but nothing pertinent comes back to me until I see the maggots squirming on her body. The thrusting motion as he enters her over and over seems to have awakened them, energized them.

Death. She is death.

Finally, the horseman before me removes its white cloak. It neighs, and this naked half-man, half-horse braying would be comical if its erect horse-cock didn't look like it would split me in half. I look away and see that the horseman plunging into Famine seems to match her in thinness. It shrinks the more it pounds into her. Both the horseman of war and his victim are glazed in each other's blood as they fight and fuck. The horseman of death is covered in maggots and flies now; insects of decomposition pour out of them, and they stink of rot. Bile rises again. I turn and puke over the side of the bed. It doesn't deter my horseman in the least. Which one is this? I can't remember. Famine. War. Death. Why can't I remember the last one?

It comes to me when the horseman sticks his jutting cock near my face. He does his best to guide it into my vomit-coated mouth with his hooves. Even more appalling than the animalistic genitals are the warts and blisters that cover it. I jerk my head away. Inflamed blisters rub against my lips. One of them bursts from the friction. The pus oozes against my mouth and drips down my chin. If I scream, he'll shove the whole thing in, so I whimper instead. I try to be strong and resist, but the stench coming from Death makes me gag. The horseman takes this opportunity to shove his disease-ridden cock inside my mouth. The blisters rip open on my teeth, spilling into my mouth. As I choke, I remember it at last.

Pestilence. I am pestilence.

I wake up drenched in sweat. The horsemen and their victims visit me every night as I wait for the test results. Waiting is the hardest part, especially when you already know what the outcome will be. I try to imagine a phone call with good news, but instead, I remember more texts.

Show me that ass again. I want to see what I'm gonna be wrecking tonight.

You should be a model. For real, you're so hot. I wish every girl had a body like you. My last girl was a skinny twig, no ass at all.

I am the skinny twig, no-ass girl he was talking about, only I wasn't his last girl when he sent that text. I was, or still am, his current girl. I haven't told him I know yet. I'm still figuring out how to go about it.

I think about confronting him at the Good Ol' Boy's Country Bar he works at. It's a family-owned bar. He'd be humiliated. But if I confronted him publicly, he'd probably say I was crazy or desperate and it would make him look like a victim or me like a pathetic wreck. They would probably laugh me out of the place. And then he'd use me as a sob story to get into the next girl's pants.

I think about stealing his phone and sending all the sexts and nudes to his family and friends. Would any of them even care? Do I even care if they care at this point?

I think about handcuffing him to the headboard and pouring acid on his sad little limp dick, watching it curl and shrivel as the chemical eats away at his flesh like salt corroding a snail. I think about this most of all. Pestilence appears beside me, nodding in approval as I allow the dark fantasy to play in my head. All it would take to lure him here are pictures of me in black lingerie and a text saying, *"Hey baby, what are you doing tonight?"*

Pestilence nods again. Its face is covered in open sores and weeping abscesses. I feel an itch between my legs. I put the phone down and hop in the shower, trying to wash this gross feeling away. I use a douche and rub a soapy loofah between my legs to get some relief. When I open the shower curtain, my visitor is gone.

I wake up clawing at my vaginal lips with my nails. I itch so badly that I scratched myself raw in my sleep. Once I'm in the shower, I try to wash away all the contamination.

I want to skin myself and sterilize the insides. I would have scrubbed my flesh with bleach if it wouldn't have left burns. Regular soap can't get me clean. Not in a way that I can feel it. I switch to hypoallergenic soap because I am washing myself several times a day, and I don't want to dry my skin out and create new problems. But lavender and vanilla-scented baby soap can't take away the feeling of disease, or the stench of Brian, perspiring and

filthy
as he moved above me, inside me, and
filthy
the repugnant odor of his testicles hovered around me
so filthy

He never showered enough, preferring to cover his stench with cheap cologne. He was scum from the start. The word repeats in my head, like the chanting you hear in Catholic church ceremonies, the ones where they anoint you with oil. Only instead of oil, mud is smeared on my face, all over my body, and all I see is

filth filth filth

Brian has been ignoring my calls and texts. I drive to the Good Ol' Boy's Country Bar and wait in the parking lot. He walks out with Jasmine, and they are all over each other. She rubs her faux leather cowgirl boots against his calf and wraps her arms around him. For a moment I think I might just go. They deserve each other, and I already feel like a crazy stalker showing up at his job unannounced. As they get closer, the light from the neon sign illuminates their faces.

He's not with Jasmine. He's with a girl I've never even seen before, and he's about to get to second base with her right here in the parking lot.

Pestilence sits in the passenger's seat. Its face is covered by a large medical mask. I can't tell if that's to protect me from it, or it from me. Its boils and blisters have multiplied since the last time I saw it, but so have mine. The red bumps between my vaginal lips, that were starting to calm down, flare up. The itching and burning intensifies. I weep, scratching my crotch as he makes out with this girl against his car.

When I get home, I put on my sexiest bra and panty set and take selfies from the neck down, still crying. The lacy material aggravates my already delicate skin, and I can't get the image of him and this new girl out of my head. I send him the pictures and a text. *Miss me?*

He sends back a gentleman's only proper response: an unfiltered dick pic and, for some reason, an unnatural emphasis on his scrotum.

See you 2nite.

When he gets to my house, two hours later, he flashes me what he believes must be an irresistible grin. I want to retch as I think about him with the girl in pink boots. His features seem almost warped now, his smile crooked and full of secrets, his eyes beady instead of warm. How did I ever find him attractive?

"I would like you to pray with me," I tell him. He laughs at me.

"Very funny." He slides his hands around my back, pressing himself against me. I gag when I smell cheap perfume, and push him away.

"We need to get our souls right with God. That's the only way to avoid his punishment."

"What's going on?" he asks. "You sent me those pics, basically asked me to come fuck you, now you're pushing me away? Are you trying to play hard to get?"

Pestilence snorts, smashes a hoof against the wall, but Brian can't see or hear my other guest.

"If we both repent, maybe we can become clean, again."

Another laugh. "This is a roleplay thing, isn't it? You're a good Catholic school girl? I'm a bad boy, coming to corrupt you?"

"Something like that." I look at the mounted horseshoe he gave me when we first started dating. I didn't know he'd stolen it from his family's country-themed bar. At the time, I thought it was cute, in a rustic way. It reminded me of when we first started dating, of twilight picnics and blanket fort movie nights. Before the lies and excuses and humiliation of having my vagina swabbed because of him. I pull the horseshoe off and turn it upside down, spilling out all the good luck it never brought me.

"What are you doing with that old thing?" he asks. The horseshoe is rusted and tarnished—I'll probably need a tetanus shot considering how hard I grab it when I bash it into the back of Brian's skull. I sigh in relief when I feel his pulse beneath my fingers. I'm not sure what I have planned will work if he dies first.

Maybe the horseshoe is good luck after all.

I rub olive oil and recite prayers over Brian's unconscious body. He comes to with a groan. His eyebrows furrow. He is confused about why he's chained to a post in my shed, with translucent plastic covering the space from floor to ceiling.

"What's going on? How did I get here?" he says.

"I had some help." Pestilence sits beside me in a yellow hazmat suit, its face obstructed by a gas mask. I'm wearing thick gloves and plastic over my clothes, not to hide evidence but because I don't want any more contact with Brian. My hands were coated in invisible grime the moment they made contact with his bare skin. I washed them several times before donning some gloves and protective clothing to shield me from him. I only wish I'd always handled him with this much caution, but, back then, I didn't know his penis was a Petri dish of bacteria and disease.

"Allison? Alli? What's going on? Is this some weird new sex game you wanna play?"

"You wish."

Pestilence tilts its head back and brays, impatient. I dab my glove into the oil and smear it against Brian's forehead.

"What are you doing?"

"Anointing you."

I unzip his jeans and pull them off. I pull out his penis and rub the oil over it. Despite his terror, and to my annoyance, he gets half-hard before I'm done.

"I'm so confused," he says.

"Don't worry. It'll be over soon." I turn on my laptop and place it within his view. A loud laugh track fills the room.

"Why are you doing this to me?" He yanks against his restraints.

"Hey, at least you get to watch *The Big Bang Theory*. That's more than I got."

"Please. *I love you baby*. Whatever this is, we can work through it."

Against my will, the good times flash before my eyes, first kisses and holidays and surprise vacations. I frown, looking over at Pestilence for support. It tilts its head as if to say, "So what?" I hesitate.

"Okay," I say at last, reaching up toward the ropes that bind him.

"Really?" His eyes close in relief.

I lean in close to him and whisper in his ear.

"Bazinga."

Before he has time to process what I said, I pull out the scalpel.

"What? What are you going to—*Oh God, don't do that—*"

The blade meets the base of his penis. With a flick of my wrist, blood sprays and the root is almost severed from his pelvis. It hangs on by a thin strand of skin and muscle. I rectify this with a second swipe, and remove the infected genitals. It isn't covered in warts and blisters like Pestilence and me, but there is no doubt in my mind that this four-inch (and I'm being generous here) innocent-looking, flaccid piece of skin and tissue is contaminated, the culprit behind my rashes and itching. I offer the afflicted organ to Pestilence, giving it the honor of destroying the cursed thing. The horseman removes its gas mask, opens its mouth, and takes it. Pestilence chomps down on it before swallowing. Bits of flesh hang between its long, yellow teeth when it smiles.

"Not how I thought you were going to get rid of it, but okay," I say. It gives a half-whine, half-laugh.

A dark red pool forms around Brian, and he passes out from the pain and blood loss. *The Big Bang Theory* laugh track plays again after Leonard makes another crack about Sheldon's antics. I chuckle along with it.

An hour later, I'm still itching. The ritual didn't work. I thought ridding the world of a proud, unapologetic disease spreader would allow my own body some mercy from my affliction, but God is angrier than I thought, or I misunderstood what I was meant to do. Perhaps Pestilence tricked me. But I don't have time to concentrate on that. I have a body to get rid of.

Dismemberment takes longer than I thought it would. Castration is easy compared to cutting through bones, even with the old hacksaw I picked up at a pawnshop. An acid composition from my biochem class does the rest, although it dissolves much slower than Google said it would.

I take his hands and gently set them inside the acid, careful that it doesn't splash, although I have goggles and a face mask on just in case it does. My phone vibrates.

"Hello, is this Allison?"

I confirm my birthday and first and last name.

"I just wanted to tell you that your results all came back negative. We recommend annual pap smears for women your age, so if you want, we can schedule your next appointment right now—"

"Excuse me. Did you say the results were negative?"

"That's right."

"All of them?" My mouth hangs open. Brian's bloody arm drips on my white shoes. His hands sizzle in the acid. An index finger seems to point at me, right before it collapses in the mush.

"Yes. It came back negative for HIV, Herpes, HPV…" she lists off every sexually transmitted disease known to man. "All negative."

"But I've been itching down there like crazy. It's all red and bumpy."

"Have you used any new soaps or detergents?"

"I don't think so. Just hypoallergenic soap, but that's, like . . . hypoallergenic."

"What about new lubricants or douches?"

I groan.

"I'm a douche."

"Excuse me?"

"I said it was probably the douche."

I try to listen to what she says next, but it's hard to focus.

"Yes, we get a lot of girls that have issues due to douches," the woman from the clinic continues. "It disrupts the pH balance and can cause yeast infections. We recommend using an over-the-counter cream, and if you'd like to come in again for an exam, we can schedule you for next week."

"I'm going to have to call you back." I stare at the top and bottom halves of my ex-boyfriend. "I'm sort of in the middle of something."

MADISON ESTES is a writer and freelance editor. She is a recipient of the 2020 Ladies of Horror Fiction grant and the Mystery Writers of America Helen McCloy scholarship. She was the editor of *Road Kill: Texas Horror by Texas Writers, Vol. 6*. She lives in southeast Texas and has three dogs. She posts reviews, writing advice, horror commentary and vlogs on her You Tube channel. You can find her on Twitter @madisonestes or Instagram @madisonpaigeestes or visit her website authormadisonestes.wordpress.com.

Ax-Squatch
Hayden Gilbert

The pipeline in Beaumont had gone up in the storm. The nights glowed red as the fire burned throughout the week. The few stragglers who had stayed during the hurricane had almost grown accustomed to the crimson nights and the smoke of flames miles away.

The storm had been a mighty thing. Louisiana had got the worst of the rain. The state was under water all the way to Lake Charles; no telling how many people lost, but the numbers would come in, sure enough. The worst of the winds, however, had hit Cotter County in East Texas, and the small hamlet of Cotter Town, the county seat, was now a wasteland of fallen timber and log. Few pine trees still spired the dusking sky, once silver at twilight or yellow after a warm rain, now streaked a pink-going-on-crimson.

Dorothy Burke sat patiently in her car, checking her rearview mirror out of habit. There was nothing to see except the downed trees. This was the first day she had been able to leave the house after the storm and she was going north to check on her sister. She was one of few old-timers who had stayed during the storm. She had weathered them all since she was a child, and no matter how many more they got every year, and no matter how much worse they were getting, she didn't intend on leaving. She was not a proud woman, but this stubborn haughtiness had been instilled in her by her father since she was a child.

Two men, a black fellow and a burly white one, were hard at work clearing the final tree on her driveway. The burly man worked the chainsaw up and down the tree's thick trunk, and the other cleared the limbs, throwing them off to the side. They were moving slowly, clearly running on fumes after a week of what had been hard work. But she was in no hurry and waved gently at them when they would look her way, sopping sweat from their brows.

Her sister didn't live far, but it would be nice to just get away from her house for a day. It had begun to feel like a prison, and she was running out of books to read since the TV was out. She had spent the last several nights sitting outside on the screened-in back porch with a candle and a wet rag for her neck, listening to the cricket songs until she felt like going to bed. The animals had started to make stranger sounds the last night, though. Odd sounds, indeed, and she thought she would not go on the back porch again.

The burly man finished cutting that last large section of tree in half, and kicked one of the halves to the side, where it rolled lazily and heavily out of the way. The black man took an ax and buried it into the belly of the last remaining hunk of timber and dragged it off.

Dorothy Burke rolled down her window.

"I appreciate you boys," she said. "What are your names?"

"Isaiah," the black man answered.

"Hound Dog," the meaty white man said.

"Is that your Christian name?" Dorothy asked.

"No, ma'am," the white man replied. "Sorry. My name's Holly. 'Hound Dog' is just a nickname."

"Well," Dorothy continued, "my name's Dorothy. It was nice to meet you both." She gave Hound Dog and Isaiah each a five-dollar bill, bid them a blessed day and pulled out on the road in front of her house, heading north.

Isaiah Brown and Hound Dog Holly were both members of the Cotter volunteer fire department. They had toughed out the storm and spent the week clearing the roads with their chainsaws and axes, first on four-wheelers, and later, after most of the roads were cleared, in Isaiah's pickup. It was comfortable, but their bodies were sore and aching from the long hours the last few days. But the truck had working A/C, while their homes, or what were left of them, would be without power for weeks. More likely, months.

They drove slowly along the cut-off from Cotter toward Wayes, swerving occasionally to avoid larger limbs and fallen squirrels. Their equipment rattled around uneasily in the bed of the truck, but they paid no mind. They enjoyed the solitude of backroads out that way. It was a scenic miles-long passage through the woodlands, and one of the few places some pines still stood perpendicular to the earth, intersecting the sky like tall, skinny totems, black against the reddening east. Nearly all the oak trees along the road were lost in the storm. Their roots grew on top of the soil, Hound Dog had said, and were easily felled in high winds. But the oaks were not the only things lost to the storm.

"It's all but gone, Isaiah," Hound Dog said.

Isaiah watched the road, listening.

"The place. My family's place. All but gone," Hound Dog said, more to himself. "Fooled myself into thinking there was something to salvage, but there ain't."

Isaiah gave him a look.

"Man, I am sorry to hear that," he offered. "Your Missus okay? Where she at again?"

"She went to stay with her sister and the kid up in Fort Worth," Hound Dog said. "But I ain't going to send for her."

A silence fell over them.

"I'm taking this as a sign to start over," Hound Dog went on. "We've known it's been finished for a while now. Us, that is. We weren't willing to admit it before, but it's over now that the house is gone. Gone with the wind. And rain."

The burly man looked out his passenger window and searched for a moon or stars in the smoky sky. Isaiah studied him. The tattoos on his broad arms danced as he clenched and unclenched his hands into fists, his beard blew as he exhaled breaths that carried a spiritual weight, leaving his body in huffs. They had never been great friends. They had gotten along fine in high school on the football team, and even better when they had both found themselves sharing shifts at the fire department, but they had never shared conversations about matters of the heart or their homelife until the last few days in the quiet lonely world of towns without people. He wanted to say something to ease Hound Dog's mind. He wanted to encourage him to talk it out with his lady, but Isaiah had never been strong at comforting others, especially other men.

Isaiah leaned his head against the window and tried to will himself to sleep. His body throbbed in dull pain and his mind felt like a thick bowl of grits, but he couldn't sleep. He stared out the window at the woods. As many trees as had fallen, there would always be more in East Texas. His friends had always tried to get him to go hunting when they were younger, and eventually he had run out of excuses and had to admit to them that he just didn't want to go. Isaiah had heard enough stories from his mother about the woods around these parts that he was scared. And when a kid from school would go missing on a scout trip, or hunting, or fishing, Isaiah wasn't surprised. When he was growing up, kids had teased him about his dad stepping out on his mom, and as he got older, he eventually came around to believing them. All he knew was what his momma had told him. She said that his dad had left early one morning to hunt hogs, and he hadn't come back. This no doubt contributed to his wariness about the woods and whatever lurked in them. He sometimes wondered why he had never left, but he supposed he was probably no different than Dorothy. It was home.

As they approached a hill, taking the curve with grace, an artificial glow, unseen for many nights, shone in the darkness.

"Well, I'll be gosh damned," Hound Dog said with a sudden spark.

The Soda Speak was a little gas, beer, and soda pop stop, and the only establishment on the road from Cotter to Wayes. And that night it wasn't an empty husk. It sat proud and pretty against the dark woods. The "open" sign buzzed, and Cooter Robicheaux's truck sat out back.

"Old Coot is a saint, indeed," said Hound Dog.

"I could go for a beer," Isaiah said. "Sounds like you might could, too."

And for the first time in several days, Hound Dog grinned.

As the truck pulled into the parking lot and they climbed out, they could hear a generator coughing loudly from around the corner. They approached the front door.

Isaiah's hand went for the handle, but he hesitated, pausing where he stood. Hound Dog didn't seem to notice, easing past him and entering the bright store, an oasis of artificial light in the encroaching darkness. Isaiah remained planted; something felt off and he was trying to decipher exactly what it was.

The humidity had been blown away by the first gusts of autumn wind, and that seemed to signal another bout of rain. But while the temperature was nice and unseasonably cool for East Texas, he could still smell smoke from the faraway flames, and the atmosphere was still surprisingly thick. It was like being underwater in the open air. And this sensation, combined with the incredible silence beyond the hum of the store's generator gave him pause. The generator hardly disturbed the eerie quietude, and it bothered Isaiah.

When he finally got a hold on himself and stepped into the white light of the Soda Speak, he saw Hound Dog carrying a twelve-pack of Lone Star and a bottle of malt liquor, stalking back and forth between the aisles of confection, candy, and condoms.

"What you looking for, Hound?"

The man didn't answer immediately. He mangled words behind his beard and finally set his drinks and a bag of pork rinds on the counter.

"Where is that old bastard?" he said finally.

Isaiah looked around and, sure as shit, Cooter was nowhere to be found. The store was completely empty and totally silent. He looked at Hound Dog and gave him a shrug.

"Watch this stuff," Hound Dog said, and walked out the front door.

Isaiah watched as he bounded around the corner, walking toward the outside restrooms. Isaiah looked the store over again. He noticed the freezers had yet to be switched back on, saving the electricity instead for the lights and an ice machine outside. He leaned over the counter, peeking beneath the hollowed-out cubby and spying just what he had expected. The riot shotgun he had always heard rumors about, but doubted the existence of. It lay cold and dangerous.

As he waited, Isaiah grabbed a bottle of lukewarm Lone Star from the twelve, uncapped it in the rough of his palm, and popped open a bag of chips. Dinner for winners, he heard his momma's voice say.

Outside the window, the sun had finally completely sunk, and the fire from down south painted the night a sullen purple. The piney stragglers that still remained vertical stirred dizzily, drunkenly, in the faintest of September winds, and the fatigue he had experienced before crept in again. His eyelids felt heavy.

As darkness began to blanket the Big Thicket, Isaiah snapped awake. He felt a chill settle in his spine again. Something about the scene outside, the gas pump or the road and the felled trees beyond, stood out and bothered him. But like the feeling he had before, he couldn't put his finger on it.

Hound Dog finally reemerged from around the corner wearing a look more worried than puzzled. He called aloud, shouting into the darkness, before once more stepping back inside. He came to Isaiah's side and took another bottle from the case.

"Where could that old man have gone to?" he said, twisting off the bottle cap and taking a warm swig.

Outside, a pair of headlights cut the night, and, like a moth to flame, a big, brand new King Ranch pulled into the parking lot. Its engine chugged in the night air, the grizzly-like rumble causing the Soda Speak's windows to vibrate. As the huge truck parked next to theirs, Isaiah suddenly wondered if this wasn't what a goldfish felt like when someone approached its bowl at night. He took another sip of his beer. He was tired and his mind was wandering.

A well-manicured man with a fiery pearl-snap shirt and white cowboy hat stepped into the Soda Speak. He took a quick look around and moseyed over. Isaiah's eyes were immediately drawn to the man's boots. They looked to be made of alligator hide and ended in the sharpest points he had ever seen on a pair of boots.

"Howdy," the man said with a wry grin. "Where can a man get a drink?"

"Help yourself," Hound Dog said. "I'd stick to what's on the warm shelf. Power went out during the storm and everything behind those doors is probably worse than warm."

The man groomed his mustache and walked with a crooked strut to the back of the Speak.

"Came down from Dallas to assess the damage to our stores out this way. Waste of time, you ask me," the man grumbled.

He perused the aisle several times before landing on a sixer of import beer.

"This place seems to be the only thing open for miles," he said with a humorless laugh.

"Likely be that way for some time," Isaiah replied. "The hurricane that came through here didn't even ask permission."

The man laughed and looked at Isaiah. Isaiah didn't return a smile.

"You boys know where the clerk might be hiding? I don't have much time to diddle-daddle."

Isaiah and Hound Dog hid their contempt as best they could. Hound Dog even managed a pleasant smile.

"No, sir, we do not," he said, taking another drink from his beer. "We were just looking for him."

The man studied them and the place where he stood for the first time, then shifted in his boots.

"It doesn't seem like he'd mind if we took these to go, then," he said, and aimed for the door.

"Come on now, partner," Hound Dog stopped him. "This ain't a place for looting. Besides, looks like you can afford a six-pack."

The man turned to them and feigned another of his dry laughs. They seemed to have taken him pretty far in his life, but they were hollow in Cotter County.

"How's about I just leave you boys with a ten-spot and we call it a night? Like I said, I gotta be getting down the road." The man placed the bill on the counter between Hound Dog and Isaiah and turned to walk out. "You can even keep the . . ."

His voice trailed off as he stopped. "Jesus Christ," he continued.

Isaiah and Hound Dog followed the man's eyes outside the window, toward the gas pump. They saw now what they had overlooked before as the sun was going down. A dusk-to-dawn light had kicked on, and there was a large, dark puddle beside the pump, and on the pole near it was a handprint in what was surely nothing other than blood.

"Christ, is that what I think it is?" the man said, and looked at them.

"How did we miss that?" Hound Dog replied, jogging outside to inspect it closer.

With Hound Dog outside again, Isaiah stood alone in the store with the man in the alligator boots. He set aside his import beer, nearly dropping it as he fumbled for his pocket with a shaky hand.

Hound Dog shouted into the night, more frantically than before, searching the edges of the parking lot for any other sign of Cooter.

"Jesus," the man in the boots blurted. "I'm calling the cops." He fingered his phone futilely for a moment or two before giving up with a frustrated grunt.

"Cell towers are down," Isaiah said, crossing behind the counter and bringing forth a corded phone. "The old man's got a landline, though." He held the phone up to his ear and heard a dial tone echoing in the void. He raised his head, gave the man in the boots a thumbs-up, and began dialing 911. It rang and he cradled it to his face. His sight fell back outside, to the handprint in browned blood. To Hound Dog calling out into the darkness. Just before Isaiah had convinced himself that no one would pick up, a woman's voice came from the other end.

"911, what's your emergency?"

Isaiah stared blankly into the night, searching for something just beyond his vision. He was sure there was something out there, something just a shade darker than the darkness it stood against, and he was sure that it was watching them.

"911, what is the nature of your emergency?" the operator repeated.

"Um, yes," Isaiah began, struggling to find the words.

The man in the boots held out a hand and gestured to give him the phone, but Isaiah held up a finger and silently mouthed I got this.

"I'm down here at the Soda Speak off 1943, between Cotter and Wayes," Isaiah reported, "and I think we've got a problem here."

"All right, we ask that you remain calm. All our officers are making house-calls because of the storm, but we have a unit close to you," she said in a voice nearly devoid of concern.

He had heard the tone before and understood its purpose, but it only made his blood rise more. The man in the boots was still fiddling with his cell phone.

"It's the store owner, Cooter—" Isaiah caught himself. "I think his name is Luther Robicheaux."

"Has anyone been injured?" She was quick with the response.

Isaiah searched outside for Hound Dog, whose muffled shouts he still managed to hear, but only barely.

"I don't know. He's gone, but I see blood outside."

"A lot of it," the man in the boots shouted over him to the voice on the other end of the phone.

There were sounds of typing and a moment of silence before the frustratingly cold voice returned on the other end. She reminded him to remain calm and asked for him to stay on the line until their officer arrived. She asked a series of questions, all of which Isaiah did not know the answers to, until finally a police car pulled in with lights flashing red and blue, and Isaiah returned the phone to its receiver.

A young police officer climbed from the seat of the car. Isaiah instinctively drew inward, his back straightening and shoulders going stiff. Hound Dog went to meet the policeman out front, and the man in the boots held the door open.

The officer looked to be around twenty-two. He stepped inside the Soda Speak and scanned the place with dark, beady eyes. Everything about his uniform fit neatly and tight, and he didn't have a hair out of place. After two passes across the inside of the store, those black marbles finally fell on Isaiah, who came around to the front of the counter.

"Officer Lee," he spoke around a stick of gum.

Isaiah nodded his head.

The officer sniffed.

"Anyone see the owner of this establishment before he left?"

"No, sir. He was gone when we got here," Hound Dog said from behind the policeman. "We came inside, wanted to get some drinks before heading home, but he wasn't anywhere to be found. That's his truck out back, though. We didn't even notice the blood out there until this man came along and pointed it out."

The officer didn't turn to look at Hound Dog. He continued eyeing Isaiah up and down, and eventually grazed over the opened case of beer on the counter.

"We've been responding to a handful of odd calls today," the officer said sternly. "Must be something in the air. That, or everyone's deciding to tie one on now that the TV's out."

"You can breathalyze us, sir, I didn't even have a sip before I saw the blood," the man in the boots said.

"You folks don't have anywhere to be, do you?" the officer said.

"We're with the fire department, officer. We've been clearing these roads all week. What's a few more hours?" Isaiah said.

The officer sucked loudly on the gum in his mouth and finally turned toward the man in the boots. The man threw out an eager hand quickly, grabbing the officer's and shaking it vigorously. The young officer lethargically returned the gesture. Isaiah couldn't help but think what might have happened if he himself had reached forward as quickly toward the officer's hand without warning.

"Anything we can do to help? Love to be of service to law enforcement," the man in the boots said.

"Not at the moment," the officer replied. "But I'm going to have a look around."

He took a long-necked flashlight from his belt and aimed the beam to where Hound Dog had pointed. He continued to chew loudly and didn't move from the door's frame with any sense of urgency.

"A lot of people go missing during these storms. More and more, recently," he observed. "Not sure what the final number will be after all's said and done with this one."

The officer gestured for Hound Dog to step back inside and, when he had done so, turned his attention back to the pump. From there, his light made a trail across the parking lot to the back of their shoddy little pick-up and the bundle of tools in the back.

"Said you're with the fire department, right?" he said.

"That's right," Hound Dog confirmed.

He studied their truck a little longer.

"You wouldn't mind if I had a look around that truck, would you?"

"Of course not," Isaiah said.

"I'll let you guys know if I need some more eyes. Sit tight."

And with that, the young police officer let the door shut in a hush behind him.

They watched as he disappeared into the darkness that had now engulfed the outside world. Only the beam from his flashlight and what it landed on floated out there in the void. It crossed the parking lot and examined the handprint on the pole, and the pool on the ground beside it. It searched the area for a trail of any kind before slowly making its way to their pickup truck.

For the first time that Isaiah noticed, the man in the boots looked at them with suspicion, but he didn't care. He only fought against another bout of sleepiness. They would probably be here for a while, and he looked behind the counter, searching for a place to nap on the cold, hard ground.

Hound Dog went back to his opened bottle of beer on the counter and took a long pull from it. The man in the alligator boots eased up a little and took a bottle from his own six-pack.

"Didn't want to be drinking and driving tonight," he said sullenly.

"This is probably the safest time in your life to drink and drive," Isaiah motioned with his own bottle at the ebony velvet of night outside, where the only things that seemed alive beyond the glow of the storefront were the headlights from the police cruiser that sat running behind their trucks.

"Looks like he doesn't want us going anywhere, anyway," the man said, commenting on how both trucks were blocked in. He knocked the bottle-cap free from its place on the edge of the counter and extended and raised his bottle for a toast.

Hound Dog and Isaiah clinked their necks against his and threw one back.

"To evenings with strangers," the man said.

"To all our yesterdays," Hound Dog mumbled.

"To whatever's next," Isaiah said, and finished his beer.

Then, the main storefront window exploded, glass raining down on them, glinting in the reflection of the light like a thousand twinkling stars. Something spun toward them, leaving a warm and viscous mess in its wake.

It was Officer Lee's head, wearing an eternal, stretched mask of terror and shroud of broken glass embedded in his pale skin. It rolled awkwardly across the tile floor until finally coming to rest at the feet of the man in the boots. His pointed right toe found itself now in between the young officer's pearly whites, and the man in the boots yelped and instinctively reared his foot back and kicked the head like a soccer ball across the tile floor where it skidded from sight. Officer Lee's gum was stuck to the man's boot tip.

Isaiah, Hound Dog, and the reluctant kicker collected themselves in the deafening silence, their bodies locked and stiff. What they saw outside, standing before the headlights of the police car, was a silhouetted figure towering easily eight feet tall. It was blacker than the night, and it was covered in clots of thick and twisted hair.

"What in God's creation is that?" the man in the boots gulped.

"Is that a goddamn bear?" Hound Dog said.

Isaiah didn't answer. Suddenly wide awake, like he'd been struck by lightning, he could only watch as the looming thing let the officer's body fall to the ground at its tremendous feet. Sinking backward, it began to melt back into the night, momentarily skirting the edge of Soda Speak's glow. Then, the night concealed it.

"Fellas," the man in the boots spoke again.

They said nothing in return.

"I think that's a goddamn bigfoot."

Isaiah immediately began disbelieving what he had just heard and seen. Excuses buzzed through his mind like a swarm of flies. He tried to grab onto any one that made an ounce of sense, but the shattered window he looked through put his desperate search for an alternative to an abrupt end. It seemed like an eternity before the other men were able to answer.

"I would laugh at the shit that just came out of your mouth," Isaiah began, "but I think you're right."

With his sight on the door, Isaiah slipped slowly behind the counter and grabbed the shotgun. He looked to Hound Dog and the man in the boots, who appeared like he wanted to say something, but under the circumstances was just glad that someone else held a gun.

Isaiah checked the magazine and saw it had two rounds loaded and was ready to fire with a pump and an easy pull of the trigger. He glanced beneath the shelf and saw no box of shells. He pulled open the drawers and still found nothing. Coot must have the other bullets stashed away, he thought. Two would have to do.

"Sonofabitch has us blocked in," Hound Dog said, looking out to the police car, still idling in the dark.

"Think we can make it to his ride?" the other man asked in a hushed voice.

"The shotgun will help buy us some time," Isaiah said. "Not sure how long we'll have to get out of here."

Isaiah swallowed his sudden doubt. The fear. He couldn't give it any room to grow. Sitting in the shop under the lights, they were sitting ducks. They couldn't wait for another police officer to get there. The three men needed to act aggressively, and fast. Any lapse of uncertainty would kill their momentum and their will to fight against that thing. The thing out there, just outside the light.

Isaiah stepped forward. He hid any sign that his grip on things was slipping. His body had ached in protest, but now his adrenaline was pumping. "Follow me close," he said in a calm voice. "We'll go around the far side of our pickup. We got our equipment in the bed. Grab something to defend yourself with if it comes down to it."

The man in the boots nodded. His eyes were wide and almost entirely enveloped by his pupils. His hair hung around his face under his hat in matted clumps from sweat. All three men mustered their composure. They crept, bent-backed and stiff-legged, over the shattered glass and out the front door. They searched for signs of something moving in the milky darkness, but nothing stirred. The cruiser sat running, the passenger side only a short distance away, but they didn't want to chance a blind run.

The three of them slid between the King Ranch and their pickup truck, holding their breath. Isaiah stood fast, his shoulders against the side of the truck's bed, and he scanned the area with the gun held tight. He motioned for the others to reach into the bed.

Hound Dog searched and withdrew the first thing he had clamped onto. It was the bulky chainsaw.

"Get the ax," he whispered to the man in the boots behind him.

The man crept forward, reached over the bed with careful trepidation, and patted around with his hand. He couldn't latch onto anything. He stood to his full height and leaned over the bed of the truck, sweeping his arm in a wide berth, his hand making no purchase

With a sudden and furious clang, the ax was brought down into the bed of the truck. It made a horrible sound as its blade sunk hot and fast into the truck bed metal. The man in the boots yelped in surprise and, in dull pain, fell backward onto the King Ranch, feeling for his arm. But it was gone. He no longer had a left arm at all. It lay dumb and heavy in a pool of crimson in the bed of the pickup truck. The monstrous thing stood tall on the other side of the truck, black against the red night sky. It growled and wrenched the ax free.

Hound Dog hollered and fell to the ground. Isaiah turned to see the commotion and immediately fired in the direction of the growling, towering creature. The gunshot lit the night like a flashbulb and they saw the figure's ghastly visage for a split second. The shot deafened them as well, silencing the screams for a moment until their hearing returned with a soft ringing.

The full blast of the shot missed its mark, but its spread peppered the creature's shoulder, sending tufts of clotted hair and a fine red mist spraying into the night. In response, the thing howled angrily and kicked the rear quarter panel of their truck. It collapsed like tinfoil and sent the back-end spinning.

Isaiah leapt out of the way. Hound Dog scrambled to his feet and nearly made it clear in time, but was clipped by the truck's revolving rear and went down holding his hip. The chainsaw flew from his grip. The man in the boots, whose name they never got, was not so lucky. While holding the bloody stump where his arm had been, the bed of the truck swung around and crushed the man as he knelt in agony between their pickup and his own King Ranch. His head cracked like an egg inside his white cowboy hat. His bones crunched and his skin split apart and blood sprayed in all directions, and for one full second after, the only sound in the night was Soda Speak's gurgling generator, which sounded like it was running on fumes.

The beast was the first to recover and wrenched the ax free from the truck bed with one furious jerk. It lurched forward, bent and bleeding, one arm hanging loose from its socket. Isaiah raised the shotgun again, pumping the second and final casing into place, but, just as he fired, realized he caught the creature in a half-swing overhead. The blade narrowly missed Isaiah's skull but made contact with the barrel of the gun as he jumped back. The swing reduced the shotgun barrel to a pinched, sawed-off plaything, and the shot missed entirely, mostly blowing a chunk from the ground and spattering into the gas pump.

Isaiah braced himself for an explosion. All his muscles tightened, his skin went cold, and his penis shrank into itself as he waited for the sudden death that would meet them all. But the pump didn't blow. Instead, steamy gasoline poured from it and began to pool on the cooling ground. The air around them was suddenly inundated with its acrid, pungent smell.

Isaiah began backing away, his arms straight out, ready to dart toward the road or the woods, and try his luck out there. But he knew he wouldn't make it. He could feel his legs giving way. His adrenaline was nearly depleted, and he was on the verge of collapse. The great beast stalked closer, raising the ax once more, as if to throw it. Isaiah could see it in the thing's burning eyes.

What a way to die, he thought. *At the hands of something no one believed in. What would they say about me? Hell, who would say it?*

He closed his eyes and began a prayer, waiting for the sweet release of a swift end and a deep sleep, when Hound Dog, down but not out, lunged forward on his one good leg and swung and drove his elbow into the injured side of the beast's abdomen with all his weight. The creature lost its footing and stumbled aside, dropping the ax and sending Hound Dog into a graceless fall.

Isaiah heard the creature hit the gravel with a thud and groan. He took the opportunity Hound Dog had bought him to seize the chainsaw lying on its side only feet away. He bent over, flicked the switch, and yanked hard at the pull-crank.

Nothing.

He tried again and tweaked something in his lower back. His muscles cramped, but he saw the creature was on its feet again and trudging toward the ax.

The chainsaw choked and coughed. It rumbled, grumbled, but refused to roar to life. Isaiah's hands held the grip and the starter-handle tightly, and he could feel the beginnings of blisters forming. "Come on, you bitch," he growled.

The saw choked and spat but lay there, stupid and dead. He risked another look up and saw the monster had retrieved the ax, the handle now impossibly long and the bloody blade matted with gravel and dirt. It turned to face him and began its lumbering shamble in a steady, long-stride gait. It's eyes were aflame with hate and murderous rage.

Isaiah's vision clouded, darkness increasing at the edges, and his body started to shut down. He shook his head violently, spat, and pumped the primer one, two, three, and seven times with his thumb, flipped the choke, and yanked one last time, nearly throwing his arm out of its socket. The chainsaw revved and finally came to life and he stood tall, erect, and back awake. He rushed forward, using his left leg like a crutch, and met the ax blade's descent with an upward thrust of the sputtering chainsaw. The point of contact was shockingly anticlimactic. The ax blade drove the chainsaw back so far that it cut into Isaiah's t-shirt and shoulder. But it gave Isaiah an opening. As the creature began another roundhouse swing, Isaiah thrust the chainsaw forward and penetrated the creature's abdomen between two ribs. The beast swatted Isaiah away, practically knocking him unconscious, and then grabbed the sputtering chainsaw blade so hard the chain seized up and the saw shut down. He gingerly extricated it from between his ribs with a painful howl and then held it up, probably planning to beat Isaiah's brains out with the handle end.

By then, Isaiah couldn't have said he blamed him. He was completely spent and on the verge of delirium, but he still crab-legged backward with his butt dragging the ground until he bumped into the King Ranch. He watched helplessly as the creature lunged forward, ready to bash him into pieces, but the police car suddenly swept in sideways and knocked the beast backward. It fell into the gas pump and slumped to the ground. The thick black fur covering its hulking body was soon matted with gasoline, but the creature wasn't out cold and it started to get back up.

Hound Dog sat in the driver's seat of the cop car, calling for Isaiah to get in. Isaiah hustled over and leapt into the passenger seat, nearly slamming his ankle in the door. The two men watched as the thing began to get to its feet, still holding the dead blade of the chainsaw in its bloody hand. Hound Dog threw the car in reverse and began peeling out backwards.

Consumed with pain and rage, the creature took one uneven step, howled in frustration, and then smashed the gas pump with the chainsaw chassis, leaving it where it lodged. It turned toward them and started to commence a mad pursuit, but the battered gas pump suddenly exploded and the underwater in open air evaporated in a swoosh pf blinding whites and yellows.

The monster, the Soda Speak, the King Ranch, and Cooter's generator exploded, one after another, and Hound Dog and Isaiah, who had careened backwards into a shallow gully, watched in disbelieving relief.

The two men pulled away and onto the road, headed God knew where. They didn't talk for a long time and instead just watched the road. Occasionally their sight drifted to the trees standing around them, hiding now what seemed to them a million dreadful things. The events that night had taught them anything could be out there. Anything they had told themselves was made-up could be true. And they could all be waiting or hating or hungry.

In the darkness of the cab, Isaiah heard something coming from the man beside him. It sounded like Hound Dog was crying. When he looked over at him, he saw tears in the man's eyes, but he wasn't crying. He was laughing. Isaiah was taken aback at first, but as the events of the night began to replay in his head, he, too, felt a fit of something bubbling up inside of him.

"Frigging ax-squatch," Hound Dog said. And the police cruiser erupted with exhausted, exasperated laughter. It was a painful laughter. Their bodies screamed against it. Their throats went chalky and sore. But they laughed until they cried.

And the world outside the car made no sound.

Their laughter came to a staggered end and their senses returned to them.

Isaiah eventually turned to Hound Dog weakly, with half-shut eyes, and spoke through struggling lips, "You good to drive?"

Hound Dog, also fatigued, but still adrenaline perked, nodded. "I'm managing." He shifted in his seat and winced against the pain in his hip. He went to say something, but Isaiah was unresponsive, his face smeared like a bug against the passenger window. Hound Dog looked back to the road unfolding before him. He started thinking about what was next. What could possibly be next? How could he possibly live the rest of his life like a normal person after something like that? His hip hurt like hell, and he was losing feeling in his left leg, but he remembered the man in the hat. He remembered Luther Robicheaux's bloody handprint. He thought about the cocksure young policeman whose car he was now driving, and he was just happy to be alive. He was happy to be a volunteer fireman for Cotter County with no house. He wondered if he would call his wife, Darby, after all, and what he would even say. He started to wonder then if he would ever get to the point where he would try to rationalize what had happened to him that night. When would this become just a horrible accident that he refused to believe?

A chill coursed through him, making him shudder. All those things would be better considered in the light of day. Right then, the only thing worth thinking about was the road ahead of him, and the road behind.

Isaiah slept dreamlessly.

On her way back home from checking on her sister, Dorothy Burke drove on the wrong side of the road, just because she could. There were no other lights on the road, and she was all alone. The boys at the fire department had been clearing the trees all week, and they had done a swell job, too. She swerved back and forth, doing her best impression of a drunk driver just because she could. She giggled at herself.

It wouldn't be like this in a month, when everyone started coming back from their homes away from home, so she decided she would enjoy the freedom of a world without people. She knew it was just an expression, nothing but a feeling you get when you were one of the few to weather a bad storm. Still, the world did feel much different after a storm like that last one. It felt like the end of days.

A chill dripped down her spine, but it didn't leave. It settled there. She waited for it to melt away, but it didn't.

As she pulled up the hill, a mile away from home, she saw a man walking down the side of the road. As she got closer, she realized his upper body was smoking.

"Oh Lord in heaven," she said. "He needs help."

This is the moment every good Christian waits for, she thought. The moment of the Good Samaritan. The moment when you must stand as a light in the darkness and help the less fortunate.

She began to slow down, but nearly screamed when she got a good look at him. He was tall. Very tall, in fact, but that wasn't the first thing she had noticed, because he was stark naked. From behind, she could see he was beaten and bloody, and good Lord was he huge. One of his arms was cradling something in front of him, and his other hung loosely at his side. The man, the giant, became aware of her and limped across the road, out of the light, and found refuge among the trees.

She stopped the car and rolled down her window, scanning the darkness.

"Hello?" she called.

There was no answer.

"Hello? Sir, are you hurt?"

Finally, Dorothy could see his head peek out from behind a tree.

"Do you need some help, sir?" she said.

As the man emerged from his hiding place and limped toward her in silence, she could smell burnt hair and roasted flesh. She froze in her seat on the side of the road. Her breath caught in her chest and her throat swelled. She saw then that he wasn't just very tall, he was remarkably tall. He was bleeding and burned badly. And his face was a mask of something unnatural. His small eyes were wild and piercing in the darkness, his flat nose bled openly. And his burnt lips were split and revealed what looked like gigantic fangs. He raised his unbroken arm high above his head, and in his hand he held an ax.

"Good God," she whispered, and pressed her foot against the gas pedal.

She watched in her rearview mirror as the strange, menacing figure shrank back into the abyss. It became nothing in the darkness, but she knew she would see that goliath when she closed her eyes to sleep. The chill in her spine lingered as she drove on into the night.

I didn't see that, she thought. *I didn't just see what I saw. It was my mind playing tricks on me. It was the fumes from the pipeline. It didn't happen.*

And she forced herself to giggle. She checked her rearview mirror.

The world was a mighty bizarre place after a storm, she thought.

HAYDEN (W. H.) GILBERT is a native of Southeast Texas, whose early years were spent watching monster movies and reading all the scary bits of Stephen King books in the library. He is a returning contributor to the *Road Kill* series and has several horror stories published in various anthologies, including *What Monsters Do For Love*, *Monsters We Forgot*, and more. If you cannot tell, he loves sad monsters.

The Grave
Katherine Anne Porter

The grandfather, dead for more than thirty years, had been twice disturbed in his long repose by the constancy and possessiveness of his widow. She removed his bones first to Louisiana and then to Texas, as if she had set out to find her own burial place, knowing well she would never return to the places she had left. In Texas she set up a small cemetery in a corner of her first farm, and as the family connection grew, and oddments of relations came over from Kentucky to settle, it contained at last about twenty graves. After the grandmother's death, part of her land was to be sold for the benefit of certain of her children, and the cemetery happened to lie in the part set aside for sale. It was necessary to take up the bodies and bury them again in the family plot in the big new public cemetery, where Grandmother had been recently buried. At long last her husband was to lie beside her for eternity, as she had planned.

The family cemetery had been a pleasant small neglected garden of tangled rose bushes and ragged cedar trees and cypress, the simple flat stones rising out of uncropped sweet-smelling wild grass. The graves were lying open and empty one burning day when Miranda and her brother Paul, who often went together to hunt rabbits and doves, propped their twenty-two Winchester rifles carefully against the rail fence, climbed over and explored among the graves. She was nine years old and he was twelve.

They peered into the pits all shaped alike with such purposeful accuracy, and looking at each other with pleased adventurous eyes, they said in solemn tones: "These were graves!" trying by words to shape a special, suitable emotion in their minds, but they felt nothing except an agreeable thrill of wonder: they were seeing a new sight, doing something they had not done before. In them both there was also a small disappointment at the entire commonplaceness of the actual spectacle. Even if it had once contained a coffin for years upon years, when the coffin was gone a grave was just a hole in the ground. Miranda leaped into the pit that had held her grandfather's bones. Scratching around aimlessly and pleasurably, as any young animal, she scooped up a lump of earth and weighed it in her palm. It had a pleasantly sweet, corrupt smell, being mixed with cedar needles and small leaves, and as the crumbs fell apart, she saw a silver dove no larger than a hazel nut, with spread wings and a neat fan-shaped tail. The breast had a deep round hollow in it. Turning it up to the fierce sunlight, she saw that the inside of the hollow was cut in little whorls. She scrambled out, over the pile of loose earth that had fallen back into one end of the grave, calling to Paul that she had found something, he must guess what. . . . His head appeared smiling over the rim of another grave. He waved a closed hand at her: "I've got something too!" They ran to compare treasures, making a game of it, so many guesses each, all wrong, and a final show-down with opened palms. Paul had found a thin wide gold ring carved with intricate flowers and leaves. Miranda was smitten at sight of the ring and wished to have it. Paul seemed more impressed by the dove. They made a trade, with some little bickering. After he had got the dove in his hand, Paul said, "Don't you know what this is? This is a screw head for a coffin! . . . I'll bet nobody else in the world has one like this!"

Miranda glanced at it without covetousness. She had the gold ring on her thumb; it fitted perfectly. "Maybe we ought to go now," she said, "maybe one of the niggers'll see us and tell somebody." They knew the land had been sold, the cemetery was no longer theirs, and they felt like trespassers. They climbed back over the fence, slung their rifles loosely under their arms—they had been shooting at targets with various kinds of firearms since they were seven years old—and set out to look for the rabbits and doves or whatever small game might happen along.

On these expeditions Miranda always followed at Paul's heels along the path, obeying instructions about handling her gun when going through fences; learning how to stand it up properly so it would not slip and fire unexpectedly; how to wait her time for a shot and not just bang away in the air without looking, spoiling shots for Paul, who really could hit things if given a chance. Now and then, in her excitement at seeing birds whizz up suddenly before her face, or a rabbit leap across her very toes, she lost her head, and almost without sighting she flung her rifle up and pulled the trigger. She hardly ever hit any sort of mark. She had no proper sense of hunting at all. Her brother would be often completely disgusted with her. "You don't care whether you get your bird or not," he said. "That's no way to hunt." Miranda could not understand his indignation. She had seen him smash his hat and yell with fury when he had missed his aim. "What I like about shooting," said Miranda, with exasperating inconsequence, "is pulling the trigger and hearing the noise."

"Then, by golly," said Paul, "whyn't you go back to the range and shoot at tin cans?"

"I'd just as soon," said Miranda, "only like this, we walk around more."

"Well, you just stay behind and stop spoiling my shots," said Paul, who, when he made a kill, wanted to be certain he had made it. Miranda, who alone brought down a bird once in twenty rounds, always claimed as her own any game they got when they fired at the same moment. It was tiresome and unfair and her brother was sick of it.

"Now, the first dove we see, or the first rabbit, is mine," he told her. "And the next will be yours. Remember that and don't get smarty."

"What about snakes?" asked Miranda idly. "Can I have the first snake?"

Waving her thumb gently and watching her gold ring glitter, Miranda lost interest in shooting. She was wearing her summer roughing outfit: dark blue overalls, a light blue shirt, a hired-man's straw hat, and rough brown sandals. Her brother had the same outfit except his was a sober hickory-nut color. Ordinarily Miranda preferred her overalls to any other dress, though it was making rather a scandal in the countryside, for the year was 1903, and in the back country the law of female decorum had teeth in it. Her father had been criticized for letting his girls dress like boys and go careering around astride barebacked horses. It was said the motherless family was running down, with the grandmother no longer there to hold it together. Miranda knew this, though she could not say how. She had met along the road old women of the kind who smoked corncob pipes, who had treated her grandmother with most sincere respect. They slanted their gummy old eyes side-ways at the granddaughter and said, "Ain't you ashamed of yo'-self, Missy? It's aginst the Scriptures to dress like that. Whut yo' Pappy thinkin' about?" Miranda, with her powerful social sense, which was like a fine set of antennae radiating from every pore of her skin, would feel ashamed because she knew well it was rude and ill-bred to shock anybody, even bad-tempered old crones; though she had faith in her father's judgment and was perfectly comfortable in the clothes. Her father had said, "They're just what you need, and they'll save your dresses for school . . . " This sounded quite simple and natural to her. She had been brought up in rigorous economy. Wastefulness was vulgar. It was also a sin. These were truths; she had heard them repeated many times and never once disputed.

Now the ring, shining with the serene purity of fine gold on her rather grubby thumb, turned her feelings against her overalls and sockless feet, toes sticking through the thick brown leather straps. She wanted to go back to the farm house, take a good cold bath, dust herself with plenty of her sister's violet talcum powder—provided she was not present to object, of course—put on the thinnest, most becoming dress she owned, with a big sash, and sit in a wicker chair under the trees . . . These things were not all she wanted, of course; she had vague stirrings of desire for luxury and a grand way of living which could not take precise form in her imagination, being founded on a family legend of past wealth and leisure. But these immediate comforts were what she could have, and she wanted them at once. She lagged rather far behind Paul, and once she thought of just turning back without a word and going home. She stopped, thinking that Paul would never do that to her, and so she would have to tell him. When a rabbit leaped, she let Paul have it without dispute. He killed it with one shot.

When she came up with him, he was already kneeling, examining the wound, the rabbit trailing from his hands. "Right through the head," he said complacently, as if he had aimed for it. He took out his sharp, competent Bowie knife and started to skin the body. He did it very cleanly and quickly. Uncle Jimbilly knew how to prepare the skins so that Miranda always had fur coats for her dolls, for though she never cared much for her dolls, she liked seeing them in fur coats. The children knelt facing each other over the dead animal. Miranda watched admiringly while her brother stripped the skin away as if he were taking off a glove. The flayed flesh emerged dark scarlet, sleek, firm; Miranda with thumb and finger felt the long fine muscles with the silvery flat strips binding them to the joints. Brother lifted the oddly bloated belly. "Look," he said, in a low, amazed voice. "It was going to have young ones."

Very carefully he slit the thin flesh from the center ribs to the flanks, and a scarlet bag appeared. He slit again and pulled the bag open, and there lay a bundle of tiny rabbits, each wrapped in a thin scarlet veil. The brother pulled these off and there they were, dark grey, their sleek wet down lying in minute even ripples, over pink skin, like a baby's head just washed; their unbelievably small delicate ears folded close, their little blind faces almost featureless.

Miranda said, "Oh, I want to see" under her breath. She looked and looked—excited but not frightened, for she was accustomed to the sight of animals killed in hunting— filled with pity and astonishment and a kind of shocked delight in the wonderful little creatures for their own sakes, they were so pretty. She touched one of them ever so carefully. "Ah, there's blood running over them," she said, and began to tremble without knowing why. Yet she wanted most deeply to see and to know. Having seen, she felt at once as if she had known all along. The very memory of her former ignorance faded, she had always known just this. No one had ever told her anything outright, she had been rather unobservant of the animal life around her because she was so accustomed to animals. They seemed simply disorderly and unaccountably rude in their habits, but altogether natural and not very interesting. Her brother had spoken as if he had known about everything all along. He may have seen all this before. He had never said a word to her, but she knew now a part at least of what he knew. She understood a little of the secret, formless intuitions in her own mind and body, which had been clearing up, taking form, so gradually and so steadily she had not realized that she was learning what she had to know. Paul said cautiously, as if he were talking about something forbidden: "They were just about ready to be born." His voice dropped on the last word. "I know," said Miranda, "like kittens. I know, like babies." She was quietly and terribly agitated, standing again with her rifle under her arm, looking down at the bloody heap. "I don't want the skin," she said, "I won't have it." Paul buried the young rabbits again in their mother's body, wrapped the skin around her, carried her to a clump of sage bushes, and hid her away. He came out again at once and said to Miranda, with an eager friendliness, a confidential tone quite unusual in him, as if he were taking her into an important secret on equal terms: "Listen now. Now you listen to me, and don't ever forget. Don't you ever tell a living soul that you saw this. Don't tell a soul. Don't tell Dad because I'll get into trouble. He'll say I'm leading you into things you ought not to do. He's always saying that. So now don't you go and forget and blab out sometime the way you're always doing... Now, that's a secret. Don't you tell."

Miranda never told, she did not even wish to tell anybody. She thought about the whole worrisome affair with confused unhappiness for a few days. Then it sank quietly into her mind and was heaped over by accumulated thousands of impressions, for nearly twenty years. One day she was picking her path among the puddles and crushed refuse of a market street in a strange city of a strange country, when, without warning, in totality, plain and clear in its true colors as if she looked through a frame upon a scene that had not stirred nor changed since the moment it happened, the episode of the far-off day leaped from its burial place before her mind's eye. She was so reasonlessly horrified she halted suddenly staring, the scene before her eyes dimmed by the vision back of them. An Indian vendor had held up before her a tray of dyed-sugar sweets, shaped like all kinds of small creatures: birds, baby chicks, baby rabbits, lambs, baby pigs. They were in gay colors and smelled of vanilla, maybe . . . It was a very hot day and the smell in the market, with its piles of raw flesh and wilting flowers, was like the mingled sweetness and corruption she had smelled that other day in the empty cemetery at home: the day she had remembered vaguely always until now as the time she and her brother had found treasure in the opened graves. Instantly upon this thought the dreadful vision faded, and she saw clearly her brother, whose childhood face she had forgotten, standing again in the blazing sunshine, again twelve years old, a pleased sober smile in his eyes, turning the silver dove over and over in his hands.

KATHERINE ANNE PORTER was born in 1890 in Indian Creek, Texas. She was a journalist, essayist, novelist, and political activist; today she is best known for her short stories in collections such as *Flowering Judas and Other Stories*; *Pale Horse, Pale Rider*, and *The Collected Stories of Katherine Anne Porter,* which earned her the 1966 Pulitzer Prize for Fiction and the 1966 National Book

Award for Fiction. Porter was nominated for the Nobel Prize for Literature in 1964, 1965, 1966, 1967 and 1968. She died in 1980.

Ambush and Blood for a Hoodoo Cowboy
Cedrick May

Freeman fell back hard on his ass after trying to stand again, holding his left hand tight against the bloody mess soaking his shirt and trousers from the bullet wound in his side. He leaned his bare head back into the hot desert sand, breathing heavy, straining his neck to look up the dusty incline leading to the cave entrance cutting into the side of the hill. Down below, he could hear the men who had ambushed him and his posse just moments ago. After they'd shot his horse out from under him, he'd managed to scramble to a rock outcrop that hid a trail up the eastern side of the valley wall to a cave entrance. He'd made it half-way up to the cave before his legs gave out.

It was then that Freeman realized he'd been shot.

Lying flat, Freeman was hidden by the face of the cliff from anyone looking up from below. Hoofbeats clopped loud against the rocky trail that centuries of runoff had worn between the two sections of what was once a single large plateau, creating the narrow valley Freeman and his crew intended to cut through on their way to Amarillo station.

"Stupid, stupid! So goddamned stupid!" Freeman hissed as he flipped over and began dragging himself over the hot sand, inching up the incline toward the cave. He suspected the gang of outlaws he and his posse had been following probably spotted them back in Briscoe County, so he should have taken better precautions when coming up on a bottleneck so ripe for an ambush, but they were tired and got sloppy.

Yeah, we got sloppy, sloppy and now dead . . .

Freeman had left seven good men dead down below, six deputized Marshals and a Seminole Lightrider (who'd once pulled his ass out of the fire back in Oklahoma), all of them shot down by sharpshooters perched on the wide overhead rocks jutting out from the canyon walls on the western side.

The bullet wound in Freeman's side throbbed like a hot poker to the beat of his pulse. He stopped for a moment to catch his breath, resting flat on his back in the blazing sun. He raised his left arm and looked at his hand to see it glistening from fingertip to elbow with his own fresh blood.

Goddamn . . .so much blood. How's there so much blood?

Freeman rolled over to drag himself further up the trail when he heard rocks being kicked by a clumsy boot from down below. He pointed the Colt revolver he'd been gripping in his right hand and fired a shot down the incline, narrowly missing the scar-faced stalker who lost his hat as he flung himself back behind the cover of the rocks at the foot of the slope. There was a flurry of laughter from beyond the rocks as the concealed stalker cursed at Freeman in Spanish. Freeman held his revolver pointed at the top corner of the dusty hat the swearing bandit had lost in his hasty retreat. The cursing eventually subsided, and on the first glimpse of movement, Freeman pulled the trigger again, narrowly missing the hand that had shot into view in an attempt to retrieve the hat. His shot sent the dirty Stetson in the opposite direction of the startled hand, that had withdrawn with haste behind the base of the rock outcrop again. There was more cursing from the aggrieved bandit and laughter from his compatriots.

"The next chicken-shit bastard gets his balls blown off!" Freeman said back in Spanish, the sound of his voice echoing through the canyon.

The laughter suddenly died down. The next voice spoke in English.

"I know you're shot, Freeman. Don't make this any harder on yourself, now."

Freeman knew this voice well.

Freeman had put Gil Dayton away eight years prior for a string of robberies and murders that left two-dozen people dead, including a sheriff, several deputies, and passengers on the Central Pacific he derailed with dynamite in Utah back in '73. Freeman had just been promoted to Deputy Marshal in '78 after serving with Bass Reeves for two years, and the Service assigned him to track down and bring Dayton in, dead or alive, after Dayton killed a bank teller during a robbery in Cheyenne. Good men died bringing that bastard to justice.

"It ain't so bad, Gil," Freeman called out, grunting hard as he pulled himself forward, leaving a bloody trail in the dirt as he dragged himself toward the cave entrance. "I'm looking at you right now," he lied. "Gonna put a hole in your head if you don't throw down your weapons and surrender."

More laughter echoed through the canyon.

Freeman knew bluffing wasn't going to work, but they were cocky now, overconfident, and he knew that might give him an edge, if only for a few moments.

"You're a right brave man, Freeman, I'll give you that," Dayton called back over his gang's laughter.

Freeman knew his odds were long and time was short. He looked down at the blood flowing between his fingers covering the wound in his side, then further down, at his boots caked with the bloody dirt he left behind.

So much blood? Where's it all come from?

Dayton was still talking to him, but all Freeman heard was a murmur as he laid his bare head down to rest for a moment. The sand burned the side of his face, but Freeman didn't mind it so much. It took his mind off the throbbing wound. As he lay there in the mean heat of the Texas sun, the hot pulsing in his side started to slow down, calming to a dull numbness, which was a relief.

Freeman jerked at the falling sensation that startled him awake. When he realized he had dropped his revolver, he grasped at the dirt in a panic until he had it in his hand again, pointing it all around in case someone had come up on him.

Stupid, stupid!

He scolded himself as his vision eased back into focus. Dayton was still talking, as was his way. Freeman remembered Dayton to be a real loudmouth but suspected he had only been out for a few moments. He braced to crawl some more when he saw the shadow cresting over the side of the cliff to his right.

Freeman swung the pistol and fired into the silhouette. A hat flew into the wind followed by a dark spray of blood and bone and brain matter blasted through the back of the figure's head. Freeman looked through the gaping hole where a human face used to be until the dead outlaw fell backward off the rocky ledge, disappearing into the valley below. Freeman heard dull thuds as the body bounced down the side of the cliff.

Freeman whipped his arm back down and squeezed off two shots toward the bottom of the incline from where two more of Dayton's gang were trying to rush him. His shots failed to find their targets, but the shooting drove the ambushers back behind the cover of the rocks. There was frenzied return fire, but the outlaws couldn't get a good bead on Freeman lying prone so far up the incline. There was more loud cursing, but this time Freeman could hear Dayton in the mix, screaming obscenities at his gang in both English and Spanish for their incompetence before turning his fury to Freeman.

"You black bastard! Look'it what you've done! I ain't playing with you no more now."

While Dayton raved, Freeman renewed his crawling, pulling himself the last several yards up the incline and into the shade of the narrow cave opening.

"You motherfucker! I'm done dickin' around with you, killing one of my boys!"

"And I'm going to kill a lot more of them, just like I did back in '78," Freeman yelled back, "Yeah, I'll do that and a lot worse if you bastards don't throw down your arms and surrender!" Leaning his shoulder against the cool rock of the cave-entrance wall, Freeman popped the cylinder of his revolver open to see only two bullets remaining, with four empty chambers staring back at him. He squeezed the cylinder shut.

"You ain't scared, are you? You ain't scared at all, you arrogant shit! Think you're so smart 'cause you caught me with my guard down one time, right? I'll show you— yeah, I'll show you something right good, *Marshal* Freeman!" Dayton's bellowing echoed through the canyon. He said something in Spanish that Freeman didn't catch, followed by the sound of shuffling boots.

Freeman looked into the cloudless blue sky. A large, black bird flew in a wide circle overhead. *A vulture? Crow?* Freeman wondered absently. Closing his eyes, he let go of the bloody wound in his side and took hold of the finger joint hanging from his mojo-bone necklace.

"You ain't never been scared for yourself, so let's see if you're so brave on somebody else's account!" Dayton said something in Spanish again just loud enough for his gang members to hear. There was a lot of scuffling about, and then a loud thud followed by a pained scream cut short by what sounded like another blow. Freeman squeezed his eyes shut tighter in the realization of who the scream belonged to.

Onacona! The Lightrider he'd befriended in Shawnee Town, Oklahoma.

"Let me tell you," Dayton continued ranting, "what I dreamed of doing to you every moment I was in that hellhole of a prison you sent me to—"

Another desperate scream echoed through the canyon. Freeman clenched the mojo-bone tighter, wincing at the sound of his friend's agony and the laughter of Dayton's goons.

"You hold on, Onacona," Freeman yelled out in Creek—or at least he *felt* like he was yelling, *"I'll get you out of there, just you hold on!"* There was more mean laughter, and Freeman couldn't be sure if Onacona could hear him, couldn't tell if his voice had enough strength in it to carry down to the canyon floor. The wound in his side became a spreading numbness that crept up into his armpits. Freeman felt his shoulders relax, even as he tried with all his might to work up the strength to pull himself back to the edge of the cliff where he could get a good bead on Dayton and do some good with the last two shots in his revolver, but he couldn't move an inch.

Freeman looked back into the blue sky and saw two more birds circling overhead with their cousin. His hand relaxed on the handle of the Colt revolver.

You hold on, Onacona . . .

The mojo-bone felt smooth and slick as he ran his thumb along its length, coating it with blood from his gunshot wound.

"While I sat in that filthy hole in Pennsylvania," Dayton continued, his voice becoming angrier with each word, "I dreamed about all the suffering I'd inflict on you, how I'd start with your ears, then cut out your eyes. Then while you were leakin' and bleed'n from your head, I'd start on your fingers and toes, making you guess which one or the other I was going to cut off next. And once I ran out of those, I'd go back to working on your head, maybe take off your nose and ears, or maybe those thick lips to wear as a trophy on my hat . . ."

The sound of Dayton's voice began to fade as Freeman fought to clear away the dark spots coming in at the edges of his vision. *Stupid . . . stupid!* he thought, gritting his teeth. *The canyon was an ambush point, clear as day . . . stupid!* Freeman pushed that useless, repeating cycle from his mind to focus on the matter at hand, to help his friend.

"Since you're so fucking *smart*, so fucking *brave*, all squirreled away up there in your hidey-hole, I'll just have to take all my creativity out on your boy down here while you listen—take off the injun's ear, Jack!"

The scream that came next was enough to raise the spirits of the dead. Freeman clenched his teeth so hard they hurt.

You hold on, Onacona . . .

The numbness crept into his wrists and Freeman felt the tips of his fingers feel like they were getting thick. He gripped the mojo-bone tighter in his left hand as his right went dead.

Hold on . . .

Freeman's mind drifted to thoughts of his great-grandmother, who had given him the necklace on her deathbed, *"Eyi yoo daabobo ọ, ọmọ mi,"* this will protect you, my child . . . The words in Yoruba sounded in his ears, as if she were there with him now. *"Máṣe gbàgbé idan ti mo ti fi fun ọ,"* do not forget the love I have given you . . .

Idan . . . Idan . . . The love? . . .The magic? The old words were blurry, out of focus—which did she mean?

The finger bone in Freeman's grip felt warm as his memory drifted to the old days, back when he was a child, enslaved on Master Singleton's Texas plantation back East, back before the war.

Freeman felt his whole body begin to float as his mind drifted back to a time when he was six—or was it seven or eight years old? It was always difficult for someone born on the plantation to know how old they were, as the servants weren't allowed to keep records, much less read or write (and Freeman had never even heard of such a thing as a "birthday" or "birthday party" until after freedom came). Master Singleton—*Marse Singleton*—was strict about his slaves staying illiterate, so keeping track of such things required a good memory for the number of seasons passing or signs. Freeman—before he became "Daniel Freeman"—remembered a time of having just lost his second front tooth, and running to show his great-grandmother, Maisie—though he and everyone else who knew her called her either Maise or (like him) Mamma Abi.

"Momma Abi, Momma Abi!" Cuffe (Freeman's name before the Freedom Days came) called out as he ran into the hot, cramped cabin where his great-grandmother was boiling a meal over the flames of the wide, stone hearth, "Lookit I've done!" He held out the bloody, little tooth that swam in a swirl of blood and slobber. His gap-toothed smile and sense of satisfaction were as wide as the hearth his great-grandmother was cooking over.

"Ooh! Lookit dat, mi Elẹwà!" she said, exaggerating her excitement while holding both hands to her cheeks. She always called Cuffe *Elẹwà*, a word from the old world, her lovely. "Here—let you Mamma Abi hab de toof," she said as she plucked the tooth from his raised palm.

Cuffe sat at the table near the hearth while she retrieved a small mortar and pestle. After rinsing the blood off the tooth, Mamma Abi sat next to Cuffe and dropped it into the mortar and began grinding it into a fine powder, just as she did with his first one. From time to time, she would pass the mortar to Cuffe so he could have a turn at grinding, the whole time they quietly recited the words to a spell in the old language that she had taught him.

"Dagba mi ga ati alagbara, bi igi Baobab . . ."

Mamma Abi and Cuffe sang the words quietly, over and again, as they ground the tooth. Mamma Abi added small sprigs of herbs to the mix—a basil leaf, some fresh moss, an acorn. They worked together kneading the finely ground up bits of tooth and herbs into a dough that she baked over the fire until they had a small, golden loaf the size of two small fists.

"Now, ye go an eat dis *whole* bread, little *Elẹwà*, an doan let *nobody else* tase it—dis a pow'ful conjure dat make a grown man wither an die, you hear? *Idan alagbara ni eyi fun ọ nikan!"*

Little Cuffe—little *Elẹwà*—understood well and did as his great-grandmother instructed, as he always did. Mamma Abi was from the old world, and her words were not to be taken lightly or for granted. She was the oldest and most respected among the other slaves on the Singleton plantation, being one of the last to arrive in the hold of a ship at age twelve.

So, when Cuffe (*Elęwà*) came into the world, she was the one who taught him the old language from the start. She had pretty much taken over raising the boy after his mother, her seventh granddaughter, died giving birth to Cuffe. Cuffe (*Elęwà*) had no brothers or sisters, though he had many cousins on this and neighboring plantations, but none of them seemed interested or able to hold on to the old tongue the way he did. Cuffe (*Elęwà*) figured it was because, unlike him, they did not have regular contact with his great-grandmother who made it a point to make sure he knew of the old language and the ways of the spirits that had followed her from the old world. She taught him the ways of the conjure women, even though he was a boy.

And it was this day, The Day of the Tooth, that came to Freeman in his floating numbness as he held the mojo-bone tight in his grip, afraid to let go until the vision of his great-grandmother, Mamma *Abiona*, played itself out. It was his last happy memory with her before late that night when neighbors came to her door with news of the terrible thing that had happened to Delilah.

The knocking startled Cuffe awake as he slept in his straw bed at the foot of his grandmother's own. After answering, Mamma Abi quickly dressed and exited the cabin with Rebecca from several cabins down the slave-quarters row. Cuffe pretended to sleep as they left, though he was awake for most of the night. He listened to the distant wails of distressed women and the anguished groans of desperate men as they drifted in on a listless summer breeze through the paneless window. The following day, he heard whispers of a terrible, nameless thing that Master Singleton had done to Delilah, something so awful that while the rest of the slaves went through the motions of tending to the plantation's daily business, some of the old women—too aged to work the fields or slow for work in the Big House—went to slaughtering an unusual number of animals that the blacks were allowed to keep out back of the quarters. It was chickens mostly, but one of the aunties slaughtered two baby pigs, another auntie a lamb. Cuffe knew that they were the best of the bunch. The blood of all these animals was drained into buckets. By noon, the old women had hauled and carted the carcasses out to a clearing, nearly a mile into the woods, where they piled them in the center and set them afire. The women all stood in a circle around the fire, silent, while Mamma Abi chanted words from the old world over the conflagration. Cuffe, crouched behind a tree at the edge of the clearing, watched the cremation of the slaughtered animals, listening, afraid.

That night, after the last candle was extinguished, a strange silence hung in the darkness throughout the slave quarters. No voices could be heard, the animals made no sounds, the crickets failed to sing their song, and the night toads had gone mute. It was then that Mamma Abi set out into the night with six of the elder women of the quarters. Cuffe snuck to their cabin window and peeked out, watching as the seven figures, led by Mamma Abi, disappeared like wisps into the darkness of the forest's edge. Each woman carried a bladder filled with animal blood.

Cuffe knew all of the aunties with Mamma Abi, all of them known or whispered to be hoodoo conjure women—though none of them knew the language from the old world the way his great-grandmother did.

Cuffe's father came a little later to take him to his cabin for the night, warning his son that, "Tonight's no night to be in a conjure-woman's house." When Cuffe said he was afraid for his great-grandmother's safety, his father said, "Now, doan' you worry none, son. She'll be back right soon enough. You jus' come stay with me a while, until things calm down around here."

That "while" turned out to be longer than Cuffe anticipated when the next morning there were screams and hollers from all around the plantation—the first ones coming from the Big House.

Master Singleton was dead.

As he lay with his face pressed hard against the rough, cool wall of the cave entrance, Freeman held the mojo-bone in a bloody grip. He could still hear the screaming down in the valley below, and the sound made him grip the finger bone tighter. He felt the piercing sting of the bone's sharp edge cutting into the palm of his hand, the only physical feeling he had left in his body as the creeping numbness overtook the rest of him. Words came into his mind. Old words, ancient words his great-grandmother had taught him as a child began to take form as he worked his mouth to conjure long-unuttered syllables, pushing air from tired, failing lungs.

"Esu . . . Eshu . . . Legba . . ." he croaked through a dry throat, finding clarity in hearing the sounds spoken out loud, *"Legba! Legba! Eshu Elegbara! Ran mi lọwọ lati wa ọna!"* As the words passed through his lips, Freeman felt the mojo-bone pulse with a beat like a red-hot throbbing sore in his hand. His eyes opened to see the black birds circling over the canyon. His vision narrowed as the sky turned red, and the flock began to revolve faster and faster, until their circling formed the impossible blur of a black ring against the redness of the swirling sky. Freeman found a sudden surge of strength and screamed out at the red sky—

"Legba! Legba! Ṣii ilẹkun si jẹ ki angẹli kọja!" Freeman felt the pulsing heat of the mojo-bone in his hand

spread through his whole body, causing him to fall over into the dust, his body throbbing with a fire from within. As he writhed in the dust of the cave floor, a vision came to him, a familiar face, a beloved ancestor, reaching her hand out to him. Freeman, burning with an internal heat that threatened to consume him, reached out to take her hand. Their fingers met just before the agony and the darkness overtook him.

Young Cuffe sat behind a tree outside his great-grandmother's cabin, hands pressed against his ears as he endured the agonized screams coming from inside.

It had been like this for three days, ever since his great-grandmother was carried in from the woods the morning Master Singleton was found torn apart, as if a pack of animals had gotten into the house and ripped him to pieces. It was whispered that Mistress Singleton was there in the bedroom with him, too, catatonic at first, and all covered in his blood. There was blood smeared all on her face and in her hair and mouth—blood *everywhere*. When the servants worked up the nerve to enter the room and give her a shake, she awoke from her stupor and started ripping her hair out in whole patches, screaming like a beast—until men from the neighboring farm came to hold her down until the doctor and constable could be fetched. The grown-up children just wept and wailed down in the parlor room.

Master Singleton's butler, who'd seen the whole thing, told some of the kitchen girls who passed it on to others that the Mistress had bloody gaps in her mouth where some of her teeth were broken or missing.

On the second day, there were more whispers that the constable and his men had found the Mistress' missing and broken teeth among her husband's remains. They said some of his bones had been gnawed on or split open by something fierce.

Cuffe wasn't allowed to go into his great-grandmother's cabin. He'd spent nearly his entire life living there, but his father didn't want him to see what had become of his great-grandmother. But, like most children who were too young to be of any good use for labor, he was left to his own devices to wander on the plantation under the general supervision of the elderly slaves. But most of the elderly who could still get around were women, and they were there, inside the cabin, tending Mamma Abi. And Pappa was, as usual, away working in the fields, trying, like the rest of the able-bodied servants, to maintain some semblance of plantation order in this time of uncertainty and chaos.

Neither his pappa nor the aunties wanted him inside the cabin, but he had resolved to disobey this day.

The screams had been terrifying enough, but what he saw as he entered the cabin threw a shock of fear through his whole body. It took all his strength to force his legs not to turn and run back out into the yard when he saw his great-grandmother, held down by six women, bucking and arching her back into impossible contortions as they struggled to hold her down. Her legs and one arm were tied to the bedposts with thick rope, but one of her arms had come lose, and now she was beating at the women—her old friends—with her fist in between what seemed painful, spontaneous contortions and incoherent yelps and screams.

The women holding her down didn't notice Cuffe, even though he had inched his way closer against every instinct in his seven-year-old body.

Between convulsions, one of the women holding Mamma Abi down with her whole body weight spotted Cuffe and yelled for him to leave the cabin. There was a sudden pause in Mamma Abi's violent thrashing as her back pounded like a hammer against the hard straw mattress and she croaked her first coherent word in almost three days.

"Mmmmnnnn . . . *no!*" She lay there, eyes wide, staring at Cuffe across the small room. Her free arm reached out to him, palm up, all five fingers splayed wide while one of the women struggled to hold the limb at bay. Cuffe could hear Mamma Abi taking hard, rasping breaths, as if her lungs were full with the consumption. "Come . . . come close, chil'," she croaked with her hand held out to him, stiff and unyielding.

When Cuffe took a step toward her, all of the women holding Mamma Abi screamed at him to stay back, to leave the cabin, but Cuffe's eyes were fixed on his great-grandmother's wild saucer eyes, and they summoned him.

Cuffe gasped when his great-grandmother's free hand darted out like a striking snake to clasp his forearm tightly. He instinctively pulled back against her powerful grip, but relaxed when he saw the softness that had come into her eyes. As he relaxed, he noticed that a powerful heat was coming off of her body, a strange fever-heat, like the fireplace when it was stoked up on a cold winter night. His fear gone, Cuffe reached up with his free hand to stroke Mamma Abi's cheek. A tear fell onto his hand as his great grandmother pressed her face into his tiny palm, her body now relaxed.

The women holding Mamma Abi scrambled to tie her free arm down until a shrill voice stopped them, dead still—

"*Duro!*" Cuffe shouted in the old tongue—"*Fi rẹ silẹ nikan!* Leave her be!"

The women froze in place, not fully in command of the words he spoke, though they understood enough to see that something had come over the boy, that he had become more than that empty, meaningless name that his master had given him at birth. Cuffe—no, *Elęwà*, the great-grandson of *Abiona Adedeji Ọyáwálé*—had earned the right to be heard. Each of Mamma Abi's attendants relaxed their grip on her tortured body.

"*Elęwà, Elęwà,* my beautiful chil'," Mamma Abi said in a deep, bone-tired voice. "Take de necklace . . ." She raised her chin as she opened the top of her blouse to reveal the mojo-bone necklace that she had always worn. Cuffe grew up fascinated by the strange little bit of bone hanging from the woven leather cord. He gently worked the necklace from under her chin and over her head. He held it up, noticing the bleached white surface of the finger bone seemed to glow with a light of its own. At that moment, Cuffe suddenly felt all the eyes in the room on him.

"*Fi si, Elęwà*—put it on," Mamma Abi said.

One of the women holding Mamma Abi's legs gasped.

"*Fi si, Elęwà . . . Fi si!*" Put it on . . .

Young Cuffe did as his great grandmother bade him and slid the mojo-bone necklace over his head, touching the finger bone as it lay low against the coarse osnaburg fabric of his shirt.

Cuffe took a step back, startled as one of the women let out a piercing scream. All six of the women began weeping into their hands and moaning sorrowful tones as they rocked and whispered prayers of protection and warding, weaving his name into their incantations over and over—"Cuffe . . . *Elęwà* . . . Cuffe . . . *Elęwà . . .*"

Cuffe stared at Mamma Abi, who smiled back at him with a wide, tired grin, a look of pride shone in her gray eyes. *"Eyi yoo daabobo ọ, ọmọ mi,* I will protect you, my child," she said to her great grandson as she gripped his left hand in hers, *"Elęwà! Elęwà! Maṣe gbagbe! Do not forget, my child! Take my hand! Take it!"* Her voice trailed off with those final strange words. But what could she mean?

Was he not already holding her hand? He gripped her hand tighter.

Her eyes seemed to stare through him now, distant, unfocused, as if peering at something far beyond him. Her eyes snapped back into focus and confusion took over. Cuffe watched as recognition faded from her eyes that suddenly grew wild with pain as she let out a scream that pierced deep into her great grandson's soul.

At that moment, her hand burned with the heat of a branding iron, searing the tender flesh of Cuffe's own left hand with an agony he had never known before. He fell to his knees, screaming, trying to jerk free without success. Cuffe's great-grandmother gripping his hand even tighter, both of them screaming into the rafters of the slave quarters, their combined voices blending into one while six conjure women, wailing chants of protection, held the convulsing, elderly woman from the old world down on the bed with all their might.

Onacona lay face down in the hot sand, blood pouring from his right ear. His heart beat hard against the inside of his chest as he turned his face toward Dayton, who was raving at the man holding a large knife in one hand and part of Onacona's right ear in the other.

"Goddamn it, Jack! I meant for you to cut off his *whole* ear, not just part!"

Jack, a dirty-looking scoundrel wearing an old Confederate frock coat, shook his head and threw the earlobe onto the ground. "I thought you wanted to do it slow-like, Day. A piece at a time—"

"I want a *whole part* of this Injun every time! Now get to it 'fore I let Fernando have 'im."

Jack looked over at the other four men standing to the side, waiting their turn, all hard men he and Dayton picked up out of Chihuahua and Juarez. Fernando had been part of Dayton's crew back in '73, and had a part in dynamiting the Central Pacific before he broke off in '77 to take care of some family business in San Guillermo. Fernando shot Jack a wink and a wide smile. Jack turned away, snarling, as he wiped blood-covered fingers on his trousers.

Onacona breathed hard into the sand, sending hot plumes of dust flying with each breath, while the outlaws bickered with one another. He forced his attention away from the pain in his ear to focus on the conversation. He had all their names now, though he had not known Fernando's until this very moment. He certainly knew of Jack, though—a new member of Dayton's crew out of Kentucky, and the reason he was riding with Marshal Freeman.

Jack was a known cattle thief and smuggler on the border between Native and Federal lands in Oklahoma. After murdering a cattle hand a few months back, the Seminole Lightriders—the Native police force on tribal lands—got serious and sent Onacona to track him and his crew down. Onacona and his posse of Lightriders managed to apprehend most of Jack's crew and their boss without incident, but Jack was a former Confederate scout, a slippery snake who had out-maneuvered them at every turn.

The Lightriders pursued him south, but once Jack crossed the border into Texas, he was out of Native jurisdiction, which put Onacona in a difficult spot—he couldn't *legally* arrest the man outside of Okahoma's Indian territory, and the federal government wasn't keen on extraditing white men into Native custody, regardless of the crimes they may have committed on the reservations. But Onacona couldn't see letting him go free and clear, so he left his posse behind and tracked Jack by himself, through a chunk of North Texas, until he met up with

Freeman in Abilene. He and Freeman had worked together on a case at Shawnee Town, near Oklahoma City, where the U.S. Marshal Service had sent Freeman as a liaison for the bureau because he spoke Creek. He'd helped the Marshal Service extradite a murderer into federal custody back then, so when Freeman heard Onacona's story, he agreed to pay back on the debt the Marshal Service owed to the Seminole Lightriders by deputizing Onacona as a temporary Federal agent, promising to help him get his man and take him back to Native territory for prosecution according to *their* laws.

Onacona knew Dayton had given Jack first dibs on him and Freeman, seeing how he hated both Negroes and Indians. And it was a test of just how savagely brutal he could be. Onacona knew this, too, as Jack stepped over and pulled him to his knees by his ponytail, arms tied tight behind his back so he couldn't reach up. Onacona screamed out at the pain.

"You hear that, Freeman!" Dayton continued yelling toward where Freeman had shot one of his men, his voice echoing throughout the canyon, "I'm gonna' cut him up! Cut off his ears, cut off his nose, take off his fingers, one by one, just so you can hear him suffer—*you hear that, you son of a bitch?*" There was no reply this time, and Onacona could see the silence was pissing Dayton off. "I know you're wounded, but don't you die yet! I got somethin' I want you to hear first!" He nodded over at Jack. "Go on, now," he instructed, pointing his gun toward the kneeling Onacona.

Jack pulled back harder on the ponytail he had wrapped in his left hand and smiled down at Onacona as he touched the cold edge of the blade against the back of his ear.

Onacona closed his eyes and gritted his teeth, bracing for what he knew was coming.

But nothing came.

Onacona felt the pressure on his scalp disappear as Jack let go of his long ponytail. Onacona opened his eyes to see that Jack had stepped back, waving his free hand frantically at something in the air in front of his face. He also saw that the sky had suddenly gone overcast.

"What the fuck is wrong with you?" Dayton growled in frustration.

"You don't see it?" Jack said, continuing to wave his hand as if batting away some tormenting pest. "Big green fucker flying in my face? Biggest horsefly I ever seen!"

"I don't see nothin' but you wavin' your arm like you're trying to take off," Dayton said back, shaking his head. "Goddamnit!" he spat, turning to the other four men who were laughing at Jack's expense. "Fernando! *Cortaste el—*" but before he could finish the order, Jack let out a scream that made everyone jump, pointing their guns in his direction. Jack was bent over, holding the side of his face.

"Holy shit!" he screamed out again in agony. "It stung me!" He continued holding the side of his face with his free hand while swinging the blade around in front of him, slicing at the air at some invisible antagonist.

"For the love of Gawd!" Dayton had become fed up with Jack's antics. *"Córtalo!"* he barked, turning to Fernando. *"Cut off the injun's goddamned ear."*

Onacona, who was closest to Jack, saw a green pus mixed with blood begin to seep from beneath Jack's hand. He looked up into the swirling, dark clouds that had come in unnoticed by Dayton and his gang. The shade had grown into a deeper darkness. He stared back at Jack, who continued his pained screaming while taking wild swings at the empty air. His wheeling and slicing had become so violent, Dayton and his other three men had become distracted and were now trying to calm him down, circling him, arms outstretched.

All except Fernando, who closed in on Onacona, smiling as he drew a long skinning knife from his belt.

Onacona looked back into the dark sky to see the clouds swirling around a central point directly above.

Strong medicine, he thought.

Jack had created a huge ruckus with all his screaming and wild flailing of his knife. Dayton and his crew were now cussing him out in English and Spanish, circling and trying to get an angle on him. He was holding the knife with both hands now, and a huge, red boil the size of a fist covered his right cheek, oozing an inordinate amount of pus and blood from a seeping pore at its apex. "Get it away from me! *Get it away!*" he kept screaming, not intending to target any of his comrades with his swings.

"There ain't nothin there!" Dayton hollered back at him as he holstered his pistol and tried to put himself in position for a tackle, without getting stabbed.

Fernando grabbed Onacona by the hair and yanked his head to the side, pressing the blade of the skinning knife against his throat.

"Maybe I should cut your throat, instead?" Fernando hissed into Onacona's good ear.

"Do as your *madre* tells you, *hijo de puta*," Onacona spat back.

Fernando slapped him so hard he fell sideways, face first, into the dust again. Onacona gritted blood-stained teeth and growled in pain as Fernando pulled him back to a kneeling position by his hair.

"I'm going to enjoy taking my time with you, *cabrón*," he said, as he pulled Onacona's head to the side and slid the skinning knife to the back of his uncut ear.

A sudden sharp scream from Dayton caused Fernando to stop what he was doing and glance over at his boss. Dayton was yelling at the top of his lungs and cursing to high heaven as he spun around like a dog trying to catch its own tail, reaching for Jack's camp knife, its blade buried half its length into the back of his left shoulder.

With a sudden surge, Onacona unfolded his legs and pushed himself upward to bury the back of his head into Fernando's chin. Onacona felt the crunch of Fernando's teeth shattering upon impact, causing the big man to yelp as he fell backward, stunned by the pain and surprise.

The Lightrider saw that Fernando had dropped his skinning knife at his feet, but with his hands tied behind his back, he knew he didn't have a chance in hell of doing anything with it before the outlaw drew his pistol and blew his brains out. He looked up to see Fernando sitting on his ass in the dirt, shaking his head in confusion as blood dribbled from his mouth through broken teeth.

Onacona glanced back over his shoulder to see Dayton cursing and trying to get at the long knife sticking out of his back, while Jack lay on the sandy trail, gagging, one hand on his throat, while his three companions struggled to hold him down. He was bucking and kicking like a man being dragged to his own hanging.

"It's in me!" Jack sputtered, holding his throat, "Oh, God, it's in me a'stingin'!"

Onacona swung back to lock eyes with Fernando as he shook off the blow he'd taken to the chin. He scowled at Onacona and reached for his pistol.

Onacona threw himself forward onto the ground and rolled, bringing his right boot down into Fernando's face, burying the shank of his spur deep into the bandit's left eye socket. Fernando screamed and grabbed Onacona's leg with both hands, but the Lightrider kicked as hard as he could to drive the long shank deep into the back of his assailant's head, causing him to go limp and fall sideways into the dirt. Breathing hard, Onacona yanked the gore-covered spur out of Fernando's head, dripping with the dead man's blood and brains.

Onacona rolled over to see Dayton had stopped trying to get at the knife sticking out of his back. He had drawn his pistol and was yelling at the guys holding Jack down to move out of the way so he could put a plug in him. Onacona looked at Fernando's gun, laying right next to his face in the dirt, then up toward the knife lying several feet away.

Knife first, then the gun . . .

Before he could start rolling for the knife, he heard the ruckus going on several yards away take a new turn. Jack had stopped screaming and Dayton was giving distressed commands in Spanish that didn't make any sense.

A chill like a cold river shot down Onacona's spine as he looked over to see that the three outlaws who'd been holding Jack down had pulled out their own blades and were butchering him—they'd already opened him up from his neck to the bottom of his belly, the one who'd been holding his legs had both arms elbows-deep in Jack's intestines. Dayton looked on in shocked distress, croaking out orders in disjointed Spanish, seeming unable to make sense of what was happening in front of him as he took a step back. When one of the outlaws yanked out a piece of Jack's lung and bit into it, Dayton fired his first shot into him.

Onacona rolled over the top of the knife and then flipped back onto his face with it in his hand, cutting desperately at the ropes binding his wrists. Another gun blast nearly caused him to drop the knife. He looked up to see Dayton had shot another one of the men eating at Jack's innards. Now, two bodies lay in contorted positions next to Jack's eviscerated corpse. The last outlaw, covered from face to feet in Jack's gore, stood and turned toward Dayton. His eyes were rolled back so far, they looked like a couple of boiled eggs. He said something in a language Onacona didn't understand. His tone was all wrong, too—like a voice coming from a distance out of a hollow cave. He took a step toward Dayton. Dayton shot him square in the chest, blasting a hole clear through the other side. The last of his outlaw gang fell on his face in the dust at Dayton's feet.

Onacona felt his ropes unravel and fall away. He scrambled to Fernando's dead body and grabbed his revolver, spinning to point it at Dayton. "Keep still, now!" he warned.

Dayton caught Onacona's movement out of the corner of his eye and swiveled to face the Lightrider. Even in the strange darkness that had come over the canyon, Onacona saw how pale Dayton had become, his eyes wide with shock.

"Whu . . . what's happenin' . . ." Dayton stammered, as he aimed his pistol at the indigenous lawman. "What in hell got into them? What kind of savagery—"

"Throw down your gun," Onacona commanded, "by the authority of the U.S. Marshal's Service, you're under arrest."

Dayton just shook his head.

"What happened? . . . Whu . . . Why would they do somthin' like that?" he muttered, turning to stare back at Jack's mutilated corpse.

"It's over, Dayton," Onacona said, taking a step forward. "Throw it down now." The whole side of the Lightrider's head, where Jack had cut off his earlobe, began to ache. The jolt from his next footstep caused a shock of pain that made him wince.

"You saw it, right?" Dayton's voice began to rise, become frantic, "You saw what they did to him, right? I ain't never . . ."

The pain in Onacona's head got worse. The gun in his hand began to get heavy. He felt the wind pick up, start to push him sideways, causing him to sway a bit.

"I'm only going to tell you one more time, Dayton . . ."

Jack's corpse jerked.

"Holy shit!" Dayton swung his gun around and pointed it at the corpse.

Onacona fell to one knee, the side of his head pounding. He held his pistol unsteadily toward Dayton, but the pounding in his head and the growing wind were throwing him off balance, causing his aim to wander.

"I saw it move!" Dayton looked back at Onacona for affirmation. *"You saw it, right?"*

"Strong medicine," Onacona muttered under his breath as his arm became too heavy to hold the pistol any longer. His head throbbed, started to spin. *Must have been the fall from my horse . . . hit my head*, he thought as he swayed slightly back and forth.

The wind had grown strong enough to throw dust into the air, swirling like the clouds through the canyon pass.

Jack's corpse jerked again, causing Dayton to jump and scream, backing away and toward Onacona. Dayton froze as the opening in the body widened and a dark, formless mass—larger than the body itself—pushed up, slow and dripping from the mangled entrails, to take the shape of a huge, winged beast standing in the wet husk of Jack's corpse. No less than seven feet tall, it loomed over the two men as the wind swirled around it, and a booming groan echoed through the canyon as it took its first deep breath. Two pairs of wings unfolded from behind its back as two glowing, red eyes popped open to stare at Dayton and Onacona standing below, side by side. It moved toward them, stepping out of the husk that was once Jack.

Dayton screamed again and emptied his pistol into the thing, the bullets bursting through the back of the still-forming, vaguely human-shaped creature.

The bullets didn't faze it one bit.

Onacona heard the clicks of Dayton's empty pistol. Dayton started backing up as the dark thing advanced. Onacona stayed put, resting on one knee, watching until the monstrous thing that had crawled out of Jack's carcass had backed Dayton against the canyon's east wall. It reached out with an enormous hand to pin him against the rocks. Onacona heard the loud cracking of bones in Dayton's chest as the dark thing flattened him against the side of the canyon. Dayton let out a faint, hissing gurgle, then fell limp, head lolling to one side.

Head still throbbing, Onacona watched as the dark thing that was pinning Dayton's lifeless body to the canyon wall turned to look back at him with eyes that burned like the white-hot fires of a furnace. It's once-featureless face now having taken shape into something—*into someone*—that he knew very well.

Freeman woke up to see Onacona sitting next to him. Looking around in confusion, he tried to sit up, but a pain in his side caused him to wince.

"Whoah! You've got to take it easy, now, my friend. Lost a lot of blood," Onacona warned, reaching for his canteen.

"Where's Dayton?"

"Dead."

"His gang?"

Onacona looked into the bright, blue sky above. The birds were gone. He unscrewed the lid of his canteen then helped Freeman sit up. "Here, take small sips." Freeman took a small swig of water.

"I had a dream," Freeman said. "Saw my great-grandmother, the one who gave me this here mojo-bone—" Freeman reached up with his left hand and winced in pain. He looked down to see that the palm of his hand had been terribly burned, as if held over an open fire. "Jesus—my hand!"

Onacona took Freeman by the wrist, held his hand palm up and poured water over the burn wound, causing him to wince again. "Goddamnit—look at me," Freeman said, noticing the blood covering his arms and clothes. "Oh, shit!" Freeman leaned forward, started feeling around his left side where the bullet had gone through. He pulled up his shirt and wiped at the dark stains. After a moment, he shot a look at Onacona.

"No, there's no hole," Onacona assured him.

"But I was shot, I know it—I think it came out the back, too, with all this blood . . ." Freeman continued feeling around until he realized the only wound on his body was the burn on the palm of his hand.

"You weren't dreaming, my friend. All that blood came from somewhere." Onacona pointed at the mojo-bone necklace. "I don't know what it is, but I saw it."

"What'd you see?"

"I saw one of the great spirits come in on the wind."

"And what else?"

"It had your face."

Freeman lowered his head.

"I haven't used thehoodoo in a long time. A very long time. Seems like a dream having ever learned it at all . . ." Freeman fell silent, thinking about Mamma Abi, and what the hoodoo had done to her. "I don't know anything about great spirits," Freeman continued. "Thing is, every time you use it to do harm, it takes something out of you. And it takes away as much as it gives." Freeman looked at the burn in the palm of his hand. "I wonder what all it took from me this time?"

"You ask questions only a Medicine Man can answer," Onacona said, helping Freeman get to his feet, bracing his arm around his neck to help steady Freeman's shaky legs. "Let's collect the horses. Find something to bandage that burn."

Although the wounds in his side were gone, Freeman groaned from the pain that continued to ache there.

"Jesus," Freeman said, noticing the side of Onacona's head. "They did some rough prunin' on your ear."

"Could have been worse."

"Sorry you won't be able to take your man back with you into custody."

"Same for you. It's a real mess down there."

Freeman stood, leaning against Onacona's shoulder, not moving, staring out of the mouth of the cave across the valley.

"You still want to ride with me, after what you saw down there today?" Freeman asked. "There's something terrible inside me I don't know can be controlled. No telling when I might have to call on it again."

"I looked into the face of Death, today," Onacona replied, "and I knew he was my friend."

Freeman studied the man holding him up by his shoulders, as if seeing him anew. He nodded, then smiled grimly, as the bloodied companions limped, supporting each other, out of the cave and into the blazing light of the hot desert sun.

CEDRICK MAY is a writer, filmmaker, and native Texan who lives and teaches in the Dallas/Fort Worth area. After nearly two decades of writing academic books and essays, he has returned to his first and foremost love—writing speculative fiction. In particular, he writes horror, supernatural thrillers, and tales of the Weird Wild West. He is currently hard at work on more stories of the Weird West and the supernatural while finishing his first independent feature film, *The Awakening*. More of his fiction can be found at *Aphelion Webzine*.

We Share Our Rage with the River
Josh Rountree

My father and I rode down to the river with Ellis to fetch him a wife. There had come a hard rain the night before, and the Brazos was angry. I had a notion that if I got too close, the river would swallow me up and carry my bones to the sea. I was ten years old and convinced all manner of mysterious creature lurked beneath the roiling brown waters. Despite my fear, I had a yearning to swim out there and discover for myself.

Maybe to keep swimming and never come back.

We dismounted, boots sinking into the mud along the bank. I helped lash the horses to cottonwood trees so they wouldn't spook. My father, my older brother Ellis, and a few of the other men waded into the river, unravelling fishing nets behind them. The Brazos wasn't deep along this stretch, but the rains made the river violent. Father shouted commands, waist deep and struggling against the current.

Mr. Bolton and a couple of the other men from the settlement remained with me on shore. They held long ropes that had been tied off to the nets, ready to pull. Mr. Bolton's shirtsleeves were rolled up, and his trousers were tucked into tall leather boots. Like all of us, he was ripe with sweat, feeling the humid air all the way to his bones. The brim of his hat drooped forward, but not enough to hide the hungry expression he wore as he watched the others fan out across the river.

The horses whickered; their hooves punched the earth.

They wanted no more to do with this than I did.

Mr. Bolton looked up, saw me comforting one of the mares with my hand on her mane.

"Don't worry, boy," he said. "We won't be here long. Water running wild like this stirs them river women into a frenzy. They'll be on the move. No better time to catch a wife than right after a hard rain."

He wasn't wrong.

We'd been there no more than ten minutes when everyone started shouting. Out in the middle of the river, one of the nets jumped. Something big splashed about, frothing the surface of the river. Part of me wondered, maybe hoped, that they'd found a knot of water moccasins, but I knew better. My father shouted as the rope in Mr. Bolton's hand went taut.

"Get to pulling!" Mr. Bolton heaved, and the others joined in.

I stood beside the two-wheeled cart we'd brought to haul our catch back to town. I felt like running, but I'm sorry to admit, my curiosity held me in sway. I watched as they dragged the woman up from the shallows, bound tight in the net and thrashing. She cut a furrow through the mud as they pulled her toward the cart. Her howls were low and throaty, like a bobcat. The men yelled and laughed and cursed as they wrestled her onto the cart and tied her down. She smelled like turned wet soil. She smelled like lightning storms. Her tail tapered into a heavy fin, and she tried to slap out with it, but the net only drew tighter. I was shocked to see her breasts, something I'd only heard older boys describe, uncovered and drawn in tight against her chest by the netting. Copper colored scales covered her body, bright as polished pennies.

She kept howling. Her mouth was crowded with teeth, slender as sewing needles. Her eyes were liquid gray, like lead poured fresh from a crucible. I could read no expression in those eyes, but I could feel her terror just the same. My breath hitched up in my chest, and my heart was thundering.

It was the first time I'd seen a river woman before she changed, and I fought back the warm tears forming in my eyes.

Ellis pushed past me, slathered in river mud and grinning. He threaded his fingers into the woman's tangled green hair, turned her head to get a better look.

"You got yourself a good one." Father stood behind Ellis, one hand on his son's shoulder. He was still winded from the struggle, and spoke in a slow, halting manner.

"You think I did?" said Ellis.

"Oh, yes. I can always tell."

Father remembered I'd come along, frowned when he saw the red in my eyes.

He had no patience for my sympathies.

My brother called his new wife Marigold, because our late mother had told him stories of a spry yellow cat called Marigold that she'd kept as a child, and Ellis had grown to fancy that name. They tied her down to the old four poster mahogany bed that had come with my parents all the way from Virginia, back when this land still belonged to Mexico. Mr. Bolton helped my father carry in a couple of armloads of cut cedar logs, and Ellis fed them one by one into the gaping fireplace.

It was high summer, and Ellis had shuttered the windows, causing the heat to blossom and suffocate. By the time he had the fire raging, standing there in the doorway made me feel like a slab of meat in a smokehouse.

Marigold thrashed and howled as the temperature climbed. The fire threw sinister shadows up the walls and colored her agony in muted orange light.

"Takes a week or so for her to dry out?" said Ellis.

"Give or take," said Father.

Mr. Bolton allowed that two of his wives had taken nearly a month to dry out, but the third was ready in just a few days.

"I hope she goes quicker than that," said Father. "Whole place will be hotter than Hell until she does."

We left her there alone, and Father instructed me to stay clear of that bedroom for the duration of her ordeal. But I couldn't help myself. I'd wander past from time to time, open the door just a crack and peer inside. I watched her change, little by little. It took three nights of screaming for her tailfin to dry up and rot off. Another three nights for her new legs to grow in, long and bone thin, like a newborn calf. Her slender gray teeth fell like pine needles, replaced by a woman's teeth, white as morning snow. Delicate, uncalloused hands replaced her sharp, elongated claws.

When he was younger, Ellis would pull the tails off the quick green lizards that sunned on the front porch, just to see how they'd regrow. Watching Marigold slowly break and come back together again put me in mind of that petty cruelty. I was disturbed every time Ellis did it, but I watched anyway. And I'd seek out those lizards, if they ever returned, wondering what kind of magic animated them.

What happened to the river wives was a different sort of magic, I suppose. But no less horrifying.

One Sunday afternoon we heard tentative footsteps coming down the stairs. Ellis helped Marigold descend, his arm around her back. She wore a blue cotton night dress that belonged to Mama Agatha, and her legs trembled uncertainly beneath her.

Mama Agatha and Mama Lisbeth were clearing dust from windowsills and cobwebs from crannies, but they abandoned their rags and watched Marigold pass through the foyer like a ghost trying to catch her breath. My late mother had ordered a bit of stained glass from St. Louis for the transom over the front door, and sunlight filtered through, casting rainbows across Marigold's long blond hair. Her head darted around, surveying her new surroundings. Marigold was a beauty; her lips were red and full, and her eyes were gray whirlpools.

Their eyes were the only things that never changed.

Father sat at the secretary desk in the corner, marking numbers into a ledger. He removed his spectacles, stood, and studied Marigold with his hands on his hips. Ellis put his palm on her cheek, turned her to face Father. They inspected Marigold like a goat ready for shearing. She was a perfect woman, carved from my brother's dreams. Father had always told us that the river women became whatever we most wanted them to be. I had no intention of ever claiming a river wife, but if I was compelled to, I feared she might become something quite unlike those ideal women conjured up by the men in our settlement.

Ellis took Marigold as his wife that very day.

There was no need for a wedding ceremony.

No God would bless their union.

Marigold joined the other wives in their daily tasks.

I'd follow them around as they swept the longleaf pine floors and dug potatoes from the garden. I'd sit at the kitchen table and watch as they pounded out bread dough with hands and forearms. One afternoon, I joined them in the chicken yard to gather eggs. Mama Lisbeth and Marigold went right to their business, but Mama Agatha was well into her decline, so I carried her basket and undertook her share of the work.

It wasn't a couple of years ago that Mother Agatha looked young as Mama Lisbeth, but all her teeth had rotted out and her hair was a thin silver thicket. Her deep brown skin had gone ashy gray, and every step set her trembling, like dry branches in a gale.

The sun burned away all the clouds, and the air turned wet and heavy. I walked down to the river where the ordinary women worked at the laundry, then snuck a bucket of water back up to the chicken yard. The river wives ladled the water in an earthenware cup and passed it between themselves, taking slow sips with their eyes closed. I kept watch so as not to get caught.

The river wives breathed in the dank odor of the stuff with tears streaking their cheeks. For a moment, they remembered everything.

There wasn't much I could do to comfort them, but I could do this.

Mrs. Harold and her daughter Sarah walked past, carrying armloads of laundry. They wore calico work dresses with the sleeves rolled up, headed for the river. Sweaty strands of hair escaped their bonnets and clung to their shoulders like river moss. They spoke in loud, happy voices, almost as if they wanted to prove to the river women that they could.

Mrs. Harold laughed at something Sarah said. The sound drew Marigold's gaze, and she made a keening noise in her throat that was easy to interpret.

Mama Lisbeth stroked Marigold's long hair, offered her another sip of the brown river water once Mrs. Harold and Sarah had disappeared into the trees. I could feel the river wives' thoughts crashing into one another like waves. I grew up imagining everyone could read what the river wives were thinking, but I learned that wasn't the case. Maybe it was my youth, and maybe it was my kindness with the water, but they trusted me, and I understood what pained them.

The river called to them like a mother's voice, but they weren't allowed to answer.

Mr. Alexander's river wife had tried to sneak down to the Brazos a few years before, deep in the middle of the night when she figured she could make it. A few of the men on the way back from an Indian patrol found her, and she spent her last months lashed to a post at the edge of town, raising dry screams in a vain attempt to chase away the vultures.

The cup of water calmed Marigold. Her gray eyes splashed about, and her muscles relaxed. I'd noticed a bit of river water had the same effect on them as a glass of whiskey had on Ellis.

When our baskets were filled with spotted brown eggs, the women started back for the house, and Mama Agatha gripped my arm with her cold hand so I could help her along. My real mother had died during my birth, as Ellis was fond of reminding me, but Mama Agatha had assumed her role. I couldn't remember a time when Agatha wasn't there, humming tunes that put me in mind of faraway places I'd never see. Her songs were enchantments. They drew the calm from deep inside the soul, and they revealed secrets.

Mama Agatha understood things about me that I wasn't yet willing to admit to myself, but she never pushed. She allowed me to grow into myself at my own pace.

I led her along the path to the house like a child, and her frailty frightened me. River women could exist on land only for so long, and though it had been a lifetime for me, Agatha's years out of water had passed with the swiftness of a runaway stallion. I imagined her blood slowing and her heart growing still. I imagined I could smell the furious decay burrowing beneath her translucent skin.

Agatha's thoughts swam in her eyes. Love for me. A bone-weary tiredness. And worst of all, a sharp desperation that I wished I could ignore. I gave thought to changing course. I could escort her the few hundred yards down to the river. The water likely wouldn't save her at this point; she was too far gone. But at the very least she might look upon the lazy flow of her river one last time, and dream of days gone by.

I knew this is what she wanted. But I still remembered the sound of Mr. Alexander's river wife, screaming from her post, and no matter how strong my love for Mama Agatha, I didn't have the nerve to free her.

Marigold and Mama Lisbeth were far ahead of us when we saw a Karankawa man watching us from the recesses of the canebrake. Not twenty feet separated us. He was lean and muscled and tattooed, wearing a deerskin breechcloth and a beaded necklace. All Father's stories about the Karankawa warned of blood and scalps, baby eating, kidnappings, and violent attacks on women.

Fear chased through me, hot and primal.

I'd seen a live Karankawa only once before. He'd been navigating a canoe up a small stream that broke off from the Brazos. Father killed him with a rifle shot from a rise overlooking the river, and the man died without ever knowing we were there. The canoe kept going, carrying his body out of sight. Father told me the man was bound for Hell anyway, and he was happy enough to help him get there faster.

I shouted for help and tried to hurry Mama Agatha away, but she used what strength she had left to plant her feet in the long grass. If I'd pulled any harder, she'd have toppled to the ground.

The Karankawa carried a wooden bow at least six feet tall, and I knew he could kill us long before we'd make it back to the house. My shouting didn't stir him. He studied Mama Agatha, taking slow steady breaths, like he was in no hurry. Men's voices filled the afternoon, answering my calls, but none of them would arrive in time.

Mama Agatha wasn't afraid. I could feel it.

She was, instead, grateful.

She locked eyes with the Karankawa, pulling at him with those gray whirlpools. She hummed one of her ancient songs. I struggled to understand the deep blue confusion of her thoughts, but finally the pure desire for death rose up from the shallows.

The man released an arrow with a motion smooth as quicksilver. It struck Mama Agatha's heart, passed clean through her, and lodged into a fence post.

The Karankawa disappeared back into the canebrake and was gone before Agatha's body touched the earth.

Father assembled a dozen men. They rode through the scrub brush, and along the cedar infested river bottoms, hunting the Karankawa. They appeared back at the settlement long after dark, bloody and drunk. A brace of Indian scalps hung from Father's saddle, but there was no way of knowing if one of them belonged to the man who felled Mama Agatha. Father was fond of killing Indians, blaming them for every fault and failure in the land. The Karankawa people had lived and fished along these river bottoms long before even the Mexicans arrived, but that made no difference to Father. To him, the Indians were obstacles to be cleared away, like stones from a field, so new life could grow.

I never hated *anyone* that much. Not even Father.

The hunting party congregated at our house, where the men offered condolences and drank whiskey. Mama Lisbeth and Marigold served them cold dinner on the porch, and I hid away in the stifling hot kitchen, small in my grief.

The men were loud and boisterous, and I heard most of what they said. Mr. Bolton barked that if you get seven solid years out of a river wife, you're doing better than most, and Agatha had been out of the water for near a dozen. Mr. Alexander agreed, but also believed it was a terrible shame, her making it that long, only to be killed by a god-cursed savage.

Father was untouched by the tragedy, other than losing something he felt belonged to him. He'd lost interest in Agatha long ago. And besides, we all knew he'd be back down at the river again with a net soon enough.

Mama Lisbeth radiated tension, and her grief hung like an added layer of heat in the kitchen. While Marigold brought more food out to the men, Lisbeth took a rest. We sat together at the table with the windows open, listening to the sounds of nightbirds and sharp, drunken laughter. We chewed hard biscuits covered in honey and shared a pitcher of buttermilk.

I fought against the intrusive, swirling nature of her thoughts. It hurt me trying to shut her out, but my misery cut deeper than hers. I'd known Agatha my whole life; she was my mother in every way but blood. And while Lisbeth mourned Agatha's death, there was something more. She wondered if Agatha's fate might not be preferable to her own. I didn't need a reminder that maybe I could have done something to save Agatha; maybe I could still do something to save Lisbeth and Marigold.

My failures and my fears were not secret to me.

I closed my eyes.

I wasn't the person to help them; I was as out of place in our world as they were.

Ellis came into the kitchen, muddy boots heavy against the floor. Lisbeth leapt into action like a startled colt.

"Why are you hiding in here?" Ellis took a seat next to me and bit into one of the biscuits. His face was sweaty and red, and I could smell the whiskey in his blood.

"I'm not hiding. Just helping."

"Helping eat all the honey and drink all the buttermilk, I guess." Ellis grinned at me, but there was something hard in his eyes that reminded me of Father. They were two of a kind. Ellis was seven years older than me, and Father had already carved him into his ideal of a man. Young and lean and strong. Eager to claim his place in the world.

Lisbeth poured him a cup of buttermilk.

Ellis put his hand on my shoulder and squeezed harder than was polite. He liked me to know how much stronger he was. He'd rinsed most of the blood from his hands and arms, but it still stained his shirt and clotted in the scruff on his cheeks.

"Real sorry about your *mother*," he said.

He always said it that way. *Mother*. Like he wanted to make it known that I'd given up all claim to our birth mother. Like caring for Agatha and Lisbeth was a weakness.

"We killed that Indian," he said.

"Looks like you killed a lot of them."

"As many as we could." Ellis patted me on the back, misunderstanding my observation for approval.

"How many?" I asked.

"Oh, I don't know for sure," he said. "But enough to keep them behaving for a while."

It snowed once, when I was five, and Ellis spent all afternoon pulling me around on a sled he'd built out of spare lumber. We waged a snowball battle with the other children and climbed skinny trees slick with ice. From the boughs of one of those trees, we watched woodsmoke climb from chimneys and infiltrate the low gray clouds.

Having an older brother to share that day with had been a fine thing, indeed, but all that had changed.

"You should come out on the porch," he said. "I'll sneak you a whiskey if you want."

"I'm okay where I am."

"It's too hot to sit in here. And besides, you're getting too big to spend all your time following old women around the kitchen."

"She's not old," I said.

"Too old to be your playmate."

Lisbeth stabbed at the fire in the hearth with an iron rod. She was heating water in a pot, maybe for tea and maybe just to keep herself occupied so she could pretend not to listen. Lisbeth's auburn hair was knotted up beneath a bonnet, but gray streaks showed in the bits that escaped. Her face had grown sharper, and wrinkles pulled at her eyes. But for all that, I never thought of her as old. More *tired*, I suppose. But time chased after the river women faster than it did the rest of us, and soon enough I'd be leading Lisbeth around by the arm and watching her wither down to bones, just like I had with Agatha.

Ellis shook his head at me, all the while cleaning dried blood from underneath his fingernails with a knife blade. "I don't care what you do, but Father doesn't like you acting this way. You come out there and show your face for a few minutes and it'll go a long way." He gave me a questioning look, like I was a wild animal with motives he couldn't predict. Maybe I'd follow him to the porch on quiet, padding feet, or maybe I'd bite.

I wasn't sure about myself anymore either.

I only knew that being around Father and the other men made me intensely uncomfortable. They expected so many things from me that couldn't be reconciled with my own desires.

Father told me time and again how the men in this world must take what they want, else they'd wind up with nothing but leftovers and regrets. When he'd moved the family here from Virginia, he hadn't bothered with Mr. Austin and the old empresario's land grants. Father encamped farther downriver, in open defiance of Mexican law, and claimed a league of rich, black soil bottomland for himself. When the revolution happened, he marched off with a musket and came back a citizen of the Republic of Texas, with all the rights of a free landowner.

This was *his* small patch of earth now, and he never lost one night of sleep worrying about how he got it.

I wanted no part of it. I didn't want to inherit his farm, and though I was still quite young, I already knew I had no interest in taking a river wife. No interest in taking *any* wife, to tell it true. Maybe that's what Father saw in me that made him hate me so much.

But what I wanted didn't matter. Time would chase me down soon enough, just like it did the river women. The prospect of growing up terrified me.

Ellis waited for me to submit, but the silence dragged on like a song we were all tired of singing.

"You've been wrong since you were born," said Ellis.

"I guess maybe I have been."

Ellis hated when I didn't react to his meanness. I figured he'd box my ears like usual, but he acted like he didn't hear me.

"Maybe if you hadn't killed our mother, you'd have more than these animals to raise you up right."

Lisbeth hissed. Her anger was a sudden spike to my brain. Ellis pushed back the chair and the legs scraped against the floor with a sound like a sawblade cutting timber.

"You will tend to your own business, Lisbeth," he said. "You hear me?"

Lisbeth couldn't respond, but she turned away from us with a flush of fear that was hot against my skin.

Ellis stood over me, hair wild and tangled. He was unsteady on his feet, and I wondered for a second if I could tackle him. Things might have escalated then and there if Marigold hadn't walked into the kitchen with an empty serving tray and stopped in her tracks, unable to stifle a sharp gasp at the unexpected presence of her husband. Ellis took the tray from her and tossed it on the table. He put an arm around her shoulders and drew her in close.

Marigold went slack at his touch, and the dull resignation she projected made the milk sit heavy in my stomach.

"You may do as you wish," Ellis said to me. "But I will take everything I've earned, and I won't apologize for it."

Ellis was talking, but the words belonged to Father.

He left then, sweeping Marigold along, and Lisbeth sat back down across from me. She made a mewling sound that was as close as she ever came to crying. I took her hands and held them. We sat together, listening until the revels died down.

And we stayed that way until daylight came rushing over the horizon.

A week later, Marigold drank too much river water.

Father and Ellis were off chasing milk cows and half-wild mustangs. I spent the morning following Marigold and Lisbeth, helping with their chores, and by early afternoon we found ourselves in the orchard, gathering peaches and pears and figs in woven baskets.

The river was close. I could hear it cutting a path toward the ocean. I could smell the lake weeds and the fish. Sunlight splashed off the water and sparkled through the trees. Only the fear of being captured kept Marigold and Lisbeth from going home.

Chances are they'd make it. But what if they didn't?

They grew melancholy, being so close. Giving them river water like I did might have made it worse, but it was a forbidden kindness I couldn't resist.

I'd fetched a full bucket while they were plucking fruit from the trees, and now it was nearly empty. Mama Lisbeth had taken only one cupful, but Marigold had indulged with a destructive fervor. Insects hummed from the shadows, and Marigold swayed like she was dancing to their strange music. I had never seen her this way. Her liquid eyes raged like storm-tossed seas, and her cheeks flushed red as new scales rippled beneath her human skin.

All of this from a half bucket of water. I wondered how quickly Marigold would regain herself if she waded into the river.

Her thoughts lashed out, slapped me like horsewhips.

She kept no secrets hidden.

Marigold spun with her arms out, her golden hair on the wind, and she showed me memories of rushing water and winding underground rivers so deep that sunlight never found them. She might live a thousand years in the cold depths of the sea, but every breath on land brought her closer to the end. Her bare feet crashed against hard soil as she danced; her legs were abominations. There was no grace in her motion. She spun like a tornado, hoping to draw all the sharp and broken things close to her and send them flying outward again, tearing apart everything here built by men. Lisbeth grew frightened, looked around to make sure no one had spotted the commotion. She grabbed Marigold and pulled her down to the ground. Marigold screeched, but Lisbeth held her tight. Marigold struggled, finally shoved Lisbeth away, and she crawled toward me, shedding alabaster skin and old secrets.

Marigold's eyes were waterfalls, pouring from their sockets, and I couldn't look away.

Memories flowed from Agatha to Lisbeth to Marigold to me. The river might keep secrets from the land, but never from those who belong to her.

Marigold showed me a woman floating down the Brazos, face up with her hair fanned out along the brown surface, dead eyes clotted with cypress leaves.

She showed me the face of my mother.

And yet, it wasn't my true mother. That much I understood. This was not a woman who'd died in childbirth. This was a woman enraged. Horrified and embarrassed that one of the creatures her husband cultivated had given him a son, just as she had. The babe could never be a brother to Ellis. She'd taken the crying child, the *unnatural* child, and swaddled it in dishtowels, secreted it away while her husband followed oxen through the field, while her young son chased frogs and lizards, while the river women worked the butter churn.

She had taken the babe to the river.

She had taken *me* there.

And it had not gone well for her.

We were drunk on memories, not keeping a watch. The men found us there on our knees in the orchard, and we never heard them coming. Marigold howled, lurched upward. Ellis had grabbed her hair and pulled her to her feet. She hissed. A few of her sharp bits had returned. Stray teeth, one long razored thumbnail. A ridge of copper scales began at her nose and traced down both cheekbones. The skin on her neck had come loose and it flapped like laundry on the line.

Father came up behind Ellis, saw Marigold covered in gray blood and fighting to regain herself. Father's face twisted up like he'd tasted something awful. Ellis backed away, afraid of his lovely young wife.

Couldn't they see Marigold had become more interesting and more beautiful than she'd ever been before?

Father saw the overturned bucket, figured out exactly what was happening. "Ellis, take your woman to the house so we can dry her out again."

Ellis had lost the color from his face. He looked younger than his seventeen years. "I don't think—"

"Take your woman to the goddamn house!"

Ellis was more afraid of Father than he was Marigold.

He advanced on her, tried to take her arm and pull her along like he always did. Marigold let him bring her close, then she tore out his throat with her teeth.

Father struck Marigold hard enough to knock her to her knees again. Ellis fell, air whistling from the empty place where his throat had been. Marigold tried to stand, and Father hit her again. Something in her jaw broke loose and slid sideways. I climbed Father's back in an effort to pull him away. He shook me loose, put me on the ground and kicked me in the ribs. One of them snapped with a sound like a tree branch breaking in a storm, and it stabbed into me with every breath.

Father loomed over me. "Should have tied you up in a grain sack when you were born and tossed you in the river."

He kicked me again, snapped one of my fingers when I tried to grab his boot to stop him.

I'm confident he'd have killed me if Mama Lisbeth hadn't taken the woven basket, heavy with pears, and hammered it against the back of his head. The blow wasn't near enough to kill him, but it was enough to topple him to the ground and momentarily steal his wits. It was enough to buy us a few seconds.

No option remained except to run.

I helped Marigold to her feet, and together we followed Mama Lisbeth past the canebrake and into the tight web of cedars that stretched from the settlement down to the river. Branches slashed and blood flowed. Marigold's fury was a living thing, casting out in all directions like a fisherman's line, catching everyone it could. She was not her true self again, not yet, but the water was empowering, and no river woman in the settlement failed to understand her pleading, her urgent command. *This* was the time; *this* was the opportunity. Everyone at once. Coordinated escape. I could hear the rasp of kitchen knives against bare throats, and the clatter of spoons against fine China as they stirred poison into black coffee. I could hear hammers collapsing skulls and powerful men screaming as they were shoved bodily into blazing hearths. Marigold shared her rage with the river, and the river shared it with us all.

We reached the water and Marigold didn't slow. She splashed through the shallows until the water was deep enough to swim. Flesh peeled away and carried downriver in a torrent of blood. Her tail tore through the remains of her human body and slapped the water.

Marigold dove beneath and was gone.

Lisbeth waded into the river with more hesitancy, as if long years of conditioning assured her that this could not possibly be happening. Knee deep in the water, she smiled as the skin on her legs split up the sides like fabric coming apart at the seams. She waved for me to follow, then swam out to deeper waters.

She called out to me. The *river* called out to me.

But how was I supposed to follow?

I'd swam here a hundred times, and the water didn't affect me. Still, the river whispered and begged, assured me there was no better life than sleeping in sunken temples and navigating barnacled shipwrecks spun with seaweed. Mama Agatha was my birth mother— I understood that now—and I belonged to the river. The river had saved me from being murdered as a babe. Had risen up and drowned my father's wife or summoned *something cold* to pry me from her hands and send her corpse floating away into oblivion.

I was a child of the river, and I belonged here.

Either that, or the river was lying.

My eyes burned and every breath was agony. No home remained for me on the land, but I was too afraid to seek a home in the water. And Father could not be far behind.

Then I heard one of the songs Mama Agatha used to sing to me. A cradle song, old as the sea itself.

Mama Lisbeth was singing me home.

I waded out up to my waist, still uncertain, until I saw children pour from the trees and splash into the water. Sarah Harold and her brother Seth. Amos and Louisa and the Noble twins, barely old enough to walk down to the river on their own. A dozen more, at least. All of them, laughing and singing along. Mama Lisbeth called out, and they came. Her song grew louder, and the children walked toward her, not bothering to swim when the water got deep, but pressing on as if their shoes were filled with lead and they could not float. Heads sank beneath the muddy flow, and the children disappeared, one by one.

The song summoned me too, and I walked until the water lapped at my chin. Mama Lisbeth watched me approach, way out in the middle of the river now. Her voice cut through my bones, gave me no choice but to wade deeper, to join the children's chorus.

Lisbeth's gray eyes drew me in and the sunlight against her scales was blinding. Her smile was sharp, and her soul was vengeance.

Did all these children belong to the river?

I didn't hold my breath and I didn't cry.

I let the Brazos swallow me up and take me home.

JOSH ROUNTREE has published over sixty stories in a wide variety of magazines and anthologies, including *Beneath Ceaseless Skies*, *Realms of Fantasy*, *The Deadlands*, *Bourbon Penn*, *PseudoPod*, *PodCastle*, *Daily Science Fiction*, and *A Punk Rock Future*. His latest short fiction collection is *Fantastic Americana: Stories from Fairwood Press*. His novel *The Legend of Charlie Fish* will be published by Tachyon Publications next year. Josh lives somewhere in the untamed wilds of Texas, and tweets about books, records, and guitars at @josh_rountree

Refugio Remembers
Carmen Gray

They said it wouldn't happen like this. Rumor was we'd make it back home eventually, Refugio thought to himself, as he trudged along the road, exhausted and hungry. They'd been waiting five long days inside the fort for their fate. He marched alongside the other men, hands tied behind his back. He thought about his novia back at home, a place he would never see again. His heart ached. His body was tired. His spirit was broken. She'd protested his voluntary enlistment in the Texian army two months ago. His hope had been to secure land for their future by fighting for Texas' independence. But now, all their hopes and dreams for a life together were dashed. He prayed to La Virgen that his death would be swift. He hoped it would all turn out to be worth it, one day.

Then, Boom!
He fell to the ground.
Everything went black.

James stepped inside Our Lady of Loreto Chapel and heard an organ playing softly in the distance. He looked around for the source of the music but found only empty pews and a few candles lit. *Must have just been my imagination*, he thought to himself. All that talk of music must have left an imprint in his mind.

He was just here for Maria. Her grandmother had asked them to drive her to present her family history slides to the townspeople of Goliad, Texas. Maria's grandmother had ancestry dating back to Goliad and La Bahía, a Roman Catholic mission established by Spain in 1722. They had driven up to Perez Road, across from La Bahía, where Maria's great-great grandmother had once lived. She had stared wistfully at the white house that still stood there. She recounted some old people's stories about her grandmother combing her mother's hair while looking at the house, as if she were reliving a moment in time.

James thought Maria was a quiet observer and a good granddaughter. When Maria was fourteen, she'd explained to him, her mother died, so her grandmother felt more like her mother. James knew the story well from when he first met Maria, two years ago. They had literally met after bumping into each other at a coffee shop at the Blue Star Arts Complex in San Antonio. He'd accidentally spilled her coffee down her shirt. Thank goodness it had been iced, so it hadn't burned her, but it made a giant stain on the bright, white shirt that she'd worn that fateful day. He was so wrapped up in the tests he'd been grading, that he wasn't paying attention. He blushed when his eyes met hers, and he realized how beautiful she was—deep brown eyes and fair skin with light freckles. He was embarrassed and had offered to buy her a new shirt. She insisted it was fine, that she'd just finished her shift at a nearby art gallery and would be headed home anyhow. They exchanged numbers and that's how the whole relationship began. As he learned more about her, he realized she had a complicated past, which made him a bit nervous. He was not one for taking risks. He liked things simple and straightforward.

Maria's mother had been in a terrible car accident during a hailstorm. She had died almost immediately in a head-on collision. It was just Maria and her father after that, but her father had fallen into such a deep depression that her grandmother had stepped in to help. Her father was in and out of the hospital for treatment for a good year following the death. Maria relied heavily on her grandmother as a parental figure. During that time, she found solace in the stories her grandmother shared with her. She became familiar with long ago ancestors while helping her grandmother write an article for a Texas music magazine. Apparently, her Perez had been musicians. They had formed a famous orchestra long ago, in the mid-1800s. She and her grandmother had carefully sorted through files of pictures, and she'd memorized the sepia faces of the men holding their instruments as they stood right in front of La Bahía. The mustached men dressed in white shirts, and the raven-haired beauties in floor-length dresses gathered together in the courtyard for a rare photo-op on the cobblestoned ground in the same place that took its name from the Goliad Massacre.

"James," Maria said softly. He turned around and she reached for his hand. He looked into her deep brown eyes. "Will you light a candle with me for my mother?"

"Of course, my love," he said. Maria knew James was not a religious man by any means, but she appreciated that he was happy to oblige her. He pulled out a dollar for the offering to light a candle in the chapel. Maria whispered a prayer. Again, he heard the organ. "Do you hear that, Maria?" he said.

"Yes, yes I do," she said quietly. They both stood still, and Maria strained to hear the sound again. "It sounds like it's coming directly from outside," she said. "Strange. But Grandmother has told me the spirits are strong here and it's not unusual to hear things or see things you can't explain."

"Oh, come on," James scoffed. He rolled his eyes and gave her a kiss. "You don't really believe that woo-woo crap, do you?"

She gave him a look.

"James, you just don't get it. You've lived an easy life with no bumps in the road. No one close to you has ever died. Spirits inhabit different realms. You know I believe it. But this place doesn't care what we believe."

He stared at her sincere, pretty face. "We can agree to disagree, my love," he said finally. And she playfully punched him in the shoulder.

Sometimes, James really got on her nerves. He was a good man. A solid boyfriend. But this side of him—the side that seemed too stubborn or rigid about the metaphysical world—that part of him she wished could be different. He would never understand the connection she had with the spirits. She and her father knew a little bit about them. They regularly felt the presence of her mother in their lives. It was a subject Maria just didn't broach with James. He always explained it away with his logic.

They walked through the heavy wooden doors leading outside to the courtyard, silently. A limestone ramp invited them to ascend to an old brass cannon that pointed toward the field.

"Imagine what this place has seen, James. So much history, here," Maria said. "You sense no vibe at all?"

"It's something we project, my love," James observed. But he knew there was a lot to learn about the place. Originally from Dallas, he didn't really know South Texas. He was somewhat familiar with the battles of the Texas Revolution, but the only one he remembered much about was the Alamo. Every Texan had learned about that one in school.

The sun was setting, and the sky had turned a beautiful shade of tangerine. Maria sighed. James reached for her hand and held it gently. They looked out into the green grass and just stood there together in soft solitude. If only they could get married here, in this spot, she mused. But James had asked her to wait one more year. He wanted to save up for a house. He had a checklist of things he insisted must happen before getting married, which she thought was just a stalling tactic. Maybe this would be the place in a year's time, she thought. Perhaps he was the one.

"Maria," called Isabella, bringing her back to the present.

"Yes, grandmother?"

"Let's go, *mija*. I must rest my feet. I need to be ready for the presentation tomorrow."

Maria and James helped Isabella get situated in her bed inside The Quarters, the historical suite onsite that they had rented for the special occasion. The rooms were dark when they arrived, but they lit a candle on the table by Isabella's bed and went into the little kitchen to make some chamomile tea for her.

James suddenly felt a shiver run down his spine, but he didn't let on. He didn't want to give in to Maria's woo-woo silliness. But the place really did have a vibe. James had listened to Maria's grandmother tell the story of the executions of so many Texian soldiers here, along with

Colonel Fannin, in March of 1836. And her ancestors had played music about it years later, when they had formed their orchestra. Isabella had played one of the songs on her grand piano in her home back in San Antonio for them—"Home, Sweet Home". It took on a bittersweet meaning here at La Bahía, as the captured Texian soldiers believed they would be granted clemency by General Jose Nicolas de Portilla and they had sung this song the night before their executions, which were ordered by Santa Anna himself. Isabella was gently singing the song to herself in the bedroom as James brought in her hot tea. Something about the melody of her voice, now that they were there, in Goliad, made James uncomfortable.

'Mid pleasures and palaces
Though I may roam
Be it ever so humble
There's no place like home
A charm from the sky
Seems to hallow us there
Which seek thro' the world
Is ne'er met with elsewhere
To thee, I'll return
Overburdened with care
The heart's dearest solace
Will smile on me there
No more from that cottage
Again I will roam
Be it ever so humble
There's no place like home"

"Here you are, Isabella," James interrupted, setting her steaming tea on the bedside table.

She looked up at him with a kind expression.

"Oh, *gracias, mijo*. You are such a dear. I'm so glad Maria has you in her life. *Buenas Noches*."

"*Buenas Noches*," James said. He'd learned a little Spanish here and there from Maria and her grandmother. He did a pretty good job, although at first he sounded pretty ridiculous, and he still couldn't roll his r's. Once upon a time, prominent Texas history figures like Stephen F Austin and Juan Seguín spoke both Spanish and English fluently. Funny how far we haven't come, James mused. He knew Maria fantasized about getting married and having children one day in the not-too-distant future, and she insisted that they would speak Spanish and English fluently. It was just an obvious advantage these days to know both—he knew that. It was a great idea.

James heard footsteps in the other room and headed there to enjoy a quiet evening with Maria. He smiled, but when he entered their room, he realized she wasn't there. "Maria?" he said.

Where had those footsteps come from? He'd just heard them from the other room. Where had she disappeared to?

James noticed that the door to the yard of La Bahía was ajar and stepped out onto the grounds. The night air was crisp. It was dark and the crickets were chirping.

Out of the corner of his eye, he noticed movement. He peered closer. It looked like Maria was dressed all in white, rounding the corner into the courtyard where they had been outside of the chapel just an hour ago. "Maria, wait up!" James called to her, but she didn't respond. She must have decided to go back to the chapel. The sky was clear and the stars were shining above him. He pushed up his glasses, as if that would somehow help his eyes adjust to the darkness. Right before he reached the spot where Maria had rounded the corner into the courtyard, he stumbled over something and fell. He rolled over on his side and straightened his glasses. Then, he heard a voice. A woman's voice.

"Stay with me, please!" she urged him. But he couldn't see her. He stood up and brushed himself off. He felt something stick on his cheek and nose. He tried to brush it away, but there was more of it than he thought, and it was almost black in the starlight. He heard the organ playing from inside the chapel.

There was no mistaking it this time. It was loud.

"Maria?" James said. But he got no response. There was no one around him. He started walking again and turned a corner just in time to see Maria going inside the chapel. *Strange*, he thought. The chapel was supposed to be locked after dark. At least that's what the guides had mentioned earlier that day as they had checked into The Quarters. When he reached the large wooden doors of the chapel, they were locked. How did Maria get in? It was ridiculous. Why was Maria doing this?

Another shiver went up his spine as he heard footsteps approaching him from behind. He felt as if he'd been submerged in an ice bath. He gasped and turned around quickly to return to The Quarters, but he was paralyzed in that spot. He couldn't move. And he noticed a man seated in a chair in the courtyard.

Was this real?

He couldn't tell. It didn't make sense. He rubbed his eyes and readjusted his glasses. The man was still there, and his hands were tied behind him. All at once, gunshots rang out over the chapel organ, and James watched in horror as the back of the man's head exploded. Unable to comprehend the scene, James fled like a child across the yard and back to The Quarters. He ran so fast, he practically flew.

Once inside the front parlor room, he caught his breath and tried to gain some sense of composure. He found

Maria in the bedroom, reading a book about Spanish architecture. She was wearing her purple robe. She looked up at him, confused.

"James, what happened to you?" He looked back at her, equally confused. Maria jumped out of bed and inspected his face. "You look awful. What on earth? Did you fall in the kitchen? You're pale as a sheet! What happened?"

"Nothing . . . I fell outside near the courtyard. I was looking for you."

Maria grabbed a couple of paper towels from the bathroom and wet them in the sink. She began cleaning the blood off his face.

"I followed you over there and I tripped and fell," James continued. "What were you doing? How did you get into the chapel? And how did you get back here so quick?!"

James realized he was speaking entirely too fast and sounded panicked. He took a deep breath. It didn't add up at all, and his brain was still processing everything that had just occurred.

"James, I don't know what you're talking about! I've been here this entire time. You took my grandmother her tea and I slipped into bed with this book. I figured you were going to check out the grounds one more time. Did you cut yourself when you fell?"

"I don't think so."

"Whose blood is this? You don't have a scratch on you."

James took a seat on the bed and rubbed his head. There had to be a simple explanation for what he'd seen. Maybe some local townspeople were playing a prank on the big-city gringo. That had to be it. He didn't want to encourage Maria's nonsensical talk of spirits, so he gathered himself and cleared his throat.

"I think I must have seen some of the locals in the courtyard or something. It's nothing. I'm fine, I was clumsy. I bloodied my nose.

"You know me, I'm not the most graceful man in the world. Otherwise, I wouldn't have met you in the first place, darling! I'm so glad that I did, because that's why I'm here with you. Now, I mean."

James was rattled. He was talking too fast again. He kissed Maria. He didn't know what else to do. She kissed him back. It was a long kiss. She was so gentle and sweet. He grew calmer. He was so glad they were together, but he would be so relieved when they could leave this place tomorrow.

They snuggled into bed. It was clear Maria wanted to make love, but James was not in the mood. He was still spooked by what he'd seen and heard. He tried to set it aside, but the image of the man's head being blown to bits remained in his mind.

"I'm so tired from the drive here, darling," James whispered in her ear. "Let me wake you up in the morning and have you for breakfast, beautiful."

Maria giggled and kissed him.

"Let's just save that moment for when we get back home," she said. "Grandmother will be awake by dawn! There will be no time for playing around in the morning." She gave him a squeeze, then he got up to brush his teeth and slid into bed, falling into a fitful rest. He tossed and turned until he heard it:

Mid pleasures and palaces
Though I may roam
Be it ever so humble
There's no place like home

It was the first lines to that damn song.

Feeling as if the temperature had dropped suddenly, James shivered. Perhaps the weather was changing. Wasn't there a cold front coming? He felt the hairs on his arms stand up as he heard someone singing more of the lyrics. They were coming from the yard of La Bahía.

A charm from the sky
Seems to hallow us there
Which seek thro' the world
Is ne'er met with elsewhere
To thee, I'll return

It was not the voice of Isabella. It was distinctly male and there was no mistake—it was not a dream. James lay still in bed to see if it would continue. He looked at his phone to check the time: 1:10 a.m. He got up to investigate.

There had to be an explanation. Maria was sound asleep, her gentle, rhythmic breathing soothing to him, even from across the room. He rummaged for his t-shirt on the floor. He grabbed his jacket for warmth and kept his phone to light his way out to the courtyard. It was pitch black out and the crickets were still chirping, evidence that the weather had not changed. It was a balmy night—like an evening at the coast. James turned on the flashlight app and shone the light around to survey his surroundings. Nothing unusual out here. Perhaps he'd been dreaming about that song, since Isabella had been singing it earlier in the evening.

"Nothing going on out here," he said to himself. "Just me and the crickets."

He turned to go back to the suite and then he saw the woman in white standing directly in front of him.

"Come with me," she said. "I'll help you get home."

A chill shot through James's bones.

"No, thank you," he replied unsurely. "I'm not lost. Who are you?"

She didn't answer him. She only turned and beckoned him to follow her into the courtyard.

"Hurry!" she cried out fervently. "There's not much time left!"

She had a distinct Spanish accent. He shined his flashlight app toward the spot where she had been and there was a strange light that reflected at him. It blinded him for a few seconds, and he dropped his phone. He reached down to pick it up and something pulled him to the ground.

"You're not getting out of here alive!" a gruff voice hissed into his ear. "*Muerto.*"

James felt the rough limestone underneath him. *Muerto.* James searched his mind for the meaning of this word. He remembered—it meant "dead" in Spanish. Again, he heard more lines from the song, but now it was coming from right above him. A young man was standing there. He was ragged-looking, with sad eyes.

Overburdened with care
The heart's dearest solace
Will smile on me there
No more from that cottage
Again I will roam

James couldn't move. He was frozen again and helpless.

"*Vamos, cabrón!*" he heard in the darkness. It made him and the ragged man both wince. But the ragged man turned and began his final march.

James heard the organ playing again. He heard the cries of babies. If only he could get back to Maria, but something held him there. The ragged man turned and made eye contact with James just before he turned the corner into the courtyard. He opened his mouth to sing the last two lines from the song.

Be it ever so humble
There's no place like home

A BOOM rang out again, and everything went black.

James found himself walking along the road. He passed by Perez Street and saw the white house where earlier that day Isabella had been recounting the story of her grandmother sitting on the porch, brushing her mother's hair. Dawn was approaching and he began to make out the shapes of the trees and the Presidio La Bahía in the distance. He didn't question how he got here now. He just knew he had to get back to Maria. He returned to The Quarters and found Maria sleeping soundly. He removed his jacket, stripped down to nothing and slipped into bed, wrapping his arms around Maria's warm body. She stirred and moaned softly as she felt him pressing up against her. He began kissing her neck and shoulders and she arched her back, letting him press harder into her. They began moving together as he led himself inside her and they made love. He covered her mouth to keep quiet when she came.

"You couldn't wait?" she whispered, and he answered hotly in her ear. "Marry me!"

She turned to face him in disbelief.

"What? Here? *Now?*"

"Yes. Let's not wait, my love. Life is uncertain. There's no place like home. We have a life to live together. There's no reason to wait."

Maria smiled sweetly.

"James, what's gotten into you? What about your unyielding plans and your schedule and all the checklists you've made? *Did you check your planner?* What's gotten into you?"

"*You.* You've gotten into me. I love you. I want to make you happy. I want to start living our dreams together now. Right now."

She hugged him tightly and pushed him onto his back, straddling him and guiding him inside her once again. The pastel colors of dawn cast a tender glow to their bodies, moving together. The organ began playing in the chapel again, but neither of them heard it. They were too wrapped up in each other at that moment.

CARMEN GRAY is a Native Texan and had her first story (science fiction) published in *Children's Digest* at age 10. Writing has always been one of her favorite forms of expression. Carmen enjoys crafting fiction, employing elements of the supernatural and magical realism. Her Mexican American heritage and the Spanish language is often reflected in the characters of her stories. You can also find her poetry on her blog: www.walkersonthejourney.com.

The Retribution of John Ramsey
Christian Riley

Florence knew the storm was coming. The signs were everywhere and not just in the sky. She heard it coming in the stolid, speechless trees, and she read it in the selfish flow of the creeks and rivers. She saw it in the long valley behind the house and on the dark hill beyond that—Cannon Hill—up where he lived, with his family, Mister John Ramsey, the John Ramsey.

She walked into the yard and looked at the Texas sky, her palm shielding her eyes from the afternoon sun. The boys hadn't come home from hunting yet, not one of them, and Florence knew well that two of them would soon take part in the storm. Its fury, at least. The very thought had her fingers tracing the seams of her blouse. Her fear was in her gut and her head, provoked by the knowledge of what may become—no, what would become—and of her horrifying trauma, which would then prevail upon the storm's aftermath. And her blessings were in her thoughts and her heart, a meager reassurance of all her many other children, and also . . . Well, the possibility of giving birth to more, when these bitter days were done and over with. Yes, it wasn't too late for that, Florence reasoned.

She stared at the yard, with its fenced-off garden, its rows upon rows of lush vegetables and melons. The corn was tall, almost ready, and so were the tomatoes. Carrots needed more time. The onions had just been planted. Greens were on the way, and the entire lot, Florence figured, could certainly use a little more nourishment.

She turned her head and gazed at the barn, her mind working its way through the rudimentary, if not primitive, calculations of prepping for the fertilizer. It was a probable thought process, part of her routine, one of many thoughts pertaining to the farm; but it was also a ruse. Florence knew full well that her mind was stalling, toiling. But what else could she do? What other choices did she have? This was John Ramsey they were up against.

The short answer was that there were no choices. No choices other than to stall, toil about, and think about what needed to get done. Florence did just that as she strolled through the wide garden, pulling weeds, and finding harmful insects that she crushed between her fingers. She threw their destroyed carcasses onto the land, adding a wee bit of nourishment for the plants.

She figured she could check on the supplies in the root cellar soon; just another thing to keep her mind working in a different gear. She could clean the canning jars and lids, get them ready for the fall harvest. She could also take an inventory of what was left, knowing that there wasn't much. And, on that thought, her mind betrayed her, thinking about the future, also knowing that immediately after the storm, there would be two fewer mouths to feed. She cringed, slid a knuckle between her teeth, and bit down hard. The human mind was truly a tough animal to keep locked up. It would look for an opportunity to wiggle free and then run off on its own. Absentmindedly, and as if to punctuate her immediate thoughts, she turned and looked again at the barn, mildly aware of the correlation.

A minute later Roy came out from behind the woodshed, a short ax in one hand, and a murdered hen in the other, the creature dangling headless and upside down, blood trailing onto the soil, feeding the land. Florence saw her husband walking toward her, and at once her mind went to the living faults of the man. It hadn't always been that way—her thinking about his shortcomings. Honestly, she rarely thought ill of Roy, as he was a good man, a proven provider, gentle and caring, except on those rare occasions when he was drunk. But Roy wasn't . . . Well, he wasn't John Ramsey, that's for sure.

Roy stopped ten feet from his wife and threw the hen on the ground beside her.

"Suppa," he said, wiping his now free hand on his overalls. "That's the one's been pecking holes in the eggs. Caught her red-handed, I did." He turned to walk away, then added, "Make soup outta the bitch. With some cornbread." He looked up, caught his wife's eye, and in that stare Florence witnessed her husband's anguish. They both knew how much their boys loved their mama's cornbread.

"I'll do just that," she confirmed, and then waited several seconds before she stopped his stride with a holler. "Roy!" Her husband looked back at her. "When do you think he'll come?" she said.

"The morning," Roy replied flatly, not skipping a beat. Then he turned and looked up at the mountain. "He's respectable like that. He'll be here in the morning."

It would be a long night for Florence, she knew. A long and ruthless night. At her husband's solid confirmation, it felt as if a sharp razor had slid across her throat. A part of her had been holding on to hope, wishing there would be another outcome. But she had been fooling herself with these thoughts. There would be no other outcome, of this she had to be sure.

John Ramsey's boy was killed, after all. His only boy. That was a sin upon sins in this land, to invoke the death of another man's son, even if it was an accident. Unless, of course, that killing was justifiable, out of warrant or necessity.

She thought about her own sons. They were also just boys, Harlen and Cooper, nineteen and eighteen-years-old, respectively. Not even Florence's oldest and they were good-hearted, the both of them. And hell, it was only an accident that had taken Ramsey's boy. A tragic accident, sure, but an accident all the same.

Florence recalled the day her sons came home, running and hollering in the yard. They knew who it was that had been killed. John Ramsey had been looking for his only son for almost two weeks, before Harlen and Cooper discovered him, drowned and dead in the distiller's water tank. Florence couldn't help to feel ill about the boy, knowing him stupid for falling into such a hole, and even more stupid for not being able to climb out. Besides, he should have known better than to come near another man's shining operation. Hell, Mister John Ramsey himself should have taught this principle to his son. Perhaps he was the one to blame for—

There she went again, allowing her evil mind to fool her, letting it till her emotions up like a plow tills the earth.

Florence picked up the dead hen, turned, and walked silently toward the root cellar, head down, as she forced her thoughts to behave themselves, and forced her will to remain strong.

Inside the root cellar, the air was cold and thick. She lit a candle sitting on a small shelf, and then stood there in the dankness for a minute, observing the quaintness of the little underground room. When she was of a younger age, Florence would come down here and sit, sometimes to cry, sometimes to think, and sometimes to do both. That was years ago, before the family got too big and the days got too long. She felt like crying now, but held it together, knowing the value of being sturdy. She knew she would come back after, though, when her boys were gone, and the pain was too much to bear.

Glancing around, Florence took rough stock of the inventory, and then picked a crate up off the ground and began filling it with empty jars and tin lids. When the crate was full, she walked back to the house and into the kitchen, setting her load onto a shelf. She repeated the process twice more, until there were three dozen jars lined out, ready for cleaning. But Florence would do that later, knowing it was time to get dinner going.

Her mind was murderous in its plotting; it wouldn't keep from focusing on how this would be the entire family's last meal together—their last supper. At this, Florence resigned herself to make her best meal ever. She dressed and plucked the dead chicken, then dropped it in a vat of water, along with spices and dried herbs, a few potatoes. Then she made cornbread batter and greased the glass crockery, in which she spread the batter delicately and evenly about. As she went to place the pan in the oven, her hands shook and she almost dropped it on the floor. Florence cursed herself for being clumsy, then sat in a chair for a minute and tried to compose herself, tears of anguish filling the lids of her eyes.

She decided to make dumplings also, and she stuffed them with chopped bacon and placed them carefully into the cooking pot along with the chicken. Then she made a pie, using the last two jars of cherries, and her grandmother's recipe for crust—a crust that no man on earth could find fault with. As she spread out the dough for the pie crust, Florence entertained a different tactic regarding John Ramsey. What if she could somehow convince the man to change his mind? Perhaps she could seduce him, use her womanly charms to broker a deal . . .

Florence shook her head; if only it were that simple. She felt shameful and guilty for her thoughts. She went back to cooking.

After two hours, the entire house smelled divine. The chicken and dumplings were ready, the cornbread was out of the oven and lathered with melted butter, and the cherry pie was sitting in the window, cooling—all the smells of heaven. But it was bittersweet for Florence, as she knew from this day forward she would associate these particular aromas with tragedy and loss.

She made a quick salad of greens and turnips tossed with oil and vinegar, and then set the table—nine plates, the number of which would be dramatically reduced by two after this night. Florence stifled her tears as she walked outside and rang the iron triangle hanging from the eave. They would all be here soon, Roy and the kids, and the anticipation kept her on edge. She was sick with nerves, and of course she had no appetite, but she would stomach the meal, if only for the two sons she would soon lose.

There was a lot of noise as everyone came in and cleaned up, then sat at the table. Roy said Grace, a moment in which Florence felt as if someone had stabbed her in the gut with a cow poker. Then the entire family methodically began dishing their plates and eating.

She could barely take her eyes off Harlen and Cooper. Conveniently, they were sitting next to each other, which made it easy for Florence to dote over them. They were both melancholy and suppressed of character, for they, too, knew what was coming. Most of the other kids also knew, and it made for a mirthless dinner, except for the few younger tots, who were lively as ever. No one said a word about the coming storm. It was as if those who knew were all in fear of Judgment Day.

After dinner, Florence sat in a rocking chair on the porch, Harlen and Cooper lingering at her side. Roy was standing in the yard, twenty feet away, smoking a pipe, glancing at the sky. The moment was awkward, as Florence wanted to say something to her boys, but dared not to, knowing that once she opened her mouth, the tears would break loose, and she would then bawl, and that's the last thing these men needed to see or hear right now.

Suddenly, Roy turned and looked at his wife. "We gonna need more slop for them hogs?" he asked.

A few seconds passed as Florence processed the question. Then she gave a silent nod, keeping her mouth shut for fear of losing her composure.

"I'll head out in a few days," Roy confirmed. "Figure I'll try the campground near Nelson City. There's sure to be a mess of city-folk over there."

Florence nodded again, then looked at her feet, her mind jumping quickly back to her sons.

"You boys give your ma a big hug before you go to bed," Roy added. "You hear me?"

"Yes, sir," Harlen and Cooper replied in unison. And then Florence gave up and cried.

She was up before the sun. She slept for maybe an hour or two, not that it mattered. A good night's rest would have done nothing to dull her sense of desperation on this day. She had snuck out of bed a few times in the night to check in on her two boys, soon to be gone. Just before she rose out of bed for the last time, Florence thought that what was left of her heart, the last piece, had been crushed like an eggshell, beyond repair.

The small hours of the morning seemed as long as the night had been. Florence crept out onto the porch and sat in the rocking chair, thinking. She rolled a smoke and drank moonshine from a mason jar, two habits she hadn't indulged in for many, many years. She contemplated the situation, knowing that there was no way out for her sons, or her. This was John Ramsey, and Florence knew how this drama would end. She did not know what would happen to Harlen and Cooper, what their fates would entail. But Florence knew she would never see or hear from her boys ever again. No one would.

She finished her smoke and the shine, then stood and walked off the porch. The sun was just below the horizon, and now the roosters were making their noise. Knowing there was nothing she could do, Florence committed herself to be strong, and dove into the routines of the farm. Like the day before, she hoped keeping busy would keep her mind and heart from spoiling, so that, when the time came, when *he* came, her true character wouldn't show.

She walked to the barn, opened the doors, and went inside. The interior was dark and stuffy, smelled of hay and manure. From one corner of the barn came a snort, old Bessie the mule, greeting Florence as she came in. There were other sounds also, the stirrings of animals as they began to wake. Florence moved slowly as she lit two lanterns near the entrance, then walked deeper into the barn, lighting more, until the inside of the building revealed itself in a gold and orange glow.

At the back of the barn was the pigpen, and the two massive hogs—Chloe and Baby—upon noticing Florence's arrival, squealed loudly. They were hungry, eager for their slop, their *prime* slop; which, after years of experience, Florence knew would end up producing the foulest of manures, the richest of fertilizers.

She went to a wall and pulled her apron off a wooden peg, fixed it around her waist, and tied it. Then she took a .22 rifle from off a shelf on the same wall, along with a bullet, opened the rifle's breech, and loaded it.

She walked over to a table near the pigpen and set the rifle down. She stood there for several long minutes, thinking about not thinking. Thinking about the days ahead. Thinking about her family, and of the farm. Looking over at the two hogs now staring back at her, and still squealing, she thought of Harlen and Cooper. Florence felt an ache inside her chest, and a buckling in her knees. She would miss her boys dearly. God, she would miss them.

The sun broke the horizon then, its rays piercing through an infinite number of cracks in the old barn. Suddenly, Florence heard the dogs outside howl, and at that sound her stomach dropped. The hounds only went on like that when they had a coon up a tree, or when someone was coming down the road. Florence knew what the reason was, and she knew damn well who was coming.

She wondered for a moment if she should just stay here and finish the job, not go outside to see that man take her boys away. Should she keep inside the barn as the storm passed? Or go out there to say goodbye, in which she knew she would break down and cry uncontrollably in front of all of them, showing her miserably soft character.

Still undecided, she picked up the rifle and raised it, aiming the sights on the largest person hanging naked and gagged from the ceiling rafters. She knew that two sets of eyeballs were pleading madly at her, a man and woman's— some poor city-folk Roy had kidnapped from a campground a few days prior—and that the two were grunting and squirming fiercely against their bindings, but Florence successfully maintained her aim anyway, and fired the round, sending the bullet through the man's right eye.

He was mostly dead, dead enough, so Florence took a cleaver and swiftly cut the rope holding him, and then his jerking body flopped down onto the table. She moved fast, thinking about Harlen and Cooper, yet trying not to think about them, hoping the task at hand would keep her mind off what was to come, what was coming. She took the cleaver and chopped away, against the frantic groans and movements from above, and against the impatient squealing of the hogs beside her, their appetites now fully whetted from the smell of blood and gore. Florence worked fiercely, madly, her actions making a mess as she tried to keep her mind in the present moment. But then . . .

Then the dogs outside barked ferociously, and that meant only one thing.

He was here.

John Ramsey was on the property, and probably with his wagon or his pickup truck, and he was here to take her boys away, and that was all Florence knew, or could handle.

She dropped the cleaver on the table and ran outside, screaming and wailing, her hands and arms dripping blood onto the ground, feeding the land. Roy intercepted her just before she reached the wagon, and she fought against her husband's firm grip, her howls of despair at once quieting the dogs.

Defiantly, Florence focused her anger and looked at John Ramsey, there on his wagon, staring back at her with an expression that eviscerated every ounce of hope. He wasn't glaring at her with eyes colder than the bottom of Boerne Lake in the dead of winter. And his eyes weren't burning white hot with fury or malice. His look was worse than any of that. John Ramsey stared back at Florence with complete indifference, his expression blasé, bereft of emotion.

Harlen and Cooper were climbing in the back of the wagon, and then they sat quietly with their hands in their laps. They kept their eyes off their ma as they stared morosely at their feet. And Roy gripped his wife tightly, wouldn't let her go, damn him, despite her fighting and screaming.

Eventually, John Ramsey looked away, slapped the reins, and whistled at the horses, and with a jolt, the wagon pulled forward. Florence went limp in Roy's arms then, crying for her lost sons, crying in absolute despair. There was nothing she could do other than cry. And after what seemed like hours, or days, of crying, as her sobs receded into a soft whimper and sank into the wake of the storm, her horrid thoughts slowly gave way to other ones. One by one, Florence's thoughts drifted in and out of despair, as her mind provided her with notions of the impending fall harvest, of the canning jars in the kitchen, the root cellar, the chickens and hogs, even old Bessie. In time, Florence's mind gave way not just to the turmoil brought on by John Ramsey, but, thankfully, to her thoughts of the farm.

CHRISTIAN RILEY was born in Houston, Texas, but he now lives near Sacramento, California. He teaches special education, writes cool stories, and hides from the blasting heat for six months of the year. He has had over one hundred short stories published in numerous magazines and anthologies, and across various genres. His debut novel, one of literary suspense, titled *The Sinking of the Angie Piper*, was published in 2017; and his debut short story collection is forthcoming, with Mount Abraxas Press. For more information, go to: www.chrisrileyauthor.com.

The Visitor
Thomas McNeely

*May 25, 198_*

I arrived at the Ranch today—a rather broken-down house in the middle of two hundred and fifty acres of Texas hill country, about an hour from Austin. The caretaker, Mrs. Gerritts, picked me up at the airport and drove me out here in her gray university-issued station wagon. She wasn't pleased I'd brought Cat—though she admitted Cat would be useful for catching the scorpions and brown spiders which infest the house. She reminded me that, before the house became the Bowie Memorial Artist's House, it had been a retreat where Mr. Bowie entertained his fellow writer friends, drinking bourbon and telling stories in the rocking chairs on the long flagstone porch. Now, she said, it is a monument, to Mr. Bowie, and to all the artists who have been invited here since he died— implying, I suppose, that I should be grateful, as well.

The house is dark and rambling, its floors uneven, its rooms seeming to appear out of nowhere; it has the stale air of a mausoleum. Mrs. Gerritts was worried that Cat would damage Mr. Bowie's artifacts: a pair of longhorns mounted above his writing desk; a pack of unfiltered Camel cigarettes, unsmoked before he died. She also pointed out a guest book kept by previous residents. They left stories, she said, of visits by Mr. Bowie's long-dead friends, and ghosts of Spanish Conquistadores and Native American warriors.

Would I be ready to welcome them? she said.

I couldn't read her tone. She eyed me strangely—or perhaps it was only her vacant blue gaze, magnified in her thick glasses, that seemed strange. I asked if she was joking. She said, her eyes not leaving mine, that the residents weren't joking about what they'd written.

Then she said, with a rather sour smile, that it was only a joke. That down here in Texas, anything might be a joke.

I felt I was being tested; and so, I answered, perhaps more sharply than I should have, that I have work to do, that I am ready to be alone.

*June 10, 198_*

In the morning, I write in a long, gallery-like room at the front of the house. In the afternoon, I edit what I have written earlier. Taking a nap in between, I make two days out of one. Nothing is wasted.

On the gallery's dark, wood-paneled walls are paintings by former residents—rough-riding cowboys, a ghostly white horse flying into moonlight-silvered clouds. There are also many, many renderings of landscapes from the Ranch's two hundred and fifty acres—watercolors and pencil drawings, oil paintings and collages—the impression is of a kind of fixedness, an obsession, as if they were trying to uncover in the landscape some secret. I looked for pictures of the ghosts that Mrs. Gerritts described. Of course, I found none, and felt foolish believing her story.

I lay out on a long wooden table the photographs and police reports, interviews with the doctors and nurses who knew my father before he disappeared, the inventory of his room, interviews with his friends—at least, people he called his friends. In the end, no one stopped him from working, even when it was clear his health was failing— what the doctors called his mental illness—how in the last days before he vanished, he said that he was visited by angels, trying to lead him out of the world we know through a tear in the fabric of our world, where he could slip into the spirit world.

*June 25, 198_*

Tonight, I saw them—or, rather, heard them speaking. I have sat many evenings on the flagstone porch in a wooden rocking chair, watching the bluff across the creek, down the hill from the house. Like many other parts of the Ranch, the bluff seems to shift, and not only in the changing light. When I walk the limestone gravel road down to the creek, the houses across the hills vanish and reappear, seeming miles away, then suddenly close; one moment, I am in a thicket of mesquite or spindly bushes, and the next, in a moonscape strewn with shell-like rocks or the bones of small animals, a dried-out ocean floor, like the rooms in a dream. I understand, now, why the artists wanted to capture the landscape, and why it eluded them. At times the bluff, striated by deep vertical gouges in its ochre dirt, as if it had been clawed out of the hillside, seems a hundred feet tall, and at others, barely taller than a house. At sunset, I watch bars of golden light shift among the trees, moving like men, like sentinels, gathering to watch me through the night; but not until tonight did I hear them, whispering among themselves.

June 27, 198 _

In 1964, in the worst snowstorm in fifty years, my father walked out of the white brick apartment building where he lived, across from Henry Ford Hospital in Detroit, where he was a cardiology resident. The door to his apartment was open, his keys and wallet on the yellow Formica-topped table where he ate all his meals. Witnesses saw him leave a side door of the building in his heavy coat, his head bowed against the driving snow. I was four years old, living in Houston with my mother—he was a distant, shimmering figure, an outline of a father, who had appeared outside my window late at night, coming home from the hospital in his white lab coat. For weeks after he vanished, police searched the streets, poking wooden dowels into snowdrifts; they searched the underpasses of the John C. Lodge Freeway and the benches of LaSalle Park, dragged the Detroit River and combed Belle Isle; but no trace of my father was ever found.

The police, my mother, his colleagues—everyone concluded that he had jumped or fallen into the river. I was too young to know what to think. But I have always believed he found some sort of loophole and slipped through it.

*July 15, 198_*

In the guest book, the residents hint at presences— Confederate and Union generals; chiefs and warriors of the

Tonkawa, Comanche, Lipan Apache, and Waco tribes; Spanish Conquistadores and Mexican generals; even Mr. Bowie himself—who visit the Ranch. The presences arrive to impart wisdom, to resolve historical disputes and controversies, fictional or real; I know too little of the history of this place to tell the difference. But I know, now, why there are no pictures of them. Like the voices in the shifting golden light on the ridge above the bluff, they are only voices, speaking out of the land itself.

*July 27, 198_*

Today I found a picture of my father as a child. He is standing with another boy his age on the bank of a winding river, dark with high reeds, probably the Brazos River near Navasota, where he grew up. The boy and my father look to be eight or nine years old. They wear straw cowboy hats and boots pulled up over blue jeans, their thin chests bare, so I can see the shadows of their ribs. They squint into the sunlight, their expressions grave, as only children's can be. They have been interrupted in a game whose meaning is clear to them but would be impossible to explain to adults. The boy is identical to a boy I had known at that age. I have no idea whether the boy was my father's friend for that summer, or a day, or his whole life. I will never know; but, for a moment, I am inside the photograph, and I cannot tell if the photograph is of my father, or myself.

*August 7, 198_*

This evening, in the shifting liquid light in the trees on the bluff, I heard my father's voice. I leaned forward in the rocking chair, listening. Even Cat, usually stalking the porch, chittering at scorpions in the eaves, was silent. I could not understand his words, though I sat, crouched over in the rocking chair, listening as his voice grew fainter and dissolved in the gathering night.

*August 20, 198_*

Tonight, I woke to the heartbeat sound of the rocking chair on the porch. I crept through the dark house to a window in the gallery. I knew what I would find. In the rocking chair, a figure in a white lab coat rocked slowly, his back to me, looking out at the bluff. I stood, trying to screw up my courage to open the door; but I stayed at the window, watching the figure, until dawn washed it away.

*August 25, 198_*

I am leaving, to find him. I have mailed a letter to Mrs. Gerritts, asking her to take care of Cat. I hope she will do her duty and be kind.

I have waited all week, listening, at sunset, to the voices in the trees on the bluff, which every day grow clearer, even my father's voice, though I can't hear his words; or rather, his words make no sense, as if he were speaking a foreign language. At night I have waited for him to reappear in the rocking chair, but he has never returned; the message is clear; I know I must find him.

I must go at night. When my father disappeared, I learned that the world is vast, and there are many places to vanish. I don't know how I will recognize the thin tear in the world I have known and slip through it, but I will know it when I see it, among the trees on the bluff, among the voices—a darkness that unfolds, and keeps unfolding, like a hall of mirrors, into a deeper darkness.

An East End Houston native, **THOMAS H. McNEELY** has published *Pictures of the Shark: Stories* (Texas Review Press, 2022) and *Ghost Horse* (winner of the Gival Press Novel Award, 2014). In a starred review, Kirkus calls *Pictures of the Shark* "an emotionally taut and often haunting collection." He has received fellowships for his writing from the National Endowment for the Arts, the Wallace Stegner Program, and the J. Frank Dobie Paisano Program, and published fiction and non-fiction in *The Atlantic*, *Texas Monthly*, *Ploughshares*, and many other magazines; his work has been noted in the *Pushcart*, *O. Henry*, and *Best American Short Stories* anthologies. He currently teaches at the Stanford Online Writing Studio and Emerson College, Boston.

Secrets That Keep Us
Patrick Torres

I was traded for a pickup truck with no air conditioning, and a rusted hood that made my diaper red when my mother put me on top of it to change me. She passed me over to a man named Cesar, who was my great uncle, the brother of my mother's father, and his wife, Thea. That's how Cesar told me it went when he sat me on his lap, while he smoked his cigars, while the lamplight made his shadow long on the wall and his eyes like slick black slits. His favorite story was about his ancestor, a Spanish conqueror with a saber hanging from his waist.

"He was in line for the throne," Cesar would tell me. Running his thumb along my temple, wiping my hair behind my ears. "He was one of the conquistadores who came to Mexico. But he didn't want to hurt the Indios, like the other Spanish men. When his commander kidnapped Chautemoc, he drew his saber and cut the commander across his chest. He tried to help Chautemoc escape. The other soldiers overpowered him and killed him, in front of the Indios. They didn't know, though, that he had been in love with a young Aztec woman, a princess who was carrying his baby." The story went on to say that when the surviving Aztecs eventually fled the Spanish, the boy's mother died in the escape, but the boy lived. Cesar would hold my face when he got to this part. He'd lock his blue eyes with my dark ones and touch my forehead to his. His skin had become loose, age and work made flesh peel off the bone. But around his eyes you could see how poorly his skin, his mask, fit. Just behind, just around the brown pupils of his eyes, was oily blue. "The last Aztec King. The first mixed baby in Mexico." He'd hold my arm out, trace the vein from my heart to my palm, and then curl my hand into a fist. "Tu sangre es la misma."

When I was young, I believed Cesar's stories. As I got older, I saw them as silly, but as I got even older, it stopped mattering to me whether these stories were real. They were true, even if they weren't real. Cesar knew that, and now I do. So take this story, not for what it is, but for what you need it to be.

Cesar and my grandfather, Antonio, were born to parents who brought them to Texas before the revolution, sensing the unrest in the country's poor. Cesar's father's intention was never to stay. Five years into the war, five years into forming his budding cotton empire, Cesar's father tried to make peace with the Rebels who looked like they would inevitably take control over Mexico. Cesar's father began a correspondence with an old friend who had taken allegiance with Zapata. Cesar's father offered to bankroll the Rebels as an act of contrition. His compadre returned his letters and agreed to arrange a meeting so that the leaders could meet their new benefactor and could find a place for him in their new government. Cesar's mother and father left their land and their two sons with a nanny whose family picked the cotton on the property. They lived on the hacienda with Cesar's family, in separate wings. The nanny was a young woman. Her name was Anna. The boys were expected to help around the property, patching fence line, loading the cotton onto trucks so they could haul it away to the gin, bringing the pickers water from the well just as they would if their parents were there to praise them for doing it. They even brought water to Anna's lame brother, Marco, who picked little cotton but came out to the field regardless.

Marco was oddly shaped. One side of his body was muscled and taut, from his toes up to his eyebrows. His other side was skinny, the bones jutted out against loose brown skin that hung on like clothes on a line blowing in the wind. They thought he was stillborn. He came out dead, they said. They had dug his grave and placed him in. Before they closed the dirt around the child's corpse, his mother saw a shooting star. She said it landed in the hole with him, his soul coming down from the cosmos. They believed in Indio things and were not waiting for heaven anyway, so she may have lied. But he lived and grew lopsidedly into adolescence. He worked in the field, though his family never asked for him to help.

Antonio and Cesar would wait for him to limp over to the truck after every other picker had drunk their fill. In silence, Cesar watched while Marco drank, water dribbling down one side of his face onto his clothes. He'd lean over toward his good side to try to get as much as he could. Some would always come out.

"Que te vaya bien," Antonio said, putting his hand on Marco's shoulder.

Anna's brother would make deep nasal noises like laughter but sounding closer to a donkey's bray. One side of his mouth curled up into a smile, while the other stayed completely unaffected. His bad eye usually drifted, watching the spirits go by.

Anna's family didn't go to mass. They didn't wear crucifixes. No bibles, no shrines to the Virgin Mary, no baptized foreheads. No guilt when she took Antonio's virginity, mounting him the night his father left to meet the rebels, pinning him down by pressing her hands into his chest. In the warmth of the bed, after she had made Antonio a man in his father's house, she drew on Antonio's chest. First, she made an X, then an arrow bisecting it. And then an eye, half-closed over the middle.

"Ya estas despierto," she said. She slipped out of bed and past Cesar's room before Antonio woke. Her bare feet were barely audible padding against the tile floor.

Four Monday trips to the gin with truckloads of cotton had passed since the brothers had seen their parents. No letters had been sent or messages relayed, and they began to fear the worst. After a week, they prayed to the angels and saints for divine intercession, to guide their parents home in safety. After three, their candles were burning out, and their hope followed suit. Antonio turned to Ana to confide in. She told him to hold onto hope, that she knew someone who could help, a curandera, a witch doctor, a healer who could help bring his parents home.

The next day, the brothers watched as the woman snapped side to side, her hands reaching out for something. She waved her hand until she grabbed onto something neither boy could see. She held her closed fist, walking to the other side of the room, her callused feet scratching the tile as she moved. She grabbed a chicken with her free hand, and with the other appeared to jam the nothing she had grabbed before into the bird. The chicken screeched and began knocking its head into the wall, faster and faster with every passing blow until the pops of a snare drum would be too slow to match it.

"Espedate," the woman said to the boys or to the chicken or to whatever she had grabbed out of the air. She had her eyes fixed on the bird. Then the chicken laid down in its cage that the woman had left open and fell silent. She lit two candles, deep red in color, and gave the boys a sack of herbs from her jars.

"Las llamas son el espíritu de tus padres. Mañana, tienes que llevar las velas a la montaña. Protegelas con su vida. La montaña es vieja. Fue hecho cuando no había ni bien ni mal. Tu cruz no te protegerá. Tendréis que protegeros unos a otros." The woman led the boys out the door by the hand. Outside the door, she stood them in a line. She took a glass jar filled with liquid and told them it was pulque and to drink it before they went to sleep. She hugged each of them and let them go back to their truck.

Antonio held the candles while Cesar drove the truck back to the rancho.

"Do you think she's telling the truth?" Cesar asked his brother, whose eyes were locked on the flames that reflected and danced in his brown eyes.

"Tenemos que creer que si."

Cesar slept that night in his bed, while Antonio piled pillows and blankets in the living room. The candles on the table in front of him. Antonio had fallen asleep, watching the candles, hoping his parents were on their way home. Anna's cries woke him up. Marco was limping down the hallway, dragging Anna. His strong side was pulling the weak side and Anna, who was pulling on him, begging him to stop. He grabbed Antonio, waking him up, his grip too strong but with no intent to harm.

"Ven." Marco croaked. "Ayudo."

Cesar came running down the hallway, pulling a shirt on as he came. He ran for Marco with his arms extended, ready to pull him off.

"Dejalo," Antonio yelled at his brother.

Marco loosened his grip. He put his arm around Anna and whispered, "Quedate." Both of his eyes, even the one that darted to and fro, were set on Anna's. She nodded, shaking. Marco touched her face and she turned away from him.

The three of them left on foot, Antonio and Cesar bringing the candles with them, lighting the way.

"Where are we going?" Cesar said, struggling to keep pace with the other two. Marco's bad leg was dragging behind him and he still was leading the group.

"Monte."

Antonio slowed to let his brother catch up. "Vamos," he said to his brother, softly.

Cesar sped up but stayed behind his brother, not daring to spearhead the group or stand too close to Marco. The fire of the candle had grown and, even in the wind, it did not waver. The three climbed up the winding dirt road, spiraling up the black mountain on the edge of Antonio's and Cesar's parent's property. At the base of the mountain were the edges of the cotton fields, where the dirt became rock, just out of reach from the cotton fields, was a cave with a boulder guarding its inner workings.

"Lleva las velas. No miras abajo." Marco wasn't wheezing anymore. "Y tus padres van a volverá. Mueve la piedra y pon las velas adentro."

Antonio had to run to keep up with Marco through the cotton fields. Cesar, being smaller, was falling behind him, losing sight of the two. He was a lonely boat at sea in the cotton.

"Where are you?" Cesar cried out.

Antonio turned back to find his brother

"Ven a mi voz. Voy a ayudar."

Cesar heard voices in the field, weeping, whispering. The wind brushing the spinas of the cotton plants against his skin. Cesar closed his eyes. He listened closely for his brother's voice, paring its direction, taking slow steps toward where he thought the voice was coming from. He was nearing the end. Antonio's voice was growing louder.

"Mijo, ayuda me," said another voice, a woman's voice, his mother's voice called from the field. Cesar spun around.

"Ama," he said softly.

"Cesar," the voice cried out.

Marco moaned, "Mentiras, no es ella," but Cesar was running into the field, calling for his mother.

"Ama!" Cesar was in the thick of the field, using his free hand to move the plants around. Antonio tried to run after him, but Marco held him by the shirt, keeping him from following. "Juntos," said Marco. The two walked back into the field together.

Cesar saw a blanket laying in the field, something was underneath it. He sprinted to the mound, calling for his mother. He knelt next to the blanket, looking for his mother's face. The roots of the plants sprung from the ground, latching themselves around his legs. He screamed as roots from the ground slid into his mouth, down his throat, inching further down, silencing the boy.

Antonio and Marco ran toward Cesar's cries. When they found him, the earth had begun swallowing his lower legs, burying them up to his ankles. The spinas from the cotton plants wrapped around his body, sliding like snakes around him, cutting gashes into his skin, spirals of blood starting from his thorny crown down to his legs, flaying the flesh. The roots snapped Cesar's limbs and forced them behind his body, so he resembled a star. Cesar's eyes had gone white and, through him, something spoke. Antonio could not remember what it said through his brother.

Falling stars lit the sky for a moment. Antonio's shirt had become heavy and wet. He saw the mark Anna made weeks ago again. It was scarred into him now; the skin was raising out of him in its shape. Voices came from the fields.

Some were chanting, some speaking Spanish and Nahuatl and languages more ancient. Growing louder, they were drawn by the mark. Antonio, the mark burning against his skin, took off his shirt and beat his chest, screaming. The symbol grew and began to glow. The people moved through the fields like grass in the wind, individually, in waves, together and apart. They encircled Antonio and Marco and Cesar's mangled body while whoever inhabited it at that moment was still inside.

Someone, a King so the story goes, held his hand above Antonio's mark. Antonio's star, that thing that animates him and all life on this world, grew into a blazing blinding light. The light pressed outward. Antonio's bones became visible, the roots of his hair inside his head could all be seen, like blades of grass growing in a glass bowl. Where his heart should be was only the mark.

The King guided Antonio's hand into Cesar's chest, moving through it like a hand through masa. The body growled and spit and shook its head in all directions. Antonio could feel the star inside the body, the King closed Antonio's fingers around it and pulled on his arm slowly.

Then, when he could feel it almost pulled out, as the chanting grew louder, Cesar's body said in Cesar's voice, "No dejes que me lleven." But then, taken over again, Cesar's thorny crown grew onto Antonio's arm, piercing it as it spiraled up further, inching toward his chest, ripping into him, binding around his arm.

He heard his brother's frightened scream before ripping his hand out. The body of Cesar fell in front of him. Cesar's heart, his star, was covered in the same thorns that covered his body, a bloody rosebud attached the thorns at the bottom of his heart. The King placed his hands on Antonio's shoulders as he held the heart in front of him, the people of the fields chanting and letting out yips and hollers. Antonio ripped the thorns off Cesar's star heart with all his might. Marco knelt before the King, and the people let out more yells, raucous cheers. A willing sacrifice was all the more noble. The King took Cesar's bleeding mangled star heart from Antonio and jammed it into Marco's body. Marco twisted and shook, and the thorns emerged from his skin, breaking the surface, and blood leaked out from the edges of the wounds. The King closed Marco's eyes, running his thumb down the mark. Marco's body erupted light, blinding light like the last gasps of a dying star. Marco, his supernova, shone out through his eyes and his ears, his mouth vomiting light. Then the King snapped his neck and the light floated into the sky. A new star took its place among the cosmos. The people in the field, ancient and the familiar recently deceased, lifted him away, moving him back into the endless, passing him from person to person further into the field, disappearing into the sea of bodies that were in celebration. His ancestors delighted in his return.

Cesar and Antonio's parents returned home the next morning, shaken from their travels but alive. Cesar peeked while his parents burned Marco's body. His body had already frozen up in death and Cesar stood behind the house watching Marco become a charred statue, his rigor mortis posing him. He asked them about it, years later, and they said it was to keep the coyotes from coming. Antonio thought his parents did it because they were scared whatever disease made him that way could pass from him into their soil and into the food they ate. Anna had left the ranch that night upon the news of her brother's death. She wept over him for a moment after Antonio carried his body down the mountain, then she packed a bag and began to walk. She knew Marco's body was not long for this world but could not remove the feelings of blame she felt toward the boys. She never found out what was done with her brother's body. The boys and their parents buried Marco's charred remains under an oak tree. The family searched for Ana, asking around town. Antonio found her eventually, but that is another story for another day.

The night Marco died, he and the boys drank the liquid and fell asleep. They woke up and the hallucinogen took over. They would make it part way up the mountain before Marco's organs failed, his body not prepared to handle the liquid the woman gave them. But he deserved a noble death, so we tell the myth until it feels more real than the truth.

PATRICK TORRES is a writer from San Antonio, Texas, whose work has been featured in *The Windward Review*. He coaches track and field at Our Lady of the Lake University in San Antonio.

The Boogie
John Kojak

When it rained in Houston, it rained hard. The drops were so large, and coming down so furiously, that it sounded like Alex Torres's Toyota Camry was being raked by machine gun fire. He pulled his car warily off the rapidly flooding street, into the empty Shell station, and scanned the lot for his passenger. There wasn't a lot of information on the user requesting a ride, not even a picture, only a name and a rating: Kyle Blackwell—zero stars. Normally he wouldn't have accepted the trip, especially on such a stormy night, but his daughter was sick and he needed the money.

As he approached the deserted pumps, the silhouette of a man appeared outlined against the fluorescent amber glow of the station's lights. Alex swung his wheel, illuminating the shadowy figure in the bright glare of his car's headlamps. The man was soaked to the bone and looked as frail as a wet cat. A large, red plastic gas can sat on the pavement beside him.

Alex pulled up next to the man and rolled down the front passenger side window. "Kyle?" he shouted over the roar of the pounding deluge.

The man stepped silently forward out of the shadows, opened the rear passenger side door, and climbed into the backseat. He placed the gas can on his lap and held onto it tightly with both hands.

"Hi. I'm Alex," the driver said, glancing back at his pitiful-looking passenger. "Did you run out of gas?"

The man looked at him blankly, "I need to go home."

"Right." Alex shrugged. It was none of his business, and he didn't really care why anyone requested a ride anyway; all he needed to know was where they were going. "1408 Fairview Street, correct?"

The man nodded, his eyes dark and unblinking as a dead fish.

Alex checked the route and pulled his aging sedan carefully back out onto the road. "Hell of a night," he said. "I usually don't go out in weather like this, but my little girl came down with a fever last week. I didn't think it was too bad, but my wife insisted on taking her to the emergency room. Not one of those strip mall places, but Texas Children's, for Christ's sake. You wouldn't believe what that cost me."

The man slid slowly over, grabbed the side of the driver's seat, and pulled himself forward until his mouth was only a few inches from Alex's ear. "We have a duty to protect our children. In the end, they're all that matters."

"Do you have kids?" Alex said. He liked to talk; it helped pass the time.

"I had a baby once, and a wife. But that's all over."

"Oh . . ." Alex replied, assuming the man meant his wife had left him and taken their child. He couldn't imagine life without his own family. "I'm sorry."

"I couldn't protect them, and now they're gone," the man said sullenly as he leaned back and clutched the gas can against his body. "There's only one thing left to do now."

Uh-oh, Alex thought. *He couldn't protect them—there's only one thing left to do.* What the hell was that supposed to mean? The driver training videos stated that the best thing to do with a potentially unstable passenger was to disengage from conversation and get them to their destination as quickly and safely as possible. He looked down at the map on his phone; they were five miles from the drop-off point. *Just shut up and drive*, he told himself.

The silence lasted less than a minute.

"The first time I saw it, I was reading to my daughter Susie . . . She was only four years old, but a real daddy's girl. Every night at bedtime, she refused to go to sleep unless I read her a story. Me, not her mom—it always had to be me." The dour man's mood seemed to brighten, even the tone of his voice changed. It had a tender warmth to it now, like maple syrup on a Sunday morning. "She always wanted me to read her those *Little Debbie Do-er* books. Does your daughter like those?"

Alex began to relax. "My daughter's five; *Debbie Do-er* and *Princess Penelope* are her favorites."

"Whenever Debbie saved the mermaids from evil polluters, or rescued those tiny tubby cats from Willie the Wild Wolf, Susie would always giggle her head off and shout, 'Do it, Debbie!'" A shattered smile spread across his face like cracking glass.

"Those books have great stories. I used to read them to my daughter every night, but not so much now that I started driving," Alex said. An unexpected wave of guilt coursed through his body. How long had it been since he was home to tuck his daughter into bed? *Two weeks—a month?*

The dark veil that had shrouded the man returned.

"I was about halfway through the story, I can't remember which one, when I saw something moving along the baseboard at the far end of her room. It was nothing really—a shadow, maybe. I don't know why it made me so uneasy, but it did. I didn't see anything else, though, so I finished reading the story and kissed my daughter goodnight. I thought that was it."

Alex nodded silently. The sense of unease he had felt about the man was returning.

"Then, a couple of nights later, I was tucking her in when I saw a dark little creature with long furry limbs scamper across the floor and disappear under her closet door. I jumped up, ran over to the closet, threw the door open, and turned on the light. Susie's little pink galoshes were on the floor next to her sneakers. Her raincoat and a few dresses were hanging above them, but that was it. Whatever it was—just disappeared."

"It was probably one of those giant, flying cockroaches. Texas is full of those things. They used to scare the crap out of me when I was a kid." Alex regretted the words as soon as they left his mouth. *Shut up and drive,* he reminded himself.

"That's what I thought." The man was animated now, waving his hands around excitedly as he spoke. "You should have seen my wife's face—her name was Elizabeth—when I told her that. 'Roaches! Not in this house, buster,' she said. Man, she was pissed!" He rocked his head back and let out a raucous laugh. "So I just let it go. I didn't really know what that thing was . . . but it was something." The man stopped talking for a moment and leaned back in his seat.

The rain was falling harder now, slapping against the car in windswept waves and overflowing the ditches that bracketed the road. Alex looked down at his phone; they were three miles from the destination.

"The next time I didn't see anything, I heard it," the man said. "It was about a week later. Susie was asleep upstairs, and Liz and I were lying on the couch, watching TV. She was sleeping when I first noticed it, a low sucking, scraping sound . . . like a dead squid being dragged across a rusty deck, *suuuck-errrarrr-squishhh-suuuck-errrarrr-squishhh*. The sound moved around the room; it was everywhere—and nowhere—all at the same time. I woke my wife up and asked her if she could hear it, but she looked at me like I was crazy. I got up and looked behind the TV, the chair, I even slid the couch away from the wall—while my wife was still laying on it!" He laughed again. "But I couldn't find anything. I wanted to call an exterminator, have the whole damn house sprayed, but my wife said the chemicals they used would be more dangerous than some 'invisible giant roach'."

The man stared out of the window at the waterlogged road. "For the record, I never said it was a giant *frigging* roach . . . but I heard something, and it was in our house."

A few moments later the soothing female voice of the navigation app broke the silence. *"In two hundred yards, turn left onto Westheimer Road."*

Alex slowed down to make the turn; the weatherman said the storm could dump up to ten inches of rain, and the roads were beginning to resemble rivers. All he wanted was to make it home to his wife and daughter, but first he had to get rid of the melancholy man in his backseat. He checked the app again, only two miles to go.

"The next weekend my wife took Susie to see her grandma in Beaumont. As soon they walked out the door, I had a guy come over and hit the place with everything he had. I told him I didn't care what it took, I wanted to kill everything that could fly, crawl, or swim. I don't know what he used, but it seemed to work. I didn't see or hear anything for a couple of weeks after that. But then, one night around 3:00 a.m., Susie screeched so loud it sounded like a steam whistle. My wife and I both leapt out of bed and ran into her room. 'The boogie, Daddy. The boogie,' Susie was shouting at me as she pointed toward her closet. My wife thought she was saying 'the buggie', but I knew better. I ran to the closet and threw open the door, but there was nothing there, just like before. When I turned back around, Liz was sitting on the side of the bed, holding Susie in her arms. My daughter had stopped crying and I thought it was over—at least for the night."

The man took the gas can off his lap and sat it down on the empty seat beside him. For a moment, Alex thought he heard him weeping.

"But then I heard that noise again, *suuuck-errrarrr-squishhh-suuuck-errrarrr-squishhh*. Only it wasn't coming from the closet; it sounded like it was coming from under the bed. Before I could move, or even open my mouth to warn my wife—a long, hairy tentacle shot out from under the bed and grabbed her by the ankles. Elizabeth was still holding Susie in her arms as they both flew off the bed and hit the floor. I can still hear the loud Thud! my daughter's head made as it bounced off the hard oak . . ."

The man's voice began to break; it sounded like the rattle of bones inside a dark hole. "My wife tried to fight it. She wasn't the type who ever went down easy, but she never had a chance. It kept pulling her further and further under the bed, until she completely disappeared."

"Shit!" Alex cried out as the car suddenly began to hydroplane on the flooded street. His foot slid off the accelerator and tapped the brake. "Sorry about that. These roads are getting pretty nasty."

The man didn't so much as blink. Once Alex had regained control, the passenger continued his story. "The bed began to jump and bounce around like crazy. I shit you not. It was like something straight out of a movie. And these wild ripping, shredding sounds screeched out from underneath it, like she was being sucked down into a giant garbage disposal. I can't tell you how long it lasted; it seemed like hours, but it was probably only a few seconds . . ."

Alex's mind shifted back and forth between horror and disbelief. He had heard a lot of stories since he started driving. But this one took the cake.

"I looked over at Susie; she was lying on the floor a few feet from the bed. A little pool of dark red blood was oozing out from a small gash on her forehead." The man's voice faltered; it was little more than a whimper now. "The worse part about the whole thing is, I probably could have saved her. I could have picked Susie up and ran out of the house. But I just stood there . . ."

Alex was sure it must have been the shadows playing tricks on his mind, but it looked like the man in the backseat had shrunk to the size of a child.

"Then another one of those hairy octopus-like arms slithered out from under the bed and grabbed Susie's leg. Her eyes suddenly flew open—they were as big as baseballs—and she began to scream, 'Boogie! The boogie, Daddy!' I tried to reach out to her, I swear I did, but I guess it was just too much. I couldn't take it. I must have passed out. I don't know for how long . . . but when I woke up, I was on the floor."

"And your daughter?" Alex asked cautiously.

"She was gone—my wife was gone—my daughter's toys, all of their clothes, everything was gone.

"I got up and called the police. I told them what I had seen: the strange sounds—those shaggy fucking tentacles. They sent a couple of uniforms over, but they didn't believe me. They said it didn't make any sense. The house was spotless, the bed was made; there wasn't even blood on the floor. Nothing. They thought my wife had left me, and I just couldn't handle it. That I had cracked up. They sent me to the nut house. Can you believe that? That's where I've been for the last three days. Locked away—like some lunatic!"

"I can't imagine," Alex said as his mind finally started to fit the pieces together. The County Psychiatric Hospital was only a few blocks away from the gas station where he picked up his passenger. The guy was crazy. It all made perfect sense now.

"You would be surprised what you can imagine . . . that's what the doctors told me. They called it a coping mechanism." The man's face shivered and big salty tears began to flow down his cheeks.

The tense silence was broken by the sterile voice of the navigation system. *"In two hundred yards, turn right onto Shepard Drive."*

"But it wasn't my imagination . . . That thing might have been able to fool those stupid cops, but I know what I saw," the man said firmly. "I know what took my wife and my little girl—and it's in that house." He lifted the gas can back onto his lap.

"In one hundred yards, turn right onto Fairview Street, then the destination is on your right."

"It's just up here, the big brick house with no lights." The man pointed toward a large two-story home situated on the corner of a nice, oak-tree lined street. Other than the lack of lights, there was nothing unusual about it. It was a nice, old house, in a nice, old neighborhood.

"You have arrived at your destination."

Alex pulled the car over to the curb. This was the point where he would normally wish his passenger a goodnight, but what do you say to someone who told you his wife and daughter were killed by a monster hiding under the bed? A man who was just released from the nuthouse. A man clutching a five-gallon can of gasoline.

"Thanks for the ride." The passenger opened the car door and stepped out into the torrential rain. He stood there for several seconds, staring at the house, before turning and giving Alex a single wave of his hand. Any sign of frailty was gone, and he looked like a man with furious purpose burning inside him.

Alex watched as the dark figure walked up the long concrete path to his front door, the gas can swinging from his arm as casually as a bag of groceries. The man opened the door, walked in, and turned on the lights. For a brief moment, Alex could see the man's silhouette framed against a large living room window. Then the lights went back out and the front door slammed violently shut.

Should he call the police?

Alex sat alone in the dark, listening to the frantic swishing of the windshield wipers as they swung frantically back and forth in their futile attempt to sweep away the cascading sheets of water. No, the man said he told the police the same story and they thought he was nuts. *But what about the gasoline?* The man never actually said he was going to burn down his house, and Alex certainly couldn't be blamed if he did. *Right?* None of this had anything to do with him, Alex told himself. He just gave the guy a ride.

Alex looked back over at the darkened home. A faint orange glow had begun to shimmer from inside the large window. Alex looked at his phone. *Should he maybe call somebody?* He was nervously fumbling with his phone when he saw the front door of the house suddenly fly open again, but there was no sign of the man. He threw his phone down and drove as quickly down the water-logged street as his car could manage. He had to get home.

He drove fast, too fast. Ploughing through the flooded streets like a ship in a stormy sea, his car throwing up huge waves of water in its wake. He blew through several intersections before finally coming to stop at a red light. That's when he thought he saw something; he wasn't sure what—a shadow maybe—moving in the back seat. He turned on the dome light and glanced back over his shoulder. Nothing. The light turned green. He continued driving, but he left the dome light on. He was just being paranoid; he was sure of it.

He pulled off the road and parked in a deserted H-E-B parking lot. He took off his seatbelt and turned fully around so he could reach into the backseat. He ran his hand over the worn velour seat covers and pulled up the small rectangular floor mats. There was nothing back there; he was sure of it now. He pulled slowly out of the parking lot and continued driving—the soft glow of the dome light shining like a lone star in the darkness.

He began to relax. He was only a few blocks from his own home now. His wife would be up; she always stayed up when he was driving late. She would bring him a beer and ask him how his night was. Sometimes he would tell her funny stories about the people he met . . . but not tonight. He didn't think he would ever tell her about the man he met tonight and his story—even though that was all it was, a story—he was sure of it.

Then, there it was again. Out of the corner of his eye he noticed something moving across the backseat. It could have just been a shadow cast by a passing streetlight or telephone pole; it could have been anything—or nothing at all. *This is ridiculous,* he thought. *Just drive!*

It wasn't much longer before he was able to turn onto his street and see his small, humble home at the end of the block. It was a tired, rundown-looking house in an old, rundown neighborhood. The only thing special about it at all was what was inside—his family. The first thing he wanted to do, even before he kissed his wife, was check on his daughter. He needed to make sure Angelina, his little angel, was safe. Then this would all be over, and the world would begin to make sense again.

Alex pulled into his driveway and pressed the button on the garage door opener clipped to the visor. As the light from inside the garage flooded into his car, he glanced over his shoulder and smiled. The guy with the gas can was a head case. That's all. No wonder his wife had left him. He eased the car into the garage, shutoff the engine, and turned off the dome light. A wave of relief swept over him as he pulled the keys out of the ignition and removed his seatbelt. He was home. But when he opened the car door to step out, he heard a strange noise—*suuuck-errrarrr-squishhh-suuuck-errrarrr-squishhh.*

A combination of panic and fear struck him like a bolt of lightning as he attempted to leap out of the car. But before he could get clear, a long hairy tentacle shot out from under the driver's seat and coiled around his right leg. He grabbed the car door with both hands and slammed it violently and repeatedly, pounding the aberration between the door and the frame of the car, but the twisting tentacle's grip only grew tighter. He looked toward the door leading into the house; his wife and daughter were inside. He bit down hard on his lip so he wouldn't cry out; he didn't want them to witness the horror as he fought, kicked, and tried to pry the creature's grip loose. But he couldn't break free. It was pulling him back into the car, just as it had pulled the man's wife and child under the bed. *I couldn't protect them—now they're gone.* The man's words thundered inside Alex's head as he watched his right leg being pulled into a dark gaping hole between the seat and the floorboard by a pair of relentlessly chomping dagger-like beaks. He gripped the roof pillar in a white-knuckled, desperate attempt to keep from getting completely sucked inside the car, but it was no use. Suddenly, the door to the kitchen opened and he could see his wife and daughter standing in their nightgowns, unaware of the evil that was dragging him deeper and deeper into the abyss. He tried to scream, tried to warn them, but his cries fell silently into the rising sea of darkness that had engulfed him. When he didn't come out of the car, Alex's daughter ran down into the garage to find her daddy, but the car was empty. There was nothing inside, just the faint smell of gasoline.

JOHN KOJAK is a Navy veteran and graduate of the University of Texas who grew up in oily little towns around Houston during the Boom-and-Bust eras of the 1970s and '80s. He still lives there, with a nice woman and a mean cat. His short stories have appeared in a variety of books and magazines, including *Pulp Modern*, *Pulp Adventures*, *Switchblade*, *EconoClash Review*, *Mystery Weekly*, *Road Kill: Texas Horror by Texas Writers Vol 5*, and *The Toilet Zone: Number Two*, among others.

The Devil Witch of Hanging Oak
Patrick C. Harrison III

In twenty-three minutes, I'll be hanged.

I won't be the first soul to be strung up from that old oak; I won't be the last either.

They'll leave my body swaying there for over three weeks, letting the crows and flies do with me what they please. Townsfolk will come and look and talk about what I did. They'll say I was the devil. They'll say I was a witch. They'll call me all the slurs they call us. When they finally cut me down, they'll burn my remains.

In thirty-six years, this little North Texas town will be renamed Hanging Oak. Decades after that, there will be a small museum explaining how that name came about, where the tree was, and all the evil individuals that hung from it. I'll be prominently featured in this museum.

Mothers, hoping to shy their children away from doing something foolish, will tell tales of me, about the things I did, saying my spirit still lurks out there, watching children, waiting for them to do something naughty. Teenagers will close their eyes in front of mirrors, saying my name, trying to summon me. People will call to me through Ouija boards and seances and black masses.

But before I became folklore, before Hanging Oak was a town name, before my eyes were plucked out by birds and my body was burned, before I was swinging dead from that oak, before I was covered in the blood of seven, there was this . . .

It was just over three months ago, with spring barely taking hold, that I arrived here—a small, scruffy town called Post Oak, for thirty-six more years—looking for work and a roof to sleep under. I found both at a farm on the outskirts.

"It's a nice spot of land you got here, Mr. Wallace," I said from the front porch, admiring the corn and cotton fields to the north, and the large garden to the west.

"Thank you, Chuck," Mr. Wallace said, puffing on his corncob and scanning the land. "We like it."

"Oh, it's Chuks, sir," I said, "with an S on the end. Chuks Barret."

"Chuks, huh?"

"Yessir. Chuks. It's a Nigerian name, given to me by my grandmother. My mother, she died during birth."

"Uh-huh. Pardon my saying, Chuks, but you're well-spoken for a former slave. You get an education on the plantation you was on?" Mr. Wallace raised his eyebrow, like he wasn't sure what to think of me.

"Well, sir," I said, smiling, "an education of sorts, I s'pose. The lady of the house was a schoolteacher there in Bossier City. I was born on the plantation and, even though I didn't attend school with the white children, she felt obligated to teach me. Taught me how to read. Taught me math. Taught me all kinds of things. My grandmother was right pleased."

"I reckon she was," Mr. Wallace said, laughing. "They were good people, huh?"

"Well," I said, shaking my head a little, "she was a fine lady. But I wasn't too upset to get away from her husband when we were freed last spring. He didn't have the same disposition she did."

"That a fact?" Mr. Wallace said, chuckling again.

He took a seat in a rocking chair and pointed to another a few feet away, indicating I could rest my legs. I nodded happily and sat, setting the burlap bag that held my few belongings between my feet. Mr. Wallace puffed on his pipe and looked out on the crops, mulling over my offer to help on the farm. After several quiet moments, he spoke.

"Chuks, I'll be straight you. I can't pay you much. I can put you in a room with a bed and I can feed you good, but . . ." He paused, looking me in the eyes. "I would pay you fair as I can. But it ain't gonna be much. If I was you, Chuks, I would go have a look at the Montgomery Ranch, south of town. It's a big farm. And Thomas Montgomery has a good deal more money than myself."

"Yessir," I said, smiling at Mr. Wallace in an amused way, "I went by the Montgomery Ranch. It's a fine place. At least, it looked like a fine place as I was running out of there. Let's just say the Montgomery folks don't take too kindly to having a Negro on their land."

"That a fact?" Mr. Wallace said. "Jesus Christ Almighty."

"Oh, I don't believe Jesus Christ has much to do with those folks."

With that we both had a good laugh. We shook hands on an agreement, and Mr. Wallace led me around the farm as afternoon turned to evening. He walked me through the crops, telling me if I knew any special prayers to make it rain, such prayers would be welcomed. He showed me the barn, where the mule I would use to plow was at, along with a couple of old dairy cows. He told me about a fence he would like to build for horses, saying there were seven girls in the house, including his wife, and every dern one of them wanted a pony.

There won't be a trial.

The sheriff who threw me in this cell said as much. He said he was locking me up and, if I was still alive in the morning, he'd take me before the judge. But the town has heard what I did. Some have even seen it. They've seen what's left of the Wallace family.

I hear a crowd forming outside.

When they come for me, the sheriff and his sole deputy can't stop them. They won't even try.

There are chants for the sheriff to unlock my cell, to bring me out. There are chants to have me disemboweled. Chants to have me slaughtered.

I hear the crackle of a fire, and its light flickers in the small, barred window of my cell.

There are people inside the sheriff's office now.

It's nineteen minutes until I hang.

Molly took to me straightaway. She was youngest of Mr. Wallace's six daughters. The first time I saw her, I was kneeling in the barn cleaning the mule's shoes with a hoof pick. A shadow stretched across the dirt and straw, and I looked up. There Molly was, pretty as a picture in a white sundress.

"Well, hey there," I said, setting the mule's hoof back down. "You must be Molly. I missed you at dinner last night. Your mama said you'd done gone to bed early."

I laughed and waited for a response, but she just shrugged and smiled. Getting up, my knees creaking, I put the hoof pick in my pocket and dusted my hands on my britches. I took a step toward her, into the sun so I could see her better.

"My name is Chuks," I said, extending a hand. "Chuks with an S on the end."

Molly shrank away from me but continued to smile.

"You don't have to shake my hand, Molly," I said politely, stuffing it in my pocket. "It's probably safer that way. Don't go shaking hands with folks you don't know too well. Say, how old are you?"

Molly giggled and shrugged, saying nothing.

"C'mon now, you know how old you are. Let me think," I said, looking up at the hay loft in mock contemplation, "I'd say you're round about twenty. You're a pretty young lady, you look very intelligent and strong enough to take down a bobcat all by yourself. Yes, I believe you're twenty."

Molly laughed, shaking her head wildly, her light hair swinging in front of her face as she did so.

"Not twenty? You're kidding me! How old are you then?"

Molly, beet-red with laughter, held up a hand with all five fingers.

"Molly, how much is that? Maybe I can't count too well. Or maybe I can't see too well. How many fingers is that you're holding up, sixty-three?"

"She can't talk," a voice from just around the corner of the barn said. Marilyn, the twelve-year-old, came walking into view, wearing a dress similar to her sister's. "She used to talk a little when she was a baby, but she hasn't in a long time."

"Oh," I said, turning back to Molly. "Well, that's okay. I was just teasing. I knew you told me you were five." I held up my hand showing her I knew the number. She smiled and nodded back to me.

"Doctor says she could if she wanted to," Marilyn said. "But she ain't said nothing since our wagon was raided by outlaws few years back."

"That a fact?" I said, looking at Marilyn and then at Molly, whose face had gone somber. "I imagine that was a traumatic event for a young girl such as yourself, Molly. You, too, Marilyn."

"Them outlaws ran off with our wagon and horses, too. That's why we ain't got any."

"That's right awful," I said. "I'll pray the good Lord takes care of those evil men." Then to Molly: "And I'll pray that you'll talk when you're good and ready, Molly."

That evening I sat once more at the Wallace dinner table. It was likely a tight fit around that old table before I came along, and it was almost uncomfortable as I sat there, squeezed between Madilyn, the oldest daughter at sixteen, and Morgan, who was nine. To Mr. and Mrs. Wallace, I offered to go eat out on the porch to make things more relaxing for the family.

"Nonsense, Mr. Barret," Mrs. Wallace said as she placed a cob of corn on her plate and then Molly's. "As long as you're here, you're part of the family. You'll eat at the table just as the rest of us."

"That's right, Chuks," Mr. Wallace said, chewing on his bite of ham. Looking down at my dinner plate, he continued, "I reckon you must not be a fan of asparagus."

I looked at my plate, smiling. I'd gotten a healthy helping of ham, bread, and corn-on-the-cob, but I'd steered clear of the asparagus.

"It's not that, Mr. Wallace," I said truthfully, "I'm allergic to it. Ate it once when I was a kid and it made my tongue swell up like a potbelly."

"You must be fooling," Mr. Wallace said, with an odd look on his face.

"No, sir. Even got to wear gloves to pick it from the garden."

Mr. and Mrs. Wallace laughed and looked at each other, and a few of the girls laughed, too, everyone acting like this was astonishing. I was plumb confused. Mr. Wallace cleared his throat and wiped food remnants from his mouth, then addressed me.

"Molly's allergic to asparagus, too, ain't ya, Molly?" he said, still smiling. "Found out last summer after I done picked our first crop of the year. She swole up, like you say, like a tick in a hound dog's ear. Couldn't hardly breathe. Thought we was gonna lose her."

Mr. Wallace looked at his daughter, a tear in his eye, smiling. I could tell the horror of that day was still fresh on his brain.

"That must have been terrifying," I said.

"It was, Chuks. It sure was."

I looked across the table at little Molly.

"Molly," I said, "I guess that makes us two peas in a pod."

Someone tells the sheriff to get the hell out of the way. I hear a brief skirmish; very brief. The chanting outside grows louder, my name and the slurs of my flesh echoing off the structures and trees of the hollow that makes up the Post Oak town square. Inside, someone yells, asking where I am, calling me Chuck, saying he's coming for me.

It's Chuks, I tell him, calling out loud enough for everyone within the sheriff's office and jailhouse to hear, with an S.

I see him round the corner of the hall before my cell and the two empty cells on either side of me. He's a young man, wiry and stubbled, with ferocity in his eyes and a club in his hand. I don't know him, but he thinks he knows me.

Coming to a stop in front of the bars that separate us, he points his club at me and tells me I'm going to die and calls me a slur.

I tell him I reckon he's right. I tell him I'm unafraid.

A second man comes around the hall corner, strolling slowly, his expensive boots clacking on the floorboards, the sheriff walking sheepishly behind him. I recognize this man, with his curly mustache. Thomas Montgomery of the lucrative Montgomery Ranch. He comes to a stop alongside the other man, his thumbs looped inside his belt, which is adorned with two shiny revolvers. He smiles.

He knew I would be trouble, he tells me. He knew it the second he saw me.

I look him in the eyes but say nothing.

No words will change the fact that I hang in fifteen minutes.

I grew close to the family. Every single one of them.

Madilyn and Margaret enjoyed literature and poetry, and we exchanged our thoughts on certain works and made suggestions on what to read next. Mariana and Morgan liked to go fishing, so we'd walk down to the creek a time or two a week to see what the good Lord would let us catch. Marilyn liked to sing. I was never any singer myself, but I sure enjoyed hearing her hit those high notes. Mrs. Wallace sat with me during breakfast and we talked about the old days. Mr. Wallace and I rested out on the porch each evening, sometimes saying not a thing, just watching the stars come out.

But it was Molly who I grew a true love for. A fatherly love, like she was my blood, flesh, and soul.

She helped me pick corn and cotton, always with a smile, that fierce Texas sun never seeming to overheat her happiness. She pulled grass out of the furrow after I ran the plow along the ground. She fed and milked the cows with me. She helped me build that fence beyond the house, the one that never would hold horses.

No matter what I was working on, Molly wanted to be in on it.

The garden was her favorite. My favorite, too. Mrs. Wallace and her girls had fashioned an impressive garden prior to my arrival. But my talented hands, with all those years of Louisiana plantation work in them, were able to work magic in the Texas black dirt. We grew fine tomatoes and peppers and herbs; zucchinis and cucumbers and watermelon; even strawberries and blackberries, when the birds and snakes would leave them alone. Molly, her favorite thing to grow and eat was spinach. It makes me laugh even still. You never can figure a little girl.

About a week before the bad thing happened, Molly and I walked the mile or so to town, to Hank's General Store, to buy pumpkin seeds for the garden and some new shoes for the mule. Mr. Wallace had given Molly a nickel to buy some hard candy. She was plumb excited.

I was no stranger to being called names by hateful folks. It was something you almost accepted as an annoyance of daily life as a Negro. Not that it didn't hurt, you understand; I had simply learned that there were battles worth fighting and battles that would only end with my head on a stick. Molly, on the other hand, was not accustomed to such things.

"Hey, look, it's Mute Molly!" some boy twice her age said as she rummaged through the candy jar at Hank's.

"Did the cat get your tongue?" another boy said, laughing.

I was sifting through a shelf of horseshoes when this began, and I looked over, seeing the two pointing at Molly, laughing and making more remarks. Molly retracted her hand from the jar, holding two colorful candy canes, her bottom lip pooching out, tears welling in her eyes.

"Are you gonna cry, Molly the Mute?" the first boy said, laughing again and elbowing his friend.

Molly sobbed and threw the candy to the floor, then ran out the batwing doors at the front of Hank's, to the complete enjoyment of those two boys.

"Molly!" I yelled, putting down the horseshoes and taking after her.

I caught her on the porch just outside the batwings, standing on the edge with her face in her hands. I grabbed her gently by the arm and pulled her close, crouching down and hugging her. I thought of saying something but in that moment, a hug was what she really needed. Picking her up, I carried her back inside the store.

The boys, going through the candy jar now, saw me coming. They saw the look in my eyes. I was never one to anger easily, but I was red-hot with them. Molly was the closest thing to a daughter I had or ever would have. Seeing her cry was tantamount to seeing her heart ripped from her chest.

The boys backed away as I came up on them. They set the jar of candy down, trembling. I turned Molly around in my arms so she could look upon them.

"Boys," I said, "you apologize to Molly right now. Make it sincere or I swear on the Holy Bible neither one of you will see the sun set tonight."

Simultaneously, the boys gasped and took another step back.

"S-sorry, Molly," the first boy said.

"Yeah, sorry," the other said. "We didn't mean nothing by it."

"Yeah," I said, turning Molly back around and laying her head on my shoulder. "Sure you didn't. If I ever catch you boys talking ugly to her again, I'll snatch your tongues out from your heads."

They gasped again as I turned away.

I bought Molly an extra few candy canes with my own earnings.

The sheriff's hand is shaking when he unlocks the cell.

He's pushed aside and Mr. Montgomery and the young, slender man come in after me, grabbing each of my arms and hauling me out. More people are filling the hall ahead of me, cheering and chanting, vowing revenge. They part as I'm led through. They spit at me and slap me over the head and call me all manner of obscenities.

I'm pushed out of the jailhouse and sheriff's office, falling into a puddle just outside the doorway. A crowd encircles me, laughing and jeering, kicking mud at my face and clothes. I'm hit in the side with a stick and my nose is mashed by someone's boot, then I'm pulled to my feet.

Mr. Montgomery tells the townsfolk to make way, that he's leading me to the hanging oak. I look up with one eye, the other matted with muck, and see the oak and the noose and the bonfire beyond. I see a sea of angry faces.

The path to my demise is not unobstructed. I'm hit with fists and clubs the entire way. Someone stabs me in the side with a knife. A rock ricochets off my head and blood dribbles from the wound.

I focus on the noose, a tear forming in my open eye.

It's nine minutes until I hang.

Early this afternoon I was in the garden, collecting the vegetables Mrs. Wallace intended to cook for dinner. Mr. Wallace had shot a possum and chicken snake the night before. He'd caught both of them in the coop, trying for their own dinner. Now, they would be ours. As side dishes, Mrs. Wallace wanted tomatoes, which she would cut fresh and sprinkle spices on, and asparagus, which she would steam in a basket over a pot in the fireplace.

"These sure are some pretty tomatoes, aren't they, Molly?" I said, picking a plump one off the vine and turning to Molly, who was grinning and nodding as she held open her burlap sack. Gingerly, I placed the tomato in the bottom so as not to bruise it.

We moved on down the line of tomato plants, picking the nine best there were. The rain had been good the month prior and the garden showed it. Molly picked cilantro leaves and chewed on them. I picked a Serrano pepper and ate it, to which she made a disgusted face. Then we moved on to the asparagus.

I'd noticed the cluster of blue asparagus for a few weeks now. Among the rows of green sticking up from the dirt like spears, here were ten or twelve that were blue as jaybirds. I ignored them at first. Nature did odd things from time to time, and this was another one of those odd things. I would look at them curiously and move on to whatever I was doing. But now, they were the healthiest and most ready to pick of all the asparagus. I'd picked a healthy helping of asparagus the week before, and all the green ones left looked thin and not fit for the dinnerplate.

But, dern it, these ones were blue . . .

"What do you reckon we should do with those blue ones?" I said, turning to Molly.

She shrugged happily, then stuck out her tongue, indicating she felt the same way about blue asparagus as she did green asparagus and Serrano peppers.

"How's it coming out here?" Mrs. Wallace said, strolling up behind us, wiping her hands on a rag. "Y'all finding us some good veggies?"

"Well," I said, standing up from my inspection of the asparagus, "I was just talking to Molly about that. The tomatoes are beautiful. They'll eat right well. But the asparagus . . . well, I don't think they're quite ready for eatin'. Unless you fancy them in odd colors, that is." I pointed to the cluster of blue.

"Yeah, I saw those the other day," Mrs. Wallace said, cocking her head to the side. "Never seen no blue asparagus before, Chuks."

"Me, neither."

"Well," she said, shrugging, "let's pick 'em and see if they're any good. If they taste like spoiled cow pies, I reckon we'll know not to eat blue asparagus anymore."

"Yes, ma'am," I said, chuckling. "I've never had spoiled cow pies, but they sound downright awful."

So, I donned my leather gloves and picked the blue asparagus and dropped them in Molly's burlap sack with the tomatoes. She cinched the sack shut and threw it over her shoulder and took them inside with her mother. She came quickly back out to help me plant the pumpkin seeds.

Little did I know, in a few hours, I would be a killer.

I'm bleeding from all over.

It pours from my mouth as numerous hands hoist me onto a rickety three-foot stool beneath the oak.

I spit out a tooth among the gore.

A whip cracks across my back, tearing through the thin cloth of my shirt, digging furrows into my flesh.

I pray to God. Not to save my life; to welcome me.

My legs are weak, trembling, but I stand firm on the stool, straightening my tortured back, bringing my head up to the crowd.

A man on a horse rides along my backside, taking ownership of the noose and lowering it over my bleeding skull.

It's two minutes until I hang.

"Chuks, the Bogarts should be here any time to pick up all that cotton they needed," Mr. Wallace said, less than six hours ago, as he walked into the dining room, the sun still peeking over the horizon through the window. "I know it's dinnertime, but you'll need to go help 'em load it in their wagon. Sal Bogart has a bad back and can't be doing it himself."

"Yessir, not a problem, Mr. Wallace," I said, nodding to him, then looking at the spread of food on the table.

"Smells amazing, hon," Mr. Wallace said, removing his old, weathered hat and hanging it on his chair, giving his wife a wink.

"Looks good, too," I said, taking my seat at the table, looking over the sliced tomatoes alongside the possum and snake meat and a loaf of fresh-baked bread. "Very good, Mrs. Wallace."

"Thank you, gentlemen," she said, seating herself as the girls came in and took their places. "It may look and smell good, but we'll have to see about tasting good."

"It'll taste good," Mr. Wallace said, grinning.

"Why is the asparagus blue?" said Margaret.

"Yeah, that's the one I'm not too sure about," Mrs. Wallace said.

"Well, they smell good," I said, looking at the steaming basket of asparagus. They looked soft and moist, and were dusted with salt and pepper. I have to admit, my stomach growled for them even though I knew I couldn't eat them. Looking across at Molly, I said, "I guess Molly and me will have to take y'all's word for it on whether it's yummy or yucky."

This brought a brief laugh from everyone. Then we grasped hands and said the blessing and loaded our plates with food. There was plenty of it. I was shocked by how much meat came off that chicken snake. Lord, it was a big sucker.

"Guess I'll try it first," Mr. Wallace said, stabbing his fork into a blue asparagus. Raising it off the plate, he sniffed it, nodded satisfaction, and deposited it in his mouth. He chewed for a brief moment, looking thoughtfully above everyone's head, then swallowed.

Suddenly, his eyes went wide and his hands went to his throat. He made a brief hacking sound, looking around the table at the rest of us, as if looking for help. A few of the girls screamed out. I stood quickly, knocking my chair over, preparing to come to his aide.

And then he laughed.

"It's wonderful," Mr. Wallace said, his face reddening with laughter.

I sighed in relief and righted my chair, shaking my head and smiling. Mrs. Wallace swatted Mr. Wallace with her hand towel and all the girls ridiculed him for his joke. They had all looked quite alarmed.

"I'm sorry," he said between giggles that kept coming. "I couldn't help myself. But it does taste wonderful. Dig in, everyone." He pointed at me and Molly. "Except you two, of course. It's a shame y'all can't eat it."

So, everyone dug in.

I had my plate nearly clear of food, enjoying every bite of it, when Mrs. Wallace spoke up.

"Bill, what are you doing?" she said, holding a fork full of tomato inches from her mouth, her eyes looking strangely at Mr. Wallace.

I looked over at Mr. Wallace, pausing my own bite of food midway to my face.

He sat there, motionless, his hands resting on the table. His mouth was slightly ajar and his eyes stared blankly over Marilyn, who sat across from him.

"Papa?" Morgan said from beside me, worry in her voice.

"He's fooling again," Madilyn said. "Right, Mama?"

"Certainly," Mrs. Wallace said meekly, without conviction.

"Mr. Wallace?" I said, setting down my fork and slowly rising to my feet. "Everything all right, sir?"

"Bill, you're scaring the children."

"Mama, look at Margaret," Mariana, the second oldest, said.

Everyone's heads whipped that way, to the end of the table where Margaret was. She, too, sat motionless, her hands limp in her lap, her mouth slightly open, her eyes fixed on nothing.

"Margaret, finish your dinner, dear," Mrs. Wallace said, her eyes wide with concern.

Margaret did nothing but continue sitting there, still as a statue.

"I'm getting sca—" Marilyn started, then fell silent.

Looking to her, I realized she, too, was suddenly frozen in place at the dinner table, stopped mid-sentence by some unknowable force, like time itself had halted for her and Margaret and Mr. Wallace. But then it was Morgan falling silent as she'd begun to cry. Followed by Madilyn, who was reaching out to shake Margaret when her arm fell limp to the table, knocking her plate to the floor. Mariana screamed but it was quickly cut short as she, too, took ownership of that blank, lifeless stare.

"What's happening, Chuks?" Mrs. Wallace said, with panic in her voice.

It was the last thing she would ever say; she, too, went the way of the others.

I stood there, wide-eyed, looking around the table, my heart throbbing like it hadn't in ages. Molly, still seated in the chair across from mine, had tears streaking down her cheeks. She and I were the only ones left unfrozen, untouched by whatever malady befell the others.

"What in the good Lord's name is going on, Molly?" I said quietly, moving around the table to where she sat.

She shook her head, sniffling.

I lifted her from her chair and held her, laying her head on my shoulder away from the rest of the family. It was then I noticed their eyes. They were changing. The whites of their eyes were no longer white, but turning blue, the same royal blue as those spears of asparagus. Each eye had puffs of that blue in the whites, like clouds of mud in clear water.

"Oh God almighty," I said, taking a step back from the dining table, looking over my shoulder at the parlor entryway and the foyer beyond, leading outside. I wasn't sure if I should kneel and pray or go running to town for the doctor. As it turned out, I wouldn't have time for either one.

Mr. Wallace suddenly shrieked, his mouth going awkwardly wide and making an almost inhuman noise, like something one might expect to hear from a large bird of prey. The other six seated around the dining table followed suit, Mrs. Wallace and the five girls screeching, still motionless, their blue-stained eyes seeming to grow wider the longer their shrills carried on.

They all silenced as one.

Molly trembled in my arms.

Sweat dribbled down my temple as I took another step backward, unable to look away from the perplexing scene.

Mr. Wallace's head slowly turned my direction, his eyes fixing on mine. Those eyes contained pure evil. Blue evil from the deepest depths of a vast ocean of evil.

With a quick, loud shriek, Mr. Wallace leapt from his chair and bounded over the table toward us, knocking two of the girls from their seats in the process, his arms outstretched like he couldn't wait to claw through our flesh. I backed away, clutching Molly tight, and sidestepped just as Mr. Wallace jumped for us. He went sprawling into the parlor, knocking over Mrs. Wallace's sewing table, sending a long crochet needle skittering across the floor.

Mr. Wallace, maddened by Satan or some wicked force of nature, was now between Molly and I and our exit. Turning back toward the dining room, I saw Molly's five sisters and her mother rising to their feet, each one of them looking at us with a mixture of anger and hunger, as if we weren't simply enemies but living meals meant to be devoured. They made fowl-like shrieking noises as they slowly took steps in our direction.

"Stand back, now!" I demanded, holding a hand out. "Just stand back! Lord Jesus, stand back!"

Mr. Wallace was on his feet again, turning to face us. I stood in the entryway between the parlor and dining room, gritting my teeth, sweat pouring from my brow. My words and Molly's sobs had no effect on halting their advance. I would have to go through the parlor to reach the foyer and the door to the porch. I would have to go through Mr. Wallace, who was not a slight man by any means.

"Let us by, Mr. Wallace," I said, trying to plead with him, not knowing if he was still capable of comprehending. "Let us by, *please!*"

Mr. Wallace charged. In the split second I had to think, I decided charging back at him was our best option. Bending at the waist, leading with my left shoulder, holding Molly tight on the right, I lunged forward. We collided hard, my shoulder connecting with Mr. Wallace's jaw with a crack, one of his teeth cutting through to the flesh beneath my shirt. We both went down, him falling beneath me from the impact and me slipping on the hard wood and tripping over his arm, collapsing atop him. I rolled off quickly, letting loose of Molly and shoving her for the door.

"Run!" I yelled at her, trying to find my feet. "Get out of the house, Molly!"

I pointed for the door and she turned and looked, frightened and unsure.

"Run!" I screamed as someone jumped on my back and Mr. Wallace struggled to get up beside me.

But she just stood there, petrified by fear.

Fingernails dug into my neck and head. I reached over and behind me with both hands, grabbing hold of the hair of whoever was on my back, and slung her off in a wide sweeping motion, sending Marilyn flying across the parlor, crashing into the painted wood wall.

Two girls flew past me, making their way for Molly. I grabbed one of them, Margaret, by the hair and brought her down, slinging her face first into an end table. I heard Molly cry as Mariana jumped atop her, biting into her arm.

I yelled for her, telling her I was coming, but the others were all over me, biting, scratching, punching, kicking. They were like wild animals, knowing nothing but the ferocious need to tear apart their prey. I threw a girl off my shoulders, falling to my knees as someone clawed at my sides and someone else struck me over the head. They were becoming too much, and I saw through a mixture of tangled body parts that Molly was taking a beating from Mariana.

Then I saw the crochet needle.

I lunged forward, stalled by the weight of bodies, but able to get just far enough. I grasped the needle as hands tore at my clothes and brought it over my head with every ounce of power I possessed, aiming for the nearest body to my face, regardless of who it was.

A pained shriek filled the room as a heavy body lurched off me, spilling blood on my head and clothes as they went. Still holding the needle, I pushed up from the floor, knocking girls off my back, gaining my knees and then my feet. It was Mr. Wallace I stuck in the neck. Spurts of blood jetted from the wound with the beat of his heart. He hacked up blood and screamed that inhuman scream, his eyes blue as ever as he fell against the wall, coming to a sitting position there as his life pumped out of him.

Madilyn, the oldest daughter, came at me with her fingers spread out like the claws of a wild cat, her teeth bared like a lion. I rammed the needle into her left eye, destroying it, turning it to a mixture of blood and jelly, pushing the needle through her socket, into her skull, into her brain. She fell limp at my feet, the crochet needle slipping from my grasp, remaining in her skull.

Mrs. Wallace was coming at me now, but I turned my focus to Molly, who was valiantly trying to fight off her older sister. Mariana was on top of her, swinging open hands down on Molly, shrieking nonwords into her face. Molly was swinging back with balled fists and kicking into her sister's gut. Grabbing Mariana from behind, I flung her off Molly, throwing her into her mother, sending them both toppling to the floor.

"Get out and run!" I yelled at Molly, helping her to her feet and pushing her toward the door. "Go, now!"

This time, she did.

As I saw her flee out the front door, leaving it open, I turned back to the oncoming Wallaces, with their maddened blue eyes. Noticing the iron fire poker leaning against the parlor woodstove, I grabbed it and held it high and got to work.

Backing toward the front door, I broke Mrs. Wallace's outstretched hands and bashed her face in. I tore out Mariana's cheek with the hook of the poker, then stabbed her in the gut and the neck. I brought the iron down hard on Margaret's head and a stream of blood shot up from the wound as she collapsed. I took out Morgan's blue eyes with two swift swings of the poker, bringing her down on the cusp of the front porch.

Only Marilyn, the twelve-year-old, was left, and she ran at me undeterred, following me onto the porch, reaching out to me, a barbaric look on her face. I brought the poker against her left temple, sending her falling hard to the wooden porch. She was still alive, moving to get up, so I delivered another blow with the iron, standing over her, hitting her again and again, splattering her skull and brain to mush across the porch. I'd gone mad, by this point, with fear and anger.

I only stopped hitting her when the wall above my head exploded in a hail of splinters.

I can't say whether Sal Bogart missed me intentionally, or whether he was a bad shot. But when I turned around, still clutching tightly to the fire poker, he was standing there by his wagon with a Henry rifle aimed at my head.

Molly stood beside him, bleeding from multiple wounds and crying.

Sal Bogart told me to throw down the iron and called me a slur.

The noose is tightened. I can feel the scratch of its fibers. I look to the heavens, to the sprawling limbs of the hanging oak and the stars beyond. Mud and blood burns one eye; tears burn the other.

Stones pelt my body. Chants of hate and revenge flood my ears.

Sal Bogart and Thomas Montgomery stand before me, yelling for my attention.

Reluctantly, I look down.

Mr. Montgomery is holding a small doll, asking if it's mine. Sal says he found it in my room at the Wallace's, under my pillow.

I nod my head slowly—*it is* mine. A voodoo doll made of burlap and straw, its face stitched with black thread, handed down to me by my aunt. A doll. A keepsake. Nothing more.

They call me a witch, a voodoo witch, a devil witch.

Torches raise and the townsfolk call for it to be done. Rifles blast into the night. The bonfire roars.

I begin to close my crying eye and wait for the end, but then I see her.

Molly is out there in the crowd. An old woman, her face creased with decades of Texas sun, holds her up shoulder high, allowing her to see my final moments. Tears are streaming down Molly's face, rolling over the scrapes and bruises inflicted by her sister. She's saying something. Screaming something. I can hear her voice for the first time.

"No! I love you, Chuks!!"

Someone knocks the stool from beneath me.

The noose was tied smartly with suitable rope, and the oak branch is plenty strong to hold me.

I reach out to Molly as the rope reaches its apex.

When it does, my neck snaps and all goes black.

Molly screams and screams.

She'll go mute again for several years.

When she finally breaks her silence, she'll attempt to explain to the townsfolk what really happened, that her family turned sour and evil and attacked the two of us. She'll tell them I was defending her.

But these claims will fall on deaf ears.

When she's nineteen, she'll move to San Antonio. She'll become a journalist for a small newspaper. She'll fall in love with a man named Mendez, a blacksmith from El Paso. They'll be married and live long happy lives and have five children, the first of which, a boy, they'll name Chuks, with an S.

Molly Mendez will never forget Chuks Barret from Post Oak.

To everyone else, I'll forever be known as the Devil Witch of Hanging Oak.

PATRICK C. HARRISON III (PC3, if you prefer) is an author of horror, splatterpunk, and all forms of speculative fiction. He is the author of perhaps the most depraved book ever written—*Grandpappy*—as well as *A Savage Breed*, *Vampire Nuns Behind Bars*, and others. His works can also be found in numerous anthologies. He is the Splatterpunk Award-winning editor (with Jarod Barbee) of *And Hell Followed*. He is the creative force that brought the world the Splatter Western series of books in 2020 and beyond. You can keep track of him and his works at pc3horror.com.

Got The Spirit but Lose The Feeling
Jonathan Louis Duckworth

Ned Cobb pulls the mortuary van into the parking lot, his exhausted body shuddering with relief at the sight of Sheriff McCaskill's cruiser under the tacky red neon sign that proclaims TIFFANY'S DINER— BEST CHICKEN FRIED STEAK IN TOWN. Tiffany's is the furthest outpost of Crumb, Texas, the last stop before the ramp to 380 and the rest of the world.

There's a good number of cars in the lot, and Ned can see people in the booths, and that relaxes him somewhat, as much as he can relax given what he's been through the last—how long has he been up now? Twenty-eight hours? Thirty-two? He takes a deep breath and closes his eyes. Breathes in, breathes out.

He turns the key and kills the engine. Crickets in the roadside bushes fill the new silence. He checks under the tarp again. Harriet Winthrop is still there, her body inert again with the wire severed; that translucent thread-like fishing line laced through her spinal cord and into her brain. He checks his face in the mirror. With his eyes bruised and ringed from exhaustion and his nose busted and swollen, he looks like a raccoon with a coke problem. His lip's cut, too. Winthrop—or the thing that turned her into a deadly marionette assassin, rather—really did a number on him back at Doc Landers' office. But at least he's alive. At least he's still in control of his body. It's been six hours, now, since he's heard from either the Doc or Deputy Barron.

"If something happens to me, find the sheriff, tell him everything," was what Deputy Barron said before driving off to investigate the Chapek farm.

So here Ned is, at Tiffany's, where the sheriff always spends his evenings.

The bell jangles as Ned steps in. He's barely set one foot down before a familiar, pale face, studded with piercings and crowned in royal purple hair, fills his vision. Doreen greets him with a smile: black lipstick, white teeth, pink gums.

"Howdy, Ned," Doreen says. "You look like dogshit. Want the usual?"

He shakes his head. Doreen's been waiting tables here since they were in high school, back when Ned had dreams of doing something more stimulating with his life than driving a van—not even a proper hearse—for a funeral home, and back when Doreen was supposed to go to art school and be the butterfly who breaks free from her small-town chrysalis. Ned and Doreen—always a little more than friends, never really a thing; just the only two kids in town who listened to Joy Division and believed President Reagan was a senile shit-for-brains.

"I gotta talk to the sheriff, Dor," Ned says, brushing past her.

It's the usual small crowd of regulars in the diner. Mrs. Tiffany, the proprietress, a slender, fifty-something auburn-haired woman who more resembles a high school principal or bank attendant than the owner of a greasy-spoon, sits at her booth, highlighting figures on a spreadsheet. The next booth over, Old Lyle Rook, knife salesman, is sharing a meal with his friend, Johnny Deale, lawyer. But the man Ned's after is at the counter, sitting high on his stool, nose buried in the day's paper. "Pres. Clinton's 100 Day Ratings Lowest Ever," the headline reads.

"Sheriff?" Ned says, coming to lean beside him.

Sheriff McCaskill lowers his newspaper and scowls. With his iron gray hair and pouting lower lip, the sheriff's always reminded Ned of a grumpier Lee Marvin. The look in the sheriff's eyes tells Ned that even all these years later, Ned's still the longhaired, pierced-nose troublemaker he caught selling weed to the other kids on prom night. Weed he got from Doreen, of course.

"Yeah?" McCaskill grunts.

Ned hesitates. He's not sure how to begin, or how not to sound crazy. Better to just show him Harriet Winthrop and the wire still dangling from her brainstem.

"Sheriff, if you'll follow me outside, I've got something I need to show you."

"Follow you? Outside?" The sheriff's already squinty eyes narrow to slits. He has such a leathery face. "This some sort of game, Cobb?"

"No, sir. *Deadly* serious. Deputy Barron told me to come to you."

McCaskill looks even more annoyed.

Ned glances around. The other patrons are watching him intently. The most irksome thing about small towns: no privacy anywhere. Doreen is smiling at him as she freshens Old Lyle's coffee. All circumstances aside, Ned can't help but smile back. How is it she's gotten prettier?

"Is this about the alien nonsense again?" McCaskill says.

Ned's not sure how to respond.

"It's that alien shit, ain't it?" Old Lyle calls out, leaning over the back of his booth, his nicotine yellow teeth shucked like an ear of sweetcorn.

"Language, Lyle," Mrs. Tiffany chides without looking up. She's finished with her spreadsheet and moved onto a crossword puzzle.

"Dan came around here a couple hours ago, spouting nonsense," McCaskill says. "Some high blue bull-mess about alien puppets and wires in folks' heads. Near about had him committed on the spot, I'll tell you."

Ned's hands are cold and clammy. The deputy was already here? But then where did he go after stopping here? Was that before or after he went to the Chapek farm?

"Ridiculous, all these rumors," Johnny Deale says, his shoulder-length gray mane flopping as he shakes his head. "Those two rotten Dufresne kids go out to shoot bottle rockets at steers and say they see a meteor, next thing everyone's seeing aliens and UFOs."

"There was a meteor," Lyle says. "I seen the pictures like everyone else."

"*Meteorite* if it hits the ground, you ignoramus. And anyway, you didn't see pictures of any meteorite, you saw pictures of a crater."

"There was no meteor when we checked it out," McCaskill says.

"*Meteorite*," Deale and Mrs. Tiffany say.

"It was just a burnt hole in the ground," McCaskill continues. "You ask me, them damn troublemaking kids just blew something up in the woods and spun a tall tale."

Ned leans against the counter and pinches his forehead. Like sharp fingers poking the inside of his skull, a headache's flaring up. It was nine days ago when the Dufresne brothers told their story about the meteor.

"What about what Mr. Chapek saw on his farm?" Doreen says.

A week back, the whole town buzzed with the story that Mr. Chapek, respected farmer and rancher, had gone crazy. Chapek said he'd watched a slimy, gray, legless creature—something like an obscene tadpole—flop its way across the pasture toward the barn.

McCaskill scoffs. "Oh, that nothing-burger. Chapek was drunk, he admitted so to me himself after we searched his barn the next morning. Nothing there."

"I've been drunk once or twice. Drunk doesn't make people see aliens," Ned says.

McCaskill's leathery face cracks with a rare smile. "For what it's worth, I wouldn't be surprised if ol Chapek was doing heavier stuff than Jim or Jack."

Ned's anxiety and exhaustion give way to frustration, and he pounds his fist on the counter, an action that hurts more than he expected. "Look, I don't care what you think you know, I've seen it for myself."

"Inside voice, son," McCaskill says. "Now, what is it you've seen?"

"Those wires Deputy Barron told you about, the ones in folks' heads? I've seen them, hell, I can show you if you'll just take a look."

"Seen them where?" McCaskill asks.

"On Harriet Winthrop and Craig Peterson."

"What about Harriet, now?" Lyle says.

"It's just horrible what happened to Craig Peterson," Mrs. Tiffany mutters. "Forty-two years old, two kids, beats cancer only to die in a pointless car wreck."

"Drunk drivers, the bane of civilization," Johnny Deale says, shaking his head.

If a drunk driver hadn't slammed into Craig Peterson's car two days ago, no one would have found out what was happening. Ned was the one who drove the body to the funeral home, was the one who found the severed wire, a translucent cord coiling from a little hole in the dead man's spine. Ned showed the body to Doc Landers, who performed a—very much unsanctioned—autopsy with his friend Deputy Barron in attendance. Landers was tracing the path of the threads through Peterson's skeletal system and musculature when frail Harriet Winthrop, the friendly old post office worker, barged into Doc Landers' office. She was maybe eighty pounds and well past seventy years, but she threw Ned across the room like he was made of packing peanuts. She'd have strangled Doc Landers were it not for Deputy Barron putting two bullets through her skull. The wire that held her in thrall then detached and burrowed its barbed tip into Barron's arm. It might have threaded into his bones and taken control had Ned not burned it out with a scalpel heated on an alcohol flame, because, as it turns out, the wires play by the same rules as deer ticks. In the eight or so hours since, Ned's been surfing a tide of adrenaline interspersed with crashes, and right now he's crashing again.

"We're not talking about drunk drivers, we're talking about aliens," Ned says. It sounds so silly, spoken out loud.

"I don't believe aliens could come here," Mrs. Tiffany says. "I'm no astrophysicist, but it seems to me we're too far away from any other star for travel to be feasible. It would take hundreds of years to get here."

"Aliens could live a really long time," Doreen says. "I mean, aren't there trees and jellyfish that live for a thousand years?"

"Trees and jellyfish can't make spaceships," Mrs. Tiffany replies. "Have you ever heard of Fermi's Paradox?"

"Oh, that's the one where you should believe in God because of hell, right?" Lyle says.

"That's Pascal's wager," Johnny Deale says.

"If there's so many stars with so many planets in the universe that can bear life, and so many of those that can develop intelligent life, why haven't we ever made contact? That's Fermi's Paradox in a nutshell," Mrs. Tiffany says.

"Aliens been here, just the government won't tell us," Lyle says.

"That's one explanation for the paradox," Mrs. Tiffany replies. "Another is the Great Filter—that intelligent life destroys itself before it can reach the stars."

"Could we please focus here?" Ned says, clapping his hands, as much to rouse himself as to get the others' attention.

"Maybe we should listen to him," Doreen says. "Ned isn't the type to just make shit up."

"Thank you," Ned says, louder than he means to.

"Well, I think I've had quite enough of this silly talk," McCaskill says, turning back toward the counter with an air of finality. "You'd think we'd stop hearing about this alien stuff after two months."

"Two months? It wasn't even two weeks ago that that meteor hit," Ned protests.

"*Meteorite*," Mrs. Tiffany, Deale, Doreen, and Lyle all say.

"What do you want us to do, Cobb?" McCaskill asks. "You want me to believe there's some space aliens turning people into puppets? You want me to get on the horn and call up President Bush and have him send the army?"

"What do you mean President Bush? It's President Clinton now. And all I want is for you to come look—"

"I think I know who the president is," McCaskill says.

Ned is about to argue when he realizes this is pointless, they're drifting from the point again. But then he sees something that makes his heart lurch. McCaskill straightens out his newspaper. The headline is different now: "Iraqi Army Invades Kuwait." And the date is different; wrong by three years.

Isn't it?

"If aliens were coming, they wouldn't come here," Johnny Deale says. "Who the hell would want to take over Crumb, Texas? No offense, Sheriff."

The sheriff only grunts, flipping his newspaper.

"Closing time in half an hour," Mrs. Tiffany announces, checking her watch. "If you want something, Ned, now's the time to order."

He doesn't answer.

"You know, Mr. Deale, why wouldn't aliens come here?" Doreen asks, leaning on the counter beside Ned now. "It's quiet, small, an easy place to start."

At least someone in here has a brain. Ned turns to her. "Dor, why don't you come and see? I need someone to believe me. I need someone to help me—we're all in danger, and Deputy Barron—"

The door jangles just as he's speaking. And in walks Sheriff's Deputy Daniel Barron, a tall young man with a neat crew cut and the ropy, rangy look of a wide receiver—which he was, back in high school.

Ned's gut relaxes, his jaw unclenches, he almost sighs audibly in relief at the sight of Deputy Barron.

"You're back," Ned says. "Thank God you're all right. When you didn't call the payphone at six like you said you would, I thought—"

"Easy there, friend," Barron says, waving his hand. His expression is relaxed, not at all the look of a man who's been up for about as long as Ned has. "You look agitated, Ned."

"I'm agitated because the sheriff won't listen," Ned says, pointing at McCaskill, who barely lifts his nose from his paper to nod at his deputy. "Why don't you tell him?"

"Tell him what?" Barron asks.

"He wants you to tell us what you already told us, I guess," Mrs. Tiffany says.

Barron chuckles. There's something weird in the sound, something not entirely organic, the rhythm too regular, the pitch too uniform. The relief in Ned turns rancid, becomes a churning, urgent apprehension again.

"Oh, Ned, I hope you haven't been telling that joke to these people," Barron says. He rolls his eyes.

"What joke? What are you—?" Ned stops. His words congeal on his tongue as he stares into Barron's eyes and recognizes the same hollow, lusterless nothing that was behind Harriet Winthrop's when she attacked Doc Landers's office. Ned's eye tracks over Barron's head, looking for the slight glimmer of the diner's lights on a wire, but he can't see anything.

"You look queasy," Doreen says, her hand touching Ned's shoulder.

"He's one of them," Ned says, pointing to Barron. "They got him—it got him."

Barron—or the puppet, rather—smiles, the folding of the skin around the lips too symmetrical to be human. "Doreen's right, Ned. You look like you need to sit down."

Ned swats his hand away. "Don't fucking touch me."

"Ned—" Doreen tries to hook her arm around his and he reacts on instinct, shoving her away. Doreen collides with the counter, and the way she grunts and the hurt, shocked glimmer of her gray-blue eyes sends a jolt of remorse through Ned.

"I'm sorry, Dor," Ned says. "I'm just—it's not safe here, we need to get out of here. Come with me, we'll drive somewhere safe, we'll . . ."

His words fail him, his chest contracts, painfully, his breaths become leaden and painful, like he's breathing from an exhaust pipe. His trembling hands are heavy as dumbbells, and he can't sense his tongue between his teeth, while the walls seem to be closing in, the people around him with their bland pink faces and gawking expressions spinning, spinning, spinning.

Is this what a heart-attack feels like?

A hand grasps his wrist. Mrs. Tiffany. Her eyes look into his, glinting with the shine and depth of a genuine human.

"You're having a panic attack, Ned," she says.

Another soft feminine hand takes his other wrist. Doreen. "Easy, Ned. Breathe in and out. Slowly. Calm yourself."

"We need, we need to—" he tries to form a sentence, but it's taking everything he has not to fall over or shake to pieces.

His ears crackle and hiss like old record players. Under that white noise, he hears Mrs. Tiffany's voice. "Look at the apple in my hand, Ned," she says. "Just ground yourself by looking at the apple in my hand."

He looks. She holds a bare palm to him.

"There's no—there's no apple in your hand."

"Sure there is," Barron says, his hateful dead face grinning.

"A shiny red delicious," Mrs. Tiffany says.

"Dark, round, and crimson, like a human heart," Lyle says.

"Hearts are gray, you dunce," Johnny Deale snaps.

He blinks rapidly. There's an apple in her hand now, and then there isn't, and then it's there again, its glossy, waxen red curves shimmering under the overhead lights.

"No, it's not, this isn't—"

"Everyone sees the apple, Ned," Mrs. Tiffany says.

"Don't you want to see the apple, Cobb?" McCaskill says, his newspaper folded on his lap now, the headline once again gloating about Clinton's low polling numbers.

"Stop it!" Doreen shouts, pulling Ned away from Mrs. Tiffany. "God, what's up with you freaks? There ain't no goddamn apple."

Ned holds tight to her, and she anchors his feet to the ground and helps him to a booth, where he sits down. "In the van," he mutters, tears rolling down his cheeks, "in the van, there's a body, there's proof . . ."

"Shh," Doreen says. "Ned, you're delirious. You're not talking sense."

"I oughta head out, the missus will be expecting me home soon," McCaskill says, standing up and walking to the rack where his coat is hanging.

"I better be going, too," Barron says, walking behind him. "Take care, Ned. You oughta go home and catch some sleep. I can tell you need it."

Don't go with him, Ned wants to yell at McCaskill, but his voice is a little shy grub in the trunk of his throat.

Doreen squeezes his hand. "Feeling any better, Ned?" Beautiful little dimples form around the silver stud piercings in her cheeks when she smiles.

Looking at her, feeling his heartbeat steady and the hairs on his arms settle, Ned remembers hot summer afternoons with the two of them sitting in her old '77 F-150 Explorer, passing a joint between them, eating bags of gummi bears half melted by the summer heat and the truck's greenhouse effect, his hand exploring the soft, fuzzy skin of her stomach, breasts, and inner thighs, his fingers sticky with sweat and sugar. She might have tattoos all over her throat and arm now, but she hasn't really changed otherwise. Her eyes are as sweet and bright as ever, and the twinkle of light in them says she's still her.

Lyle and Johnny Deale are paying their check, getting ready to go. The light is out in the kitchen behind the counter—the cook gone, if the cook was ever there to begin with.

"You all right to close, Doreen?" Mrs. Tiffany says.

Doreen nods in answer. And now it's just Ned and Doreen. Doreen wipes down the counters and turns out the lights. "So tell me about these aliens. What are we dealing with?"

Her tone is serious, sober.

"Do you believe me?" he asks, tracking her as she wipes down the counter with a rag. As he watches her cleaning, he wonders when they—it?—got Deputy Barron. Wonders if McCaskill is a puppet by now. And what about the rest? Probably all of them are, or will be soon.

Doreen tosses the rag into a cleaning bucket, then removes her apron and folds it up. "Don't know yet, but I figure you wouldn't make an ass of yourself if you didn't believe something was happening, and I don't think you're on anything. Are you?"

Ned shakes his head. "No. Three months sober."

She sits down across from him in the booth, leaning forward on her elbows. "Clean, too?"

"Yeah, uhh—" he stops, wondering why she's asking about him being clean. Her eyes still shimmer, humanlike, and yet . . . "Dor, I need to ask you something."

"What?"

"Can I . . . feel behind your neck?"

She tilts her head, like a cat. The dimples appear again around her cheek studs. "This some kind of put-on?"

"I'm serious."

She rolls her eyes. "Sure. Knock yourself out." His hands tremble as he reaches across the booth, grazing her cheek and flicking past the fleshy lobes of her ears with their huge black gauges. He feels the bumps of her neck and spine, up to the base of her skull, down toward the neckline. "Feel anything interesting?"

No wire. No wire in her. He sags with relief. "Oh God, you're still you. You're still—"

She leans in, presses her lips to his. His tired eyes flutter. He tastes the menthols she smokes on her breaks.

His eyes open, and they're not in the diner anymore. His shoes crunch into a litter of old receipts and empty cigarette packets, and his back sinks into the familiar seat cushions of Doreen's old Ford. From the truck's crummy stereo, "Disorder" by Joy Division threads out, grainy and faint, like he's listening to the song through a seashell.

Doreen sits beside him, in the driver's seat. Whiskers of pale smoke waft from the tip of a lit joint tweezed between her tattooed fingers. "You feeling better?" she asks.

He nods his head, slowly. Yes, he feels better. Safe, relaxed, all the aches gone.

"So, why do you think these aliens came here, Neddy?"

He shrugs his shoulders. "I don't know. To conquer, I guess. Isn't that what invasions are about?"

Doreen slips the joint between Ned's lips, and Ned takes a puff. It's nasty stuff that makes him cough, and that discomfort is almost enough to make him believe this is real.

"I don't know, Neddy," she says. "Maybe they think they can help. Maybe they see a reckless species going off the rails, and they're here to steady the proverbial wheel. Or maybe that's just some bullshit they tell themselves. Maybe it's just fun to see what you can do to lesser creatures."

Doreen brushes her hand through her hair, and when her fingers emerge, delicate silver wires slither from under her black nails. The song on the stereo hits its crescendo: Stephen Morris starts massacring the drums and Ian Curtis launches into immortal refrain.

"What will it feel like?" Ned asks.

"What do you mean?"

"I mean, will it hurt when the wires burrow into me?"

She rests her hand on Ned's wrist, her fingers sticky with the grime of evaporated soda that coats the armrest. The wires coil around Ned's arm; they're not smooth, as they appear, rather edged in tiny bristles like what grow on cat's ear leaves.

"Oh, Neddy." Her voice is so perfectly inflected, so unmistakably her own. "Haven't you figured it out? They already have."

"But when? When did they, when did you—?"

She presses a finger to his lips. "Relax. Just listen to the music, and don't worry about what your body's doing without you."

JONATHAN LOUIS DUCKWORTH is a completely normal, entirely human person with the right number of heads and everything. He received his MFA from Florida International University. His speculative fiction work appears in or is forthcoming in *Magazine of Fantasy & Science Fiction*, *Pseudopod*, *Beneath Ceaseless Skies*, *Southwest Review*, *Flash Fiction Online*, and elsewhere. He is a PhD student at University of North Texas where he serves as the interviews editor at *American Literary Review*, and he is also an active HWA member.

Blue Moon
Jacklyn Baker

The moon had come a second time this month.

It was large in the sky, bright and full. But it was silver in color, not blue. Adriana had never understood why they called it a "blue moon."

She stared at it while waiting for the 6:58 bus to arrive. It was past 9:00 now—the bus had broken down and, according to the announcement online, the other busses that had already finished their daily circuits were working to complete Route 4 now.

When the bus finally did come, it would pick her up from Speight Avenue and take her six stops to 11th Street, to her tiny apartment on the ground floor of a thirty-year-old building that needed a paint job and a new HVAC system. She would unlock her door and shuffle her heavy bag off her shoulder without taking more than two steps into the living room. She would change into comfy pants, take off her bra, and heat up some form of microwavable dinner. Then she would sit on the couch and study her Organic Chemistry book until she couldn't see straight anymore. Then she would wake up at 5:30 a.m., go to her shift at the coffee shop, then her classes, then her shift at the library. And then she'd wait for the 6:58, and do it all over again.

It was just bad luck that it hadn't happened that way today.

A bus finally rolled to a stop in front of her, creaking on its axles and hissing at her as if to warn her away from it. It certainly felt like some beast come to swallow her whole.

Adriana stared at the moon until the vehicle's doors opened. A fleeting thought about running away with the man in the moon crossed her mind and then she dismissed it for the flight of fancy it was.

The thing about running away with any man was the inevitable consequences that came with it.

Adriana woke six days after the night of the blue moon, threw up into her bedside trashcan, and immediately knew she was pregnant. She couldn't explain how she knew—some strange sense that she was no longer alone maybe—but she knew. A trip to the Student Life Center clinic, at the cost of a missed Anatomy class confirmed this. She was two weeks into an unexpected pregnancy.

She didn't know what to do.

More importantly, she didn't know how it was possible in the first place.

She hadn't had sex in the two months since the semester started. She didn't have the time for it.

When the doctor kindly tried to discuss her options, Adriana dismissed her. She rose from the examination table, paper sheet crinkling loudly, picked up her purse, and walked out of the room.

Sitting on the lumpy couch in her apartment, Adriana wrestled with her dilemma alone. She loathed the thought of telling her mother. Although the woman was only thirty minutes outside of Waco, she would offer no comfort, and certainly no assistance. Her classmates and coworkers were friendly, but not friends. Adriana knew she couldn't keep the baby, but she also knew she couldn't go through with the act of getting rid of it. She'd have to give it away. There was really no other choice.

She waited until after midterms—she owed herself that much at least after all her hard work—and then she went to a doctor off-campus. This one was a proper OB/GYN. She picked a man in his late forties called Dr. Moorjani, who officed in the Women's and Children's Center of the Hillcrest Hospital for no other reason than that he had a time slot available during her Anatomy class, which was quickly becoming the go-to class to skip for doctor's appointments.

Adriana waited an unreasonable amount of time for the doctor to finally see her, sitting in the sterile, beige room and staring at a diagram of a uterus for nearly an hour after her appointment was due to start. Too bad that wasn't the section they were covering in Anatomy right now.

When Dr. Moorjani finally concluded the examination, the results were the same, except that this doctor told her she was closer to two months into her pregnancy rather than, according to the initial doctor, what would be just over four weeks now. That made more sense. The S.L.C. doctors just weren't equipped to properly evaluate a pregnancy, that was all. This pregnancy must be from before school started and she'd had some spotting that she thought was her period last month. She questioned the doctor about it, but he told her everything was normal and a little bleeding early-on isn't unheard of. The baby was fine.

When Dr. Moorjani asked if she knew who the father might be, Adriana had to admit that she didn't. Her last sexual encounter had been a one-night stand. She hadn't gotten a number or even a last name.

"Baby Lawrence, then," Dr. Moorjani said with an easy acceptance, making a note in mother and baby's file.

But it didn't sit right with Adriana when she knew she wouldn't be keeping it.

Three weeks later, Adriana was showing. Her belly had swollen overnight. She stood in the full-length mirror on the back of her bedroom door for fifteen minutes, turned sideways and staring at the . . . growth. It was beginning to feel less like a baby was in there and more like a parasite, like her belly would just swell and swell until it burst like a balloon and whatever was inside crawled out and left her hollow and bloodless.

Adriana gasped. She stopped that train of thought right there. That was ridiculous. The possibility of a more realistic complication, however, was not ridiculous. She forced herself away from the mirror.

Throughout the morning her coworkers offered their congratulations, asking her why she hadn't told them. The answer was simple. She'd thought she had more time to do it.

The minute his office opened, Adriana called and moved her next visit with Dr. Moorjani up to his earliest available time. He saw her that afternoon (Anatomy class, again).

The doctor's brow furrowed to see her belly and arranged for an ultrasound immediately. He spread the cold gel over her stomach, creating involuntary spasms in Adriana's muscles, then moved the wand around until he found what he was looking for.

Then he turned the machine off and sat there silently.

"Dr. Moorjani?" Adriana said with a hint of alarm. This morning's vision of her stomach bursting apart came back in a flash of remembrance.

He shook his head.

"I'm sorry, Miss Lawrence. The baby looks perfectly fine, but . . . let me just look at your file again."

He did and he came away from it confused.

"It's a boy," he told her, but he still looked completely flummoxed.

"Okay. And?"

"And I shouldn't be able to determine the sex yet. It should be another two weeks before we can tell, but . . . well, you look to be about sixteen weeks along now."

Adriana jerked, her elbow knocking into the ultrasound machine. "Sixteen—! How can that be? I was only nine weeks along *three* weeks ago."

The man looked down at the papers again and flipped one over. "Perhaps I was mistaken."

Adriana couldn't help the flare of anger. "Mistaken? Do you think you could maybe not be mistaken, please?"

The doctor blinked, then lowered the file to give her his full attention. "Yes. Yes, of course, I apologize, Miss Lawrence. I didn't mean to upset you. Let me make some phone calls. Come back the same time next week?"

Why not? Adriana thought. *I'm already failing Anatomy anyway.*

When it first kicked, Adriana dropped a cup of coffee.

It was such a strong kick, it startled her as much as the ceiling falling down might have.

The loud clatter of the paper cup and the *slosh* of liquid against tile drew the attention of patrons and employees, alike. The steaming coffee was all over the floor. Some of it had splashed up and was scalding the skin beneath Adriana's pant leg.

"Adriana?" came the concerned voice of her shift manager, Elizabeth. "Are you all right?"

"I—" Adriana swallowed, her sentence cut short by another rattling kick. "Yeah. Yeah, fine."

Elizabeth frowned, unconvinced. "Why don't you sit down for a few minutes? I'll remake that drink. Okay?"

When Elizabeth put her hand on her arm, Adriana noticed the steadiness of her touch against her own shaking limbs. Sitting might not be so bad an idea after all. She nodded. "Okay."

Adriana caught the eye of the customer whose drink she had dropped as Elizabeth ushered her out of the workspace. He was giving her a look like there was something wrong with her.

Maybe there was.

At their follow-up appointment, Dr. Moorjani had called in a second doctor to consult on her visit.

"It's not that we think that there's anything to worry about, but I'd like a second opinion," Dr. Moorjani explained. "So we can be absolutely certain nothing's wrong. No mistakes. Is it all right if Dr. Dillihunt examines you as well?"

Dr. Dillihunt, a woman with graying blonde hair, smiled pleasantly at her. Adriana didn't like the sound of "second opinion," but gave her permission.

The conclusion was not good.

The baby had reached what her doctor *and* the consulting doctor both deemed to be eighteen weeks.

"It's only been one week!" Adriana exclaimed. "How could it be two weeks further along?"

Her OB/GYN shook his head.

"I don't know. We'll want to run some tests . . ." he prodded gently.

Dr. Dillihunt was rapidly flipping back and forth between the pages in her file, a look like fascination on her face.

Adriana pressed her palms into her eyes. "Fine. Do what you have to."

By the following week, Adriana was twenty weeks along, according to both Dr. Moorjani and Dr. Dillihunt.

A whole team of doctors was brought in to poke and prod at her, but not one held any more answers for the unusual growth rate than the last. Adriana spent more time in a doctor's office than she did in a classroom. They ran blood panels and performed scans and went over her family's medical history with a fine-tooth comb. They picked apart her diet and shined a light in her eye more times than she thought was strictly necessary. They monitored her for seventy-two hours straight and recorded every move she made.

The school marked all of her courses as Incompletes. It was for the best. She was going to have to reconsider her field of study anyway. Working in research held a lot less appeal now, after being given the guinea pig treatment and listening to doctors talk about the medical journals they would publish in about *her*.

Her belly continued to swell. It protruded past her breasts now. Her back was beginning to ache. Her clothes were getting tighter.

She took down the mirror in her bedroom.

Three weeks later and all the medical experts could tell her was that there was nothing wrong with her and that the baby was a perfectly healthy boy, twenty-six weeks along.

Adriana was tired of the doctors.

She went to a medicine woman. To be honest, "witch" felt like a more accurate word for the strange woman who resided forty minutes outside of town, in a shack tucked against one muddy bank of the Brazos River. The solitary house was creepy, at best, a possible crime scene, at worst. Twelve weeks ago, Adriana would never have pictured herself going to such a person. But twelve weeks ago she wasn't twenty-six weeks pregnant.

It was her mother who suggested it. When Adriana had finally acquiesced and called her to tell her what was going on, all her mother, a born and bred local, had had to say was, "Bad luck. Better see the river woman."

It was perhaps the only valuable piece of advice her mother had ever given her. But that had yet to be seen as she'd only just knocked on the door of the "river woman."

The person who answered the door looked to be as old as the Brazos itself. She was short and round and frowning. The combination gave Adriana the impression of a bullfrog.

"Yes?" the woman said, her voice surprisingly strong for her wizened appearance.

"Hello, my name is Adriana Lawrence. I have a problem I was told you might be able to help me with."

"What problem?"

Adriana almost started to tell her about the abnormal pregnancy, but she paused, remembering what her mother had said on the phone.

"Bad luck," she said, instead.

The river woman nodded and let her in.

The home was as dingy and shabby inside as it was outside. It smelled like dirt and dead plants and it was certainly a change of pace from the disinfectant and bright, gleaming white of the doctor's offices and hospital rooms. The maroon threadbare couch she sat on was almost a welcome reprieve, even if Adriana still felt uncertain about being there.

The woman introduced herself as Cora, and Adriana told her about the baby.

Cora raised a hand toward Adriana's belly. "May I?"

"Yes."

The river woman reached out with both hands then, as if she were preparing to pick up something fragile.

Adriana didn't know what she was hoping for, exactly, but it certainly wasn't what she got.

The baby squirmed, a churning, uncomfortable twist that had its mother gasping and bowing in half.

A sharp kick landed on Cora's hands and the woman jerked back, eyes wide and glued to Adriana's stomach.

The force of the kick lanced through Adriana's abdomen, keeping her doubled over. She breathed through her mouth until the pain passed, then righted herself.

The baby stilled.

"What just happened?" Adriana asked.

Cora's wild gaze settled on Adriana's pale face. "You looked at the blue moon."

Adriana shook her head, not understanding. "Everyone looks at the blue moon."

Cora's gaze was heavy on her. "Not long enough for the moon to look back."

Adriana's spine stiffened.

"There is a legend. That any woman who stares at the blue moon too long will become pregnant with the moon's child."

Adriana's jaw dropped. "You can't be serious. Are you trying to tell me that the moon got me pregnant?"

"I am not telling you that at all. It is only a legend. But there is always some truth in legends."

"What else does the legend say?"

"Supposedly, blue-moon mothers give birth to demon children," said Cora, "but this is not true."

Adriana's eyebrows climbed into her hairline.

"Then what . . ." Adriana didn't want to ask, but she had to. "What is it?"

Cora paused, then said, "Celestial."

"It's not . . . It's not human?"

Cora shook her head.

Dread welled in Adriana's stomach, alongside the unnatural spawn there. It sounded crazy. And yet. What other explanation did Adriana have? Science had been stumped by it. If folklore and old wives' tales were all she had to go on, then so be it.

"What do I do?"

"You carry the child to term. It is your only option."

Adriana wrung the fabric of her shirt between her fingers. Her belly sat bulging under her hands. "Am I . . . am I going to be okay?"

The river woman eyed her for a long moment, something strained in her expression. Her reply was: "You know what Brazos means? The river's name?"

The question threw her, but Adriana answered. "Yes. It means "arms" in Spanish."

"That's right. This is the *Río de los Brazos de Dios*. And here in the "Arms of God" it will all work out."

With that small comfort, Adriana went back home and waited.

The expectant mother's belly grew.

She felt enormous. Her feet were swollen and she waddled when she walked, back bowed to compensate for the boulder attached to her midsection.

Adriana continued seeing Dr. Moorjani, who assured her with every ultrasound that the baby looked perfectly healthy. That made one of them. Dr. Moorjani started to make a lot of noises about bed rest and not straining herself and risk of hypertension.

Week fourteen of her pregnancy, Adriana officially quit her jobs at the coffee shop and library and moved back in with her mother.

She didn't apply for the spring semester of school because she couldn't be certain of her due date.

She sat in her mother's backyard and stared up at the moon every night.

Her belly finally stopped growing.

The contractions started as the sun went down.

It had been only seventeen weeks since the night of the blue moon.

And on this night, it came again.

Its presence filled the small space, as doctors and nurses rushed around Adriana and her mother. She knew its touch like anyone who spent time dreaming did. It was nearly the shape of a man now, swathed in brilliant light, almost too bright to look at with human eyes. But, then again, Adriana wasn't so sure she was even occupying her human body anymore, even though she could feel her mother's hand in hers, even though she could feel herself squinting, even though she could feel her body splitting in half. Her mind felt separate. Apart.

As her eyes adjusted to the light, Adriana realized it wasn't the shape of a man the moon had taken. It was that of a woman.

Adriana watched as the celestial figure watched her. It was waiting patiently for the baby to be born.

It was then that Adriana understood.

The moon could bear no children of her own. And so, she sought out surrogates to carry her children. It had never been Adriana's child growing inside her. It had always been the moon's.

Now the child was ready, ready to be born, and the moon was here to collect it.

Adriana only had one last thing to do before she was free of them both.

The pain was blinding in a way that even the light of the moon standing beside her could never match. There was so much noise around her, the doctor, her mother, the nurses, all clamoring. All except the silent, watchful moon.

Adriana cried out—screamed until she ran out of breath.

When she fell silent, the moon approached, arms outstretched.

The arms of God . . .

Adriana reached out a hand.

But the moon reached for the child.

The clatter of tools, the voices of deliverers, the angry alarm of machines, and finally, the moment frozen in time when a child's cry never comes.

It really had all just been bad luck.

Adriana's hand fell limp. Her skin drained of color, her body drained of blood. Everything around her faded away, until only one thing remained.

The light of the moon—

—blue—

And then, nothing.

JACKLYN BAKER is a graduate of Baylor University currently living in the Dallas area with her dog, two cats, and a ghost that refuses to leave. Her short stories "Southern Hospitality," "2908 Porch Swing Lane," and

"The Teeth" appear in volumes two, three, and six of *Road Kill: Texas Horror by Texas Writers*, respectively. When not writing, she can be found bringing nightmares to life at Dark Hour Haunted House and a variety of conventions. You can find her on Instagram and Twitter at @I_Am_The_Baker.

The Old Man of the Ground
Nathan Machart

Some weeks ago, I heard Mrs. Parsons was at the old File Room land on the northwest side of town, having a nervous breakdown. I found her kneeling in a yellow nightgown, her hands boring a hole in the earth, the black soil this part of Texas is famous for caked under her eyes. She said her daughter had stayed the night with her, drank a cup of tea at the breakfast table, and, at three in the morning, had gotten up and walked out. Mrs. Parsons said she had followed her here, where she'd disappeared in the early morning light. I drove the woman home and cooked some eggs in her kitchen while one of our department admins looked up the number for a trauma counselor. At her table, Mrs. Parsons relayed the story to me, again, of what happened out at the File Room, and brought down Melody's diary from her room.

"I'm not cracking up," she told me. "I swear I did see her. I spoke to her."

Mrs. Parsons's daughter, Melody, had been dead seven years.

I'd met the girl only once, at a Fourth of July BBQ at a church—one of these where I drop by and hand out deputy stickers to kids. I'd just settled down at a picnic table with a hamburger and potato salad when she slinked up, tall in a t-shirt tied around her mid-rift so that her belly button winked at my shoulder, and quietly started speaking. I know that seventeen is about when young women settle into how they're going to look as adults—my own daughter wouldn't grow out of her own mousiness for some years— but Melody was beautiful, had been ever since she could stand, and it was clear she would've stayed that way.

"There's a man staying in the File Room that's not supposed to be there," she said, over me. "I saw him yesterday."

I'd only been in town a couple of years at that point, trying to figure out life with my daughter in a new place, but I was trying to be a good cop, so that night I drove out to the File Room and looked around, shined my flashlight in windows. I didn't see a thing, but it was only two days later the accident happened, and after all this time, I still don't know what I think about it—whether it was just a strange coincidence, so seemingly unrelated. How could a man staying where he shouldn't result in all that?

Couple weeks ago, after I took Mrs. Parsons home, I had my laptop with Melody's school picture up, to see her again, my daughter eating dinner beside me on the couch, and an old movie on that we knew a million times over. Kelsey leaned over, swallowed and said, "That's who I saw today."

"Who?" I said, looking at the movie for the actor she must be talking about.

"That girl. She was out front."

"This one?" I pointed to the screen, Melody's bright smile from seven years back. "You saw this girl?"

"She was out front, looking at our yard. At the grass."

"No. This is someone different, kiddo." I would not tell my daughter, who at ten couldn't even watch some scenes from *The Wizard of Oz* without hiding her face, that this girl she thought she'd seen was dead and gone.

But it was this, and what Mrs. Parsons said on her knees clawing that dirt, that did it. What I'd seen in Melody's diary—after her mother pointed out certain entries. I couldn't help but wonder if she was still alive. Out there, somewhere, looking for help. The cop in me had been waiting for a mystery like this all my life.

I borrowed the diary and made copies first thing. In it, the girl wrote almost as if she knew what was coming, that her words might shed light on something later—it was the first time, too, I felt Melody was more than just a pretty small-town girl. About the building she wrote: *The squat, two-story structure sits halfway down a winding, industrial road that ends in a lonely cement products yard, so that the only traffic—apart from the medical record keepers that come Mondays—is these eighteen wheelers blubbering around the curve like Junebugs, past a stand of pecan trees and out of sight.*

It took some weeks of digging, as Melody's former boss, Tomas Maron, had left town a year after the incident. He was one of these post-Patriot Act types that recorded everything, even the audio, uploading footage to a secure database before that was a normal thing. But I gained access, made my copies, and started through them, file after file of high-quality video, lining up dates and times with what Melody described in her entries about the coffee cup and that last day. I've never been much of a spiritual person, apart from whispering a quick prayer when I think a call might get dicey, but all this—it made me wonder.

She'd gotten the summer job there through a friend. This place would be obsolete, now, and should've been then. But it sometimes took years to digitize paper records, especially back then. So they had a building secured by fence and lock, and information stored inside rows and rows of cardboard boxes on metal shelves filled with insurance claims, contracts, medical records, and protected all those cameras. *Clients make the drive from the city to request a file or two, sometimes a box, which is pulled. They must be re-filed when they're returned to us. That is what I do. I'm a re-filer.*

Tomas shows up in the footage most days before eight, but Melody not until eleven. *The File Room has no air conditioning, because why spend money to cool a building of boxes and paper. This is Tomas' thinking. Most days he's gone by noon, so I'm by myself. He tries to get me to come earlier, because it's cooler then and he says I can do more work, but I like to be alone—no one can see what I do.*

Of course, I see what she does, these years later, and there's a feeling I don't like in it, like it's a violation, what makes me uncomfortable watching this, because she wears sleeveless shirts cut off at her stomach or tied like at the BBQ, and always little shorts. I can understand it, I think, as it had to be brutally hot in there. She said so herself: *It's stupid hot. So immensely fricking hot. I'm hauling these same stupid boxes back and forth. Lift with your legs! And sometimes I really think Tomas is watching me through all these cameras, but it's sort-of fun all the same, being watched by someone. Scintillating. This is the hardest work I've ever done, but I refuse to be insulted by Angela Battern again at the pool. I'm going to look so deliciously hot for once when I finally get to A&M, and Angela will be stuck here, no doubt impregnated by then and married miserably to Dick Newspitt.*

Afternoons she sits and eats a sandwich in a spot she calls section 177, where I can see a stack of her re-files and a metal folding chair for sorting them. *It's cold between row*

177F and 177H, for some reason. I can sit and cool off. Every so often, I forget about it and walk through with a stack of folders, and suddenly I can't stop shivering. There is no 177G. Tomas says he must've forgotten it while doing the labeling.

It's not there, but section 191 is where she first writes about things changing, starting with a box in the aisle. She lifts it onto its shelf and the next day it's down in the aisle. *Tomas must be pulling from it and keeps leaving it for me. Maybe he's messing with me. Trying to get me to talk to him.* I should be able to see what happens in the recordings, but the lights are out at night, and in the morning, when the sunlight comes in the windows, the box is there again.

In July—the day before the BBQ—she's loading a dolly in section 124, downstairs, the tight room, as she describes it. It's cramped, the aisles so narrow it's difficult to get boxes in and out, and the dolly won't fit, so she leaves it in the corridor. The temperature that day—I checked an archival website—reached one hundred and three degrees, so I can't imagine what it was inside with all those windows. Drinking water would be important, but Melody's soda is probably all sugar. She works and I can see sweat on her neck, her arms, and working this way, sweating so much, wearing what she does, I believe what she writes about herself: *It's like I feel alive working that hard. Like I'm an animal. Sometimes I think about the fact that I'm alone, or with only Tomas there, though he's married, older—somewhat gross. But can I let you in on a secret, diary? I've never been kissed by anyone other than Mom and Dad.*

There comes a thump at the window you can hear in the recording, and in the narrow aisle, Melody freezes. *Three weeks into a job where I work all alone in an empty building this size, I thought I'd come to terms with how creepy it could be.* She sets the stack of files down and goes to the row. It's a cardinal outside the floor to ceiling windows, in the weeds and oak leaves from last fall. She stands at the glass, watching the bird to see if it will move and it does. *It was hurt. It's little wing retracted, each articulated feather drawing in like a Japanese fan. I wanted to bring it home with me—if it lived.*

In the center of the building sits a foyer with a skylight and a little pool that looks empty. It may have been a trickling fountain once upon a time, or a water garden, but the water's gone. She goes past it and out, around the corner where the brush and trees lean against the building, and there bends under overgrown branches, moves along the length of the windows, sneakers crunching leaves. *It was standing. It's little red breast pumping fast.* She bends and takes it in her hands and turns, speaking to it, though I can't hear what, as the outside cameras don't collect sound. It's then she sees something, back through the window glass, and because of the light she holds the bird and puts her face to the glass and then she can see what I have already seen on the interior footage, that someone is there, a man, standing in the corridor beside her dolly.

Watching this the first time, I remember cursing out-loud. Seven years ago, she'd come to me for help. I should've done more.

In the video, she squats outside the window, a hand pressed to the glass to shade her eyes instead of cup the bird. The man is tall, like Melody, but thin, dark brown skin under a long white shirt. Melody moves, now, along the windows, back around to the front door. *I'm seventeen*, she writes, *all alone in there, dressed like I'm headed to yoga, and while I don't buy the stereotype, the black rapist bullcrap, going back in, I felt like I might as well be an all-you-can-eat buffet.*

It seems she doesn't think about the bird until she gets to the foyer with the empty pool, and only there sets it down in a planter with a small tree, something that might even be plastic. She sneaks near the restrooms and drinking fountain where the corridor starts to the tight room and calls down it, "Hey, listen." The audio is seven years old but good, and she sounds strong, with an authority that comes from working there, or that she was born with. "You're not supposed to be in here."

The corridor stands empty now. The loaded dolly, one file pitched over and spilled onto the industrial carpet, her fountain drink on top of the boxes, sweating onto the cardboard. "You need to get out of here," she calls again and waits.

The rest of that afternoon she stays as quiet as she can, pausing every so often to listen in case the man is still there. He is. I track him through the camera views, up the foyer stairs as she's coming inside with the bird, into one of the second-floor corridors, the only one that doesn't have a security camera. And I lose him there.

Tomas returns at four—she watches him park from the second-floor windows and meets him in the little office downstairs. He switches on the AC unit that serves only the office as she describes what's happened. It's hard not to dislike him, watching this. What sort of man leaves a teenager to work alone in a place like that?

"You brought the bird inside?" he says on the video.

"It's not about the bird."

Tomas is short and thick; he turns and leans against a desk, looking Melody over. He does this at times, seemingly thinking but always with his eyes on her. I've started to care about her, I realize, watching this and reading her words.

"I'll walk around later," he says. "If he's still here, he's a squatter. I'll kick him out." He looks at her, like he's doing it to make her uncomfortable. "If you kept the doors locked when you're here, you'd be fine."

He treats me like a child. I kept the doors locked. And why would a squatter choose this hell hole? I didn't say as much to him, though, because he's an asshole.

The next day she doesn't arrive until after lunch, when Tomas is gone. She unlocks the door and locks it behind her. There's a coffee cup she uses for water, and she takes it to the second floor and begins in section 164, next to the maze—this is what she calls it. It's the only office suite in the building that doesn't have boxes, because it was built—as she describes it—*with little turns and cubbies and tight corners, as if meant for a game of laser-tag.* It's also the only area in the building without cameras. *There are no boxes,* she writes. *I don't go in there.*

She's worn a longer shirt today, but after two hours of filing she sweats through it and ties it in a knot at her ribs. I don't know how to feel about it. Her entry for this day is the longest in her diary: *More and more I think about telling Tomas I'm quitting this place and picking up work at the mall. I lost the coffee cup. That's what started it. Then someone started whistling.*

In the video I can hear it, and it does sound like a man whistling. Section 164 and the maze are down from the foyer, through one of the corner suites with big windows, and so she goes through and stands on the second-floor balcony overlooking the empty pool. Below, the sound seems to echo off the tile. I check the other views. No one is down there, but by then I'd recognized it. *It was just the bird. Took me forever to figure it out. God, what a fricking horrible place this is. The bird was down there, and it was singing. It would've been better if it had died.*

She goes back, past the bright windows and afternoon light, and looks at the maze where the lights are off, but what she hears now—and what I hear in the tape—comes from the other way, down the long side suite, section 177. She described it in her diary better than I ever could: *There was a high ring in it, like an airplane's engines far away, which is what I thought it was at first. I'd heard them before on the long approach into the city. They throttle up or down. Dad was a pilot in the navy, lest you forget, and he calls this remaining in the glideslope. But this sound didn't throttle up or down.* She listens to it for a time. *It was just so consistent. It could not be branches against windows. It could not be a raccoon in the walls. It sounded too mechanical, as if it were some device driven by a battery.*

She follows the long corridor down the suite, against the inner wall. There is the folding chair and the pile of boxes and folders she needs to focus on, and there is the sound, coming into the audio of the camera—objective sound—from the aisle.

Of course, it would be coming from 177F. There was a box down the aisle, my coffee cup full of water on top of it. The one I'd misplaced. I hadn't been down there all that afternoon. Not once, so I don't know how the cup—but the sound had stopped already.

In the footage, she stares at the box and the mug. The mug is ceramic, off-white, little words on the side. She comes down the aisle and is hit with a rush of cold—I can see it, how she's hit and suddenly trembles; she'd forgotten again. Nearer to the box, I can see her breath. She notices, too, and doesn't believe it at first, but she puts a hand in front of it, testing it. She looks up, as if for an air conditioning vent. Her teeth chatter. She lifts the cup and sets it back down. *It was freezing. Like no fricking joke, freezing. The water frozen solid. Screw that place right up its ass.*

She turns and leaves the aisle, going on a few feet. *I'm quitting, I thought. Done. None of this is worth seven dollars an hour. I'd seen too many movies.*

In the video, the sound starts again. The tiny far-away airplane. It's the mug on the box—she knows it—must know it now. She's stopped outside of the aisle and now she turns, but she's shaking, cold. *I knew if I looked at the mug it would not be moving, would not be turning. That whatever it was was playing with me, and that after a few more days of this crap it would murder me, turn me into paper or something, or follow me home and suck me into another dimension. I should've left.* The sound is so mechanical, so precise and perfect, and it is the mug. She knows it, knows it cannot be anything else, and also that it cannot be that.

She steps forward in the video and goes around the corner. The other view shows the aisle and that the mug is turning—does turn. It rotates, the handle and the little words sliding round and round. She stares at it, hands on her elbows. Her breath comes like a sputtering draft. She is of sound mind, she must think. Not hallucinating. I was not either, watching it. *Tomas said that sometimes, after he's worked in the heat too long, he's hallucinated, but I'd only been there a couple of hours.* The mug keeps turning. It turns, and it is ice cold.

When it stops, she flinches—I flinched, too, watching it. It's the mug stopping that makes her flinch. Up and down the long corridor it is still. There is nothing. No sound but the change in her breath, which I can see coming from her. She stares at the mug and her lips move, but there is no sound. *It was like I was willing myself to leave.*

Her shirt looks wet, but I could tell she's freezing. A few steps down the corridor and it's as if a wall of hot air slaps her, sauna hot, ninety-five degrees hot. *It felt so good, so real again, but then I saw the maze.*

The lights are off in there. She stands and looks for a long time, almost three whole minutes of run-time. *I'm not sure why I went that way, save that this was where I'd been working before the sound—before the cup. I never bring a bag in, and I had my keys in my back pocket of my shorts. I was leaving. Just down to the foyer, out and away. But I couldn't. In dreams you know when something will happen before it does, and it was like that. I knew something was going to happen. I had to hold it, keep from peeing. In the dark of the maze someone was breathing, coming out. Be Tomas, I thought, but it wasn't. It was the man, black hair, that white shirt too big for him. Pants, too. He looked like he'd been working, like he was sweating the same as I was, but even in the great heat, I felt cold.*

He comes out looking exhausted, leaning against the wall. *If it weren't for the coffee mug I would've spoken to him, or I would've run.* Instead, she stands her ground, jaw clenched, teeth tapping together. The man grips his hand as if it pains him. He's speaking to her, but there's no sound that comes through the video. Then he raises a hand—he has fingers as long and thick as a billy club—and touches his long throat, and I could see—she can see—inside the wide collar of his too-big shirt, a bruise, discolored and purple, in a tight ring around his neck. He speaks and she can hear it. She steps nearer. He looks real in the video, though his eyes are stark gold.

He said the word mistake. I heard it. I know it was that. I should've left, but I couldn't. I waited. I would've been better for leaving, I think. He looked at me, not like Tomas does, but as if deeper. Then he said I looked like Miss Annie, his voice hoarse. I asked him what he needed here. I'd seen movies. They come with a purpose. Something that will bring peace to disturbed rest.

In the footage, he looks around the corridor, the space between the interior wall and all the many shelves of boxes. The ceiling tiles have been removed there and part of the building's unused air conditioning duct hangs through with a pad of foam insulation. He seems to be staring at this, studying it. *He was looking for rafters. He said the word rafters. This, too, in a whisper, as if he had no voice. Then he said he needed to sit down.*

He comes forward—Melody backs up—and bends, as if weary from all the work, and sits in the folding chair, sits as if he's real enough. Melody doesn't move. *He said there was a barn here, but that this was different. Not a barn. I was freezing still, and warm. Both. I told him it was a file room, and he asked what for?* Files, I said. He hunched over his knees in the video and he's looking over the folders and boxes on the floor. *Seems like paper, he said, and I asked who he was, and he said Eddie. Then he told me—but he was real, I swear, sitting right in front of me— he told me they hung him in the barn. They thought he'd done something he hadn't. To Miss Annie. And she, he told me, was too scared to tell the truth about it.* You can watch the footage and see her leaning, speaking, and he speaking to her. *I asked him if he was dead, and he seemed to think about this a long time before he nodded. He swallowed and it seemed to hurt past that scar. Then I asked him if he was going to hurt me, and he said he'd never hurt anyone all his life. Least of all Miss Annie, or someone that looked like her. It was the Old Man, he said, that had them hang him from the barn.*

The next day was the Fourth of July, the day she spoke to me. I went out there, looked in some of the windows, but it seemed like nothing, like nothing would come of it. It would have been easy, that morning or the next, for Melody to call up Tomas and quit, but what happened, I think, made her curious, and so she shows up in the video again on the fifth.

After he came that way, out of the maze as if out of nothing—but had it been out of nothing, or was he just a squatter, playing a joke?—I just couldn't work anymore. The cold, the mug. They couldn't be tricks. I want to know the answer. I've weighed the risks. He said the Old Man— this is what Eddie called him—cannot do more than what he has. In tormenting Miss Annie all those years ago. In driving her near insane, and that what he'd done, Eddie now, had been only to preach against him—the Old Man— preach against his power. But that the Old Man had his last laugh, to get those white men to hang a free man from the rafters. And even that amounted to—Eddie said—a killing of the body and not the soul. Over the soul, the Old Man had no power, save to hold a while—a long while, some hundred years in Eddie's case—if I am to believe anything he said.

It didn't make sense to me. It still doesn't. I'm not sure it made sense to her. In the foyer with the empty pool, she stops and listens. The building is quiet, Tomas gone, the bird quiet, no eighteen wheelers along the bending road. She walks along the second floor, in and around the suites of boxes, looking to see—I think—if Eddie has come but she does not find him. 177F is warm—no vapor out of her mouth—as the entire building seems bright and warm, as if all of it were but the hallucinations Tomas warned her about.

She picks up on her work, the stacks to be re-filed. By noon she's sweating, the heat in from the windows oppressive, the air humid like in a giant greenhouse. She wipes her brow and cheeks and goes by the maze, but not in it, as the lights are off inside. Nothing comes of it, out of it, so she leaves for lunch in town and, coming back, finds Tomas in the office.

They speak awhile, Melody at a desk that seems to have once hosted a secretary, laying out her sandwich. There is a client coming in the morning to pick up boxes to digitize and Tomas asks her to start the next day earlier than normal to help.

"Has anything weird ever happened here?" she says in the video.

Tomas has a file open in his lap and he's smoking a cigarette. "Listen to this. This kid. They found cancer behind his eyeballs and took them out. The eyes."

"Like, I mean, really weird."

Tomas props his sneakers on his desk, cluttered with folders and a phone. He looks at her awhile. "There's a few files with pictures of botched surgeries," he says. "Stuff you shouldn't see, but once you do, you can't stop looking at it. You mean weirder stuff than this kid with the eyeballs?"

She says something but it's garbled by the sound of her sandwich paper. Tomas blows smoke from his cigarette, drops the butt in an ashtray on his desk.

"Listen, this place can get to you," he says. "It can be creepy, working here alone. You should come when I'm here. Are you drinking enough water?"

"It's not the water."

"I thought it might not work out," he says. "A girl, you know? If you're not able to keep up, we should talk about it. This place—it isn't for everyone."

"I can keep up," she says, and draws her sandwich and drink up to go.

He takes out another cigarette, lights it. "I'm taking off soon, but I'll be back tomorrow morning for thatclient. Nine a.m.. You should be here."

She stands. "I've got work to do."

She files into the afternoon, drenched and hot. There's no sign of Eddie. Nor is there any shift in temperature from what I can tell—no vapor or chills. She must wonder, as I do watching her, if that is all it is going to be, all it will be, and, if so, whether she should walk out before anything more happens. Of course, I know better, what's coming. I look for something else, some footage capturing her leaving before nightfall, sneaking out through a rear door, or away by other means, something, so I could go back to her mother and say her daughter is alive. That the girl she saw—that my daughter saw—is Melody.

It's near five when she looks ready to call it a day. The light has changed—she notices it, too. It looks different without the blaring sun in the skylight over the foyer. I watch her at the door. It's locked. The door to the office, too—they're both locked and she doesn't seem to have her keys. There she is on the video, patting pockets, turning in a circle. She glances back at the empty pool.

There's a sound now, something she hadn't noticed before. It feels to me as if whatever it is, whatever all this is, might be seizing an opportunity, and as if something is watching her walk around the empty pool, under the soft light. The tiles of the foyer seem wet. Her sneakers pat into it—she looks down, lifts a foot—and the sound seems to be water running, a sink. In the corridor where the restrooms are, it's trickling from under one of the doors, as if Tomas left a faucet on, but it comes from the women's bathroom. I hear it inside.

The light in the foyer is soft. She's being drawn into the bathroom, I know, as she was drawn into the aisle with the mug, but still, she reaches out and takes the knob. She's agreed to this—I think—all the while, agreeing.

Tomas has a camera in the women's bathroom. That should tell you more about him than I can. It shows three stalls. Two sinks. The first runs over, water spilling onto the floor with loud slaps. In the footage Melody steps in, water sloshing as she moves. She gasps as if it's freezing, water reaching up past the rubber soles and into the fabric of her sneakers and into her socks. It feels freezing, even as I watch. She turns the faucet off and touches what's in the sink. Water, in this town, in the summer, is never cold.

She looks at herself in the mirror, at the nectarine tank top, her hair braided but matted with sweat. There's nothing now, no sound but the droplets sliding down the porcelain and into the water on the dirty floor. I wonder, of course, what she's thinking, but there are no entries in her diary beyond the day before. Only blank pages. At the door we hear it, the faucet's knob. The slow squeak. Threads and calcium deposits and a rubber gasket. It's like before, she must feel it. I certainly do, watching. He will come now. She looks at it, sees it turning, water coming at a trickle and then a stream and then a rush into the sink where it has pooled, and then onto the floor again.

She goes into the corridor, unwilling to turn it off again. She must be thinking about going by now, about breaking a window and leaving. Splashes of her shoes. She reaches the pool. The water on the floor seeps in somehow, there, a crack in the concrete, another in the pool so that it fills. Already there stands a stagnant circle of earthy water, scummy brown and barely trembling as beads slip out of the crack and down. Melody moves up the stairs to the second-floor balcony, into 177—I think she is looking for her keys, but they aren't there. The seat is. The files. The coffee mug.

She goes down again, as if all of a sudden she knows where they are, goes right to the door of the office, where she started to eat with Tomas. I've done the work she will be unable to do soon, going through the footage of her sitting in there. She slipped the mass of keys and keychains out of her pocket, set them on the desk as she spoke to Tomas, and forgot them when she left with her drink and sandwich. The office is locked with her keys inside.

She says something I can't hear, with the noise from the water, and then thumps the door. She can break a window, she must think, but can't get into her car. She can't get away.

Padding through the water, she returns and watches the pool fill. There is the soft sound of trickling in the foyer, and a lumbering big rig leaves the industrial concrete yard out on the winding road. The last one. I wonder if she realizes it—that she's missed the last one. Had she broken the window, she might've caught it. The glow in the skylight is so dim now, the entire foyer looks blue. There is a new sound in the video, and I see a chill, like an electric current, run through her shoulders. She turns, and I wonder if she's thinking that it must now be him, that he must have finally come, but it's not. It's the bird. The cardinal is in the water on the ground flapping and spinning. From the angle of the camera, it makes rings in the water, as if the bird is a stone dropped into the center of a pond. She comes to it and it flaps, as if trying to leap into flight, but it looks soaked on its side, wings slapping. She lifts it and to me it looks drowned, its eyes black and its little beak open, its chest and lungs gasping and full.

Above her, over the balcony, there is a thud, as if someone has dropped a box of files, or a cinder block. I hear it in the recording over the sound of the water. Melody straightens, holding the bird, water running around her tennis shoes, between them.

"Eddie?" she says—calls. The sound of the sink in the bathroom goes on, the water beading through the crack into the pool, and it feels deafening in the recording, though I'm sure it's not. Every time I watch this part, I have the volume as high as it can go.

She climbs the stairs, holding the bird. Blue light from the ceiling bends into the foyer below and ripples against the water in the pool so that now there are globes of light about the walls and ceiling, wobbling globes of flickering light, the entire room seemingly under water, all of it dancing.

He sits outside the maze, an entrance I never even knew was there, a door into it from the balcony, that I never saw Melody open—so many doors there, so many ways. He sits against the wall on the floor, just under a camera, his long legs in those too large pants. His head, that black hair—now blue—painted over with coruscating light from the evening sky and the water. She comes to him, holding the bird.

"Eddie?" she says, and his eyes are wet, or all of him wet—it's hard to tell in the video. He lifts his great, long fingers, wipes them, saying something I can't make out. "What?" she says, and he starts shaking, speaking again. His voice is so small, so slight, but I can hear the breath behind it—that he draws breath, that he moves air. He apologizes for something, over and over. His lips working the same way.

"Eddie," she says. "What about the water?"

"Water," he says, and it's because his lips move that I can tell what he says. He doesn't understand what she's talking about.

"The sink. The water."

He stares, blinks once, slow.

"You turned on the water."

He turns, muttering, but I can't hear what it is he says.

"Him," she says, repeating it, I think. "Eddie, who is it?" She looks over the balcony at the pool, and at the light shimmering up and over the ceiling as if all of it were in a cave. "What about the mug? Was that you? Or him?"

He speaks, lifts himself. Then he puts his hand, with those long fingers, to the door, which is cracked and leads into the maze, but he slides in, halfway in. He mutters, and I have the volume so high, but I can't hear it.

"Do what again?" she says.

In the door he turns. I can hear his breath, the way he seems to weep. He says something now about Miss Annie. I hear that much. Miss Annie. Something about hanging him from rafters again, but it's not clear. I've watched it ten times. A hundred times. I've hooked it up to all sorts of different speakers and headphones, but I can't get it.

She says, "What did you save her from? What did you save her from? What can't you do again?" But he's already gone, into the maze again, where it's dark. Melody is alone, and I am left alone with those words to puzzle this out.

It's quiet a moment, in the shimmering water-light, and then a new sound—like some great dragging thing. And here is the accident. What we've thought of as an accident for years.

The sound is like that of an anchor released from a ship, all that weight and length of links of chain. It thrums through the speakers I've turned up, thrums and hums, so distorted because it's louder than the microphones can handle. Melody stands, her chest rising and falling, hands at her elbows. She's dropped the bird without even thinking of it—I can see it, dead on the ground by her feet. Now I see her breath, so I know it's cold, and I feel it, watching it, how cold it is, even where I am. The sound ceases, but the ring of it, metallic, is left in the air. She breathes out and sees it in front of her face. She has to get out, she thinks—she must think. Things have changed, she has to feel.

I have never been aboard a ship, never been in the Arctic where the ice cracks and bends and makes a sound like the world is breaking, but I can imagine that the sounds I hear—that she hears—are like that, the cracking whine of something great moving, shifting. The camera shakes as if the floor trembles, and Melody puts her hands out to steady her, as if the entire building turns, as if the building were now the coffee mug over the box, turning, the building shaking, the foundation dragged across the ground.

She goes down the stairs and splashes through the water to the doors, but they're not there anymore. The sound rises, ice cracking. No doors, no walls. She stares at it as if through great panes of glass, and beyond, what she sees—what I see—feels impossible. It's not actually what I see—it cannot be—because what it seems to show are things in a dark shifting, writhing earth, great moving blubbering things, whales if whales could drive in the deep of the ground, tentacles if octopi lived in an earthy underworld. They fade in and out in sliding soil, in and out of such darkness. In the video, Melody turns and tries to steady herself against the tremors of the foundation, all the files of medical facts and social security numbers and pictures of botched surgeries, filed in such particular order, shaking over the plywood and metal shelves. She lurches back to the pool and its water coils as if something lay within it, under the surface. The sound of ice bending and snapping feels deafening, and she holds to her place, the building shaking, boxes toppling in the camera angles. There is no light now, but what seems to be only a dim glow from above, as if the skylight is run over with dirt, clops of it falling, broken earth clouding the panes of glass, as if this were a grave, a glassy sinking grave, and she looking up at what was her life.

This is where all the videos stop. At this exact moment. Seven minutes after six o'clock. What we believe—have believed—about the town, what can be relayed to any visitor in our bar, after all these years, is that a sinkhole opened beneath the file room and sucked it two hundred feet down, straight to the water table. Millions of medical files bleeding through with mud. No body was ever recovered, despite teams digging two months, looking for Melody. No body of a seventeen-year-old girl, nor the unidentified man who appears in the security footage.

I went out there again. I drove FM 347 and parked outside the great nothingness that sits in the middle of the twisted and broken parking lot, amidst all those pecan trees, where Mrs. Parsons had been kneeling. The eighteen wheelers still lumber by, and the space has been filled with dirt, grass growing in places. I almost wish I might see her, Melody, standing in the evening light, but it's not there. Not then.

It was in the middle of the night, last night, that I heard my daughter speaking in her room. I sat up, listening, trying to rouse myself enough from sleep to go. It felt cold, but it was night, and nights are always cold. Kelsey spoke and waited, spoke again, but I couldn't tell what she was saying in whatever dream she was having. I moved down the hallway of our little one-story, past the bathroom, and stood outside her door, listening. I heard her say go away.

I can't tell you what I expected, opening the door. Kelsey sat in her bed, the nightlight on and turning so that little stars played out over her ceiling—something she still loved, though she should've outgrown it by then. The girl stood on the other side, near the closet, wet through and caked in mud, but it was her. Clearly her.

"Kelsey," I said, and drew out my hand, and she came to me, out of bed, and took it. I put her behind me, drew her into the hallway, but by then the girl near the closet was gone. I held the door open, Kelsey behind me, and looked into the little room with the turning stars. I knew then why she'd come, and what she would be back for. I knew who she'd brought with her.

NATHAN MACHART is a graduate of the University of Iowa Writer's Workshop. His work has appeared in *The Carolina Quarterly* and *December Magazine*. He teaches Creative Writing at Sam Houston State University and lives with his wife and children in Cut-n-Shoot, Texas.

Definitive Act
Tytus Berry

Eladio had scoped the mailbox out for three days. It sat on the edge of the barrio in the vicinity of several boarded-up businesses. There wasn't much traffic and there were no working pay phones anywhere close. He worried about being seen, falling into the street or somehow making it to a working pay phone.

This would be Eladio's *acto definitivo*. For as long as he remembered, he had dreamed of doing something remarkable, something that when people studied the map of his shitty life, they would point to this moment and say that this was who Eladio Segura was. Not the drugs or the gang stuff, or the trouble that always seemed to follow him around. He would redraw the lines of his existence. People would know who he really was. The beginning and the middle wouldn't matter. Only the end.

Eladio was certain that the police would think his death was just another instance of senseless street violence. That he was just another *pendejo del barrio* dead at the scene. He was also pretty sure his Abuela might get microphones stuck in her face for comment, and he felt bad about that. But he knew what her answer would be. She would be on TV saying her grandson never had an enemy in the world.

It didn't matter.

By the time they figured out what had happened, it would be too late. But it would also be okay, too.

Eladio placed a 12X9" manilla envelope on the top of the faded blue, graffiti-splotched USPS mailbox around 1:30 in the afternoon. He had skipped breakfast, school, and lunch. He'd heard too many stories about people shitting their pants when they died. He didn't like it, and, even as ridiculous as it sounded, he felt it was unbecoming of *un acto definitivo*.

The envelope was not the normal kind. When he bought it, he made sure it was self-adhesive because he wouldn't be able to lick it. He thought about rereading the note, but he'd poured over it for hours and reread it a dozen times. It said what it needed to say.

Eladio pulled a red bandana out of his back pocket and wrapped it around his upper left bicep. He looped a granny knot in the bandana, and pulled it as tight as he could using his front teeth and his free right hand. Then, he pulled a new razor out of his shirt pocket and removed the protective cardboard sheath that covered the blade.

Eladio knew he had to move fast. Even with the bandana around his arm, he would bleed like *un cerdo atascado* . . . and that might give him away. His only other concern was the letter getting caught at the post office. But the manilla envelope was thick-stock and he had inserted a piece of thin cardboard that he removed from the back of his sketch pad. He was sure the letter would make it through. It had to.

He removed the adhesive strip from the envelope but left it open. He placed the razor between the thumb and index finger of his right hand and then surveyed his surroundings. There was no one in sight.

He turned his left wrist up and held it out and away from his body. He dug the razor blade into the left side of his wrist where it met his hand and slashed inward and diagonally across. Blood jutted from the slit.

Still holding his slit wrist away from his body and the mailbox, he loosened the hand-made tourniquet and draped it over the wound. Then, he placed the razor blade in the envelope and sealed it with his right hand. He dropped it through the drop slot and began walking away. He held the bandana in place. He didn't want to lose too much blood near the mailbox.

After Eladio had walked a half-block, he removed the bandana and let his wrist bleed freely. The blood still came in small spurts.

When he knelt to drop the bloody bandana into a gutter slot, he almost fell over. He was scared for a moment, but he had known he would be. He had planned well. No close pay phones was a great idea—but not because he was changing his mind.

It wasn't so bad. And he was going to pull it off.

The Rio Grande Valley sun suddenly seemed hotter, and he felt a little dizzy. His mouth was dry and his whole body seemed to droop, but he wanted to remain lucid. He started to jog. His stride was drunken and he stumbled, barely recovering. He thought about his girlfriend, Julie. He knew his letter would make it. He began to cry, but he was not afraid.

Eladio's blood was barely dribbling from his wound now, and his skin was turning gray. His moment was gone.

The sun seemed less oppressive and he grew cold. He collapsed to his knees and fell forward. His head came to rest on a patch of dingy grass just off the cracked sidewalk. He turned his face toward the mailbox. No one was near it.

His breath was short. His shallow puffs shook the grass near his lips. He didn't have much time. His muscles leadened, but he turned his head to face the sun. He stared at it for as long as he could.

His eyes never closed.

Eladio was right. And lucky.

A short spring rain came later that afternoon, washing away some of his blood. And the police ruled his death a homicide. They said there appeared to have been a struggle and Eladio, wounded, had fled. And though they had no suspects and hadn't found a murder weapon, the investigation was ongoing. One of the police detectives recognized Eladio and said he wasn't surprised.

Eladio's friends and classmates were stunned. A few were quick to tell reporters that Eladio had really seemed to be turning things around. When the news got to Julie at school, she ran into a bathroom and threw up. She refused to come out of the bathroom stall.

Julie hadn't heard from Eladio in a few days. Her father had threatened Eladio and ran him off. She had pled with her father and begged him to reconsider, but he wouldn't be swayed. The thought of his daughter going with a "wetback" (as he called Eladio), and a troublemaking wetback at that, made his stomach sink. He decided Julie simply had to move on.

Julie hovered over the toilet, sobbing lightly. Her friends took turns trying to coax her out, but she refused to respond.

It took three days for Eladio's letter to make it through the postal system. It did so undetected.

The letter arrived at Julie's house just after Eladio's funeral. Julie's mother and father had attended the service, and her father—even as much as he disliked Eladio—felt bad about the boy's death and tried his best to support his daughter. It was easier to support her with Eladio gone.

The funeral was a large, outdoor affair, with half the high school in attendance. This surprised Julie's father, but he didn't let on. Father Gonzalez from the historic Immaculate Conception Cathedral said a few words about tragedy and forgiveness and salvation, but kept things brief. It was hot and there was very little shade. The Rio Grande Valley sun bore down on the funeral service as if through a magnifying glass.

Tears trickled down Julie's cheeks, but she kept her composure. Her father was surprised by the depth of her grief. In a brief moment of panic, it occurred to him that Eladio might have taken his daughter's innocence, but he refused to accept this possibility. And if he was wrong, he didn't want to know. Still, he took one of her hands and squeezed it, expecting to get her attention.

Julie didn't acknowledge him, and he released her hand.

Eladio's abbreviated family was situated almost opposite of Julie's through the entire ceremony. They seemed more irritated than agonized, and ignored Julie entirely. She wondered if Eladio had encountered resistance to their relationship as well.

Eladio's grandmother's eyes were sad but dark and stern, like his. Julie couldn't help but stare at her, but never for very long. She was afraid Eladio's grandmother would catch her.

Eladio's grandmother wept quietly, gently dabbing her eyes with a white handkerchief and occasionally shaking her head and peering up into the sky.

After the funeral, Julie and her parents returned home in silence. Julie's dad had decided that the best way to respect her grief would be not to be a hypocrite. He despised hypocrites more than anything else. He wouldn't speak of Eladio unless Julie initiated it. And he hoped she wouldn't.

Julie's brother had skipped the funeral and arrived home from school before the rest of the family. He got the mail and placed Julie's new *Miss* magazine and a manilla envelope on her bed.

When Julie got to her room, she pushed the magazine and the envelope to the side of her bed and laid face down in her pillow. She closed her eyes and began to cry. Her mother heard her muted whimpers and closed her daughter's door.

Eladio had made Julie feel special. Eladio had made her feel like a better person than she knew she was. When someone thinks of you in that way, you try to live up to it. You try to be that person. You want to be better—and she wanted to be better. She and Eladio talked about all the things they would do, where they would go. Eladio made her feel perfect, and her dad ran him off. Her father made a choice for her, and now the one person who made her feel really special was dead.

After a while, Julie rolled over and opened her eyes. Her cheeks were red and wet with tears. She felt the magazine under her elbow and retrieved it. Once she discovered what it was, she flung it across the room. She grabbed the envelope and held it up. No return address. It looked like junk mail. She started to throw it as well, but dropped it on her chest instead. She wiped her tears and tried to compose herself.

She picked the manilla envelope back up and opened it. She examined the thin cardboard stock inside and noticed a speck of deep scarlet, almost black. There was a letter written on notebook paper. She removed it and gasped. She recognized Eladio's handwriting immediately. She sat up and tears began streaming down her cheeks again.

Julie read Eladio's letter in shocked silence. She noticed dried specks of blood in the upper righthand corner. She began crying again and didn't stop for a long time. When she did, her lips still quivered, but she managed a strange smile.

Julie read the letter again and again and then held it over her face. Her tears made the ink run.

She would never let another boy talk to her the way Eladio had. And she would never talk to another boy the way she talked to Eladio. And if her father wasn't going to allow her to have a say, what was the point in having a voice?

Julie turned the envelope upside down and the razor dropped into her lap. It had a trace of rust and dried blood on it. She held it flat against her cheek. Then, holding the blade side between her fingers, she slid the blunt side down her cheek to her neck and across a jugular vein. Fresh tears came again.

The razor felt warm.

When Julie entered the living room, her dad was sitting is his recliner watching cable news, and her mother was reading a book on the couch. Neither looked up.

If they had, they would have noticed the bloody footprints that trailed Julie on their light-colored, Berber carpet.

Julie had the blood-soaked manilla envelope in her left hand and she was carrying it by the envelope flap.

By the time her dad looked up, she was standing over him. Her face was flushed and blood was running down her chin. Her cheeks were puffed out like a chipmunk's and the front of the dress she'd worn to the funeral was covered in blood.

"Julie!" he cried. "What happened? What's wrong?"

Julie's mother looked up and began screaming.

Julie tipped the blood-soaked manilla envelope upside down and dumped her tongue into her father's lap.

He squirmed away from it and fell out of his recliner. Her mother stood up, still screaming, and tried to help him.

Julie smiled.

When the blood that filled her cheeks drained out of her smile, you could almost see the whites of her teeth.

TYTUS BERRY is a retired newspaper morgue attendant trying to live off the grid in Texas. He occasionally works as an adjunct professor at a dusty community college and spins fantastical yarns at night.

The Book Sniffer
Bret A. McCormick

"Book sniffer's back," Terence said, a mouthful of sandwich impeding his enunciation.

"Book sniffer?" This was the first time I'd heard the phrase.

"Yeah, I saw him yesterday at the opening preview," Sally said. She swept the hair out of her eyes and looked up at the sky.

The three of us were eating lunch, seated under a pathetic little tree that grew up out of a small planting bed in the parking lot outside the warehouse. We worked for Discount Books, at the flagship store in North Dallas. The annual purge was underway, and via a well-publicized two-day sale, we were liquidating 200,000 books from our inventory. Lots of small-time book dealers looked forward to the event. They could quickly snatch up a lot of merchandise from a single source, at super low prices, then hawk their acquisitions through various on-line outlets.

"So, who's this book sniffer?" I said. I wasn't going to volunteer the information, but I enjoyed sniffing old paperbacks.

"This strange old guy who comes around a lot," Terence offered, again speaking through a mouthful of food.

"He's been coming here for years." Sally had worked for Discount Books longer than the rest of us.

"So, he sniffs books?" I said. "What's the big deal?"

Vintage paperbacks from the 1960s and '70s always carried an olfactory summary of their surroundings: a hint of tobacco, a touch of cooking oil, a female reader's favorite perfume, cedar paneling . . . It was amazing how much information could be had for the astute book sniffer.

"You've just got to see this guy for yourself," Terence said with a laugh that sent a few particles of food flying. I pretended not to notice.

I'd been sniffing books for as long as I could remember, probably for as long as I had been reading. I remembered the sterile, institutional smell of the slick pages in my elementary school textbooks. To me, the smell of a book was just an added dimension to the already enjoyable process of reading.

"I've even caught the guy in our warehouse after hours," Sally said.

"After hours?" That struck me as more than a little odd.

"Yeah. One night I was locking up. We'd been closed for half an hour. When I went in the warehouse to shut off the lights, there he was, sniffing away at some old mystery novels."

Sally shook her head with disdain and daintily popped a grape into her mouth.

"What did you do?" I said. Sally is small; I'd guess she weighs less than 110 pounds, but she gives the impression of being able to take care of herself

"I told him he needed to leave immediately if he didn't want to spend the night in the warehouse."

"What did he say?"

Sally's forehead wrinkled as she searched her memory. "I don't think he said anything. He didn't argue, just stared at me."

"Sounds creepy."

"Not really. I went on to the loading dock and shut off the lights there. When I came back, he was gone."

"What's this guy look like?" I said.

"Old. Maybe in his sixties. Heavyset." Sally snorted a derisive little laugh through her nose. "He's always overdressed."

"Really? How so?"

"He looks like something out of a British television show. Overcoats, ties, hats, the whole nine yards. And his clothes don't look like they came from a thrift store. He wears expensive stuff."

"Does he speak with an accent?" This talk of the book sniffer had captured my imagination.

Sally considered my question.

"I don't think so. I don't know, for sure. I don't think he's ever really spoken to me. Maybe a word here or there. No real sentences."

Terence stood up, crumpling his brown paper lunch bag into a wad and emitting a hearty belch.

Sally peered up at him, shading her eyes from the sun with one hand. "Terence, you come across as a real pig sometimes, you know that?"

"At least I don't sniff books." Terence guffawed, as if he thought he'd said something clever.

With soft sarcasm, Sally replied, "And that would be so much worse."

"Come on," Terence said, tossing his head, "I'll show you the book sniffer."

Inside the warehouse was bedlam. We had a record turnout of book buyers and they were making a shambles of the inventory, digging through boxes and dropping books on the floor, carrying books from one category to another and leaving them in piles in inappropriate places. I don't claim to be the most orderly person in the world, but these booklovers were as oblivious as sharks in a feeding frenzy. I felt grateful that the sale would end at five, but that meant four hours to go, and maybe an hour clean-up afterwards.

I followed Terence into the maze of cardboard boxes.

"Where is he?" I said.

Terence planted his feet, did a full 360 of the entire warehouse, and shrugged. "I don't see him. Maybe he left. He could be in the restroom."

Before either of us could say anything further, Dan Martin, the General Manager of the facility, called us over to help load a pickup truck with about twenty cartons of books. After that, Terence went one way and I went another, responding to the ebb and flow of the sale, answering questions, cleaning up messes, and watching the clock.

It was 5:35 and we'd finally gotten the stragglers out of the warehouse. I was closing and securing the bays on the loading dock and thanking God I'd be home and grabbing a hot shower in the foreseeable future.

Sally's strained voice came over the PA system. "The Annual Discount Books Clearance Sale is now officially concluded. We are locking the doors. Unless you work here, you need to move toward the nearest exit." The exasperation was evident in her voice. As a shift leader, she'd dealt with a lot more nonsense from the customers than I had. Employees referred to the Shift Leaders as 'Shit' Leaders for good reason. There was seemingly no end to the minutiae of complaints a stingy bibliophile could generate. Some of our customers would take up a quarter hour or more of an employee's time over a purchase of less than two dollars.

When I reentered the warehouse floor from the loading dock, there he was.

I knew it was him. He was pretty much as Sally had described him, Cashmere overcoat, expensive-looking hat from a bygone era. The man had horn-rimmed glasses and a flabby face, jowly, with large bags under his eyes. But the dead giveaway was that he was sniffing an old paperback.

I walked toward him, observing the odd fellow in detail. His shoes were shiny and expensive-looking, like the rest of his clothing. He held the open book close to his face and inhaled with exaggerated gusto. His demeanor reminded me of a coffee aficionado, or a chef checking a particularly savory broth. I started to call out to him, but changed my mind, opting instead to approach and make a more personal request for his departure.

Walking toward the man, I experienced an odd fluctuation in my senses. I noticed it at the time but attributed it to fatigue. The light in the warehouse became dimmer, except that the area immediately around the man remained illumined, something like special lighting for a movie. The sounds outside, traffic noises, the voices of departing customers, became increasingly muffled. The air in the warehouse took on a crisp, almost crackly quality, and the temperature felt cooler with every step I took toward the stranger. Finally, as I was directly behind him, I felt I was the one dressed inappropriately. There were goosebumps on my arms and the moisture from my own perspiration felt uncomfortably chilly.

"Sir . . ." I ventured. At first, he did not respond. "It's time to leave, sir."

He lowered the book away from his face and turned toward me, fixing me with a distracted gaze. My immediate impression was that he was suffering from a sort of brain fog. Perhaps he did not even know where he was. Then a grin formed on his face.

"Are you a fellow traveler?" he said.

I had no clue what he meant. I started to repeat my request for his departure, but he suddenly raised a hand and placed it on my shoulder.

"This is a really good one," he said. I noted that he did have a slightly British accent. But I had no time to linger on that observation as he thrust the book, a tattered Western novel by an author I did not recognize, toward my face. "Smell it!"

I inhaled, not so much to smell the book that occupied the space an inch or two from my nose, but simply as a matter of breathing. I smelled peppermints, cigarettes, potatoes boiling and pork frying. Then I heard sounds growing louder, as if someone was increasing the volume on a TV set.

It seems crazy. Insane. Even to me. But next, I was standing alongside the book sniffer in a modest home much like the one my great aunt, Margaret Anne, used to have in Mesquite, Texas. Overcome with confusion, I looked from the man to the room before us. We were standing in a kitchen, behind a countertop with a view directly into the living room. Or maybe they would've called it the den. A television was on. A woman stood with her back toward us, drying her hands on a pale blue apron she was wearing. Beyond her, a man sat in a recliner with his feet up, watching the TV.

I looked to the book sniffer for an explanation. His eyes were gleeful. Quickly, he raised a finger to his lips, warning me to remain silent, then he pointed at a book on the coffee table near the man. It was the same book he held in his hand. He grinned at me and nodded eagerly.

"Why would anyone do such a thing?" the woman cried out, her voice cracking with emotional distress.

"World's gone crazy," the man muttered, taking a deep draw from the cigarette between his fingers.

It was only then that I noticed the programming airing on the TV. It was coverage of the Kennedy assassination. *Live coverage*. I looked around the house. It was a perfect example of a lower middle-class home from 1963. I saw not one thing that might've been manufactured after 1963. On the countertop in front of me were assorted magazines, all from the early '60s.

I turned and looked at the large pot of potatoes boiling away on the range. Pork chops were sizzling in a cast iron frying pan.

"I told you this was a good one," my companion whispered enthusiastically.

"I don't want to burn the chops," the woman said with a sense of both urgency and weariness. She turned abruptly and her eyes fell on us. She stared blankly for just an instant, then her expression filled with terror and she screamed. The man in the recliner jumped and dropped his cigarette. The woman's hands went to her face.

"Pardon us, madam," the book sniffer muttered.

Then he laid his hand on my shoulder and my head swam.

When my vision cleared, I was on the floor, lying between tattered cardboard cartons of books in the warehouse, staring up at the ceiling. The book sniffer smiled benignly down at me. He sighed heavily, "Ah, delightful!" he exclaimed.

"What . . ." I was unable to finish my question. I don't even know what question I was trying to formulate. I was as bewildered as I have ever been in my life. I wasn't even certain I was awake.

Rubbing his palms together, the book sniffer dramatically observed, "How frugal is the chariot that bears a human soul!" Then, he chuckled and walked away.

I tried to shake off the uncertainty of my mental state. About the time the book sniffer was stepping through one of the side exits, I made it to my feet. Behind me, I heard Terence say, "So, you met the book sniffer!"

Terence's expression shifted to concern as he approached. "You okay?" he said. "You don't look so good."

"I think I'm all right," I answered, looking toward the exit door the book sniffer had just disappeared through.

"Did you talk to him?" Terence asked. He was eager for more information about our mysterious customer.

"Not really." I answered.

"Weird, huh?"

"Very weird."

That was three months ago.

I haven't seen the book sniffer since then. But I'm keeping my eyes open for the guy. Every day I bring an old paperback copy of a Nero Wolfe mystery with me. The book belonged to my Aunt Margaret. I loved that lady. She encouraged me in my appreciation of reading, and I spent a great deal of time at her house during summer breaks.

The book I carry in my hip pocket smells of tea and the vanilla candles Aunt Margaret always burned in her home. Aunt Margaret told me, more than once, that she believed in ghosts. I wonder what it would be like to show up as a ghost and visit her back in those days before she died. When the book sniffer returns, I'll be ready.

Maybe I can learn his technique.

BRET McCORMICK is an author, artist and filmmaker based in Bedford, Texas. He was the co-creator of *Road Kill: Texas Horror by Texas Writers*, and his schlock cinema offering *The Abomination* (1986) has an international cult following. In real life, McCormick is an unapologetic book sniffer.

About the Editor

WILLIAM JENSEN is the author of the novel *Cities of Men*, and his short fiction has appeared in *North Dakota Quarterly*, *The Texas Review*, *Tinge Magazine*, and elsewhere. Mr. Jensen teaches at Texas State University, where is the editor of *Southwestern American Literature* and *Texas Books in Review*. He lives in Kyle, Texas, with his wife and stepdaughters. You can learn more about him at williamjensenwrites.com.

ROAD KILL: TEXAS HORROR BY TEXAS WRITERS - VOL 4

For four years now, Bret McCormick and E. R. Bills have been beating the bushes and peering into abandoned wells to seek out the most terrifying tales the Lone Star State has to offer. They have left no stone unturned, no attic unexplored, and no grave undesecrated. And boy howdy, their diligence has paid off! Road Kill Volume 4 is the best and grimmest yet!

You hold in your hands a grand collection of 16 goose-flesh-inducing prose. But, don't just take our word for it; these sixteen stories speak – or perhaps scream – for themselves.

Featuring tales of Texas terror from:

Corey Lamb, E. R. Bills, James H Longmore, William Jensen, Patrick C. Harrison III, W. H. Gilbert, Jeremy Hepler, Dan Fields, Thomas Kearnes, Sylvia Ney , Mark A. Nobles, Russell C. Connor, Elliott Baxter, Ralph Robert Moore, Carmen Gray, and Andrew Kozma

HellBound Books Publishing LLC

ROAD KILL: TEXAS HORROR BY TEXAS WRITERS - VOL 3

Everything is bigger in Texas - including the horror!

A Piney woods meth dealer clones Adolph Hitler. A nightmare exorcist meets an inexorable fined. An eyeball collector gets collected. The apparition of a lynching victim tracks down his executioners. A Texas lawman is undone by shades of his past. A Baphomet recruits converts as a local summer camp. The tales of the baker's dozen who appear in this anthology demonstrate why everything is scarier in Texas...

Including tales of terror from

Jeremy Hepler

Madison Estes

Bret McCormick

James H Longmore

ER Bills

Shawna Borman

And many more...

AVAILABLE on AMAZON.COM

Road Kill: Texas Horror by Texas Writers: Vol 1

An ancient demon plays cowboy and *takes on* the Texas Rangers. Three teenage girls sneak into a "body farm." An aging African American couple defies the Grim Reaper. An FBI agent discovers an entire city that's gone to the "dogs." A handyman learns that the fixer-upper he's working on has a doorway to the past that's way out of square. And a pack of possums burrow into the body politic. Join seventeen Texas authors for a harrowing spin on the twisting freeways and dark back roads that wind through the Lone Star State. Includes works from Joe R. Lansdale, David Bowles, Anna L. Davis, Stephen Patrick, Carmen Gray, Russell C. Connor, Michael H. Price, Tom Bont, Ernie Lee, David Robledo, Alan Beauvais, Michael Baldwin, Glen Coburn, Joe McKinney, Tom Alexander, Bret McCormick and E. R. Bills.

Road Kill: Texas Horror by Texas Writers: Vol 2

A hanging tree takes the law into its own limbs in "The Tree Servant." A mother's love is tested by the walking, crawling and thumb-sucking dead in "Mama's Babies." A famous author lays his process bare in "A Writer's Lot." Not for the faint of heart, this terrifying batch of Texas horror fiction delivers a host of literary demons who will be hard to shake once they get comfortable.

The second volume of the critically acclaimed *Road Kill Series* from Eakin Press, featuring seventeen Texas writers. Some of the writers are established and have been published in a variety of mediums, while others are upcoming writers who bring a wealth of talent and imagination. Edited by E. R. Bills and Bret McCormick, this collection of horror stories is sure to bring chills and make the imagination run wild. Writers include Jacklyn Baker, Andrew Kozma, Ralph Robert Moore, Jeremy Hepler, R. J. Joseph, James H. Longmore, Mario E. Martinez, E. R. Bills, Summer Baker, Dennis Pitts, Keith West, S. Kay Nash, Bryce Wilson, Bonnie Jo Stufflebeam, Stephen Patrick, Crystal Brinkerhoff and Hayden Gilbert.

Road Kill Texas: Horror by Texas Writers Vol 7

**A HellBound Books LLC
Publication**

http://www.hellboundbookspublishing.com

Printed in the United States of America

www.ingramcontent.com/pod-product-compliance
Lightning Source LLC
Chambersburg PA
CBHW030349200726
48286CB00013B/635